Children of the Age

CHILDREN OF THE AGE

(Børn av Tiden)

Knut Hamsun

Translated from the Norwegian by J. S. Scott

Tough Poets Press
Arlington, Massachusetts

Original title: *Børn av Tiden*

Translated from the Norwegian by J. S. Scott

Cover art: "Larvik by Moonlight" (detail) by
Norwegian artist Johan Christian Dahl (1788-1857)

Back cover photo: Knut Hamsun in 1927
(Source: National Library of Norway)

ISBN 978-0-578-64570-4

This edition published in 2020 by:

Tough Poets Press
Arlington, Massachusetts 02476
U.S.A.

www.toughpoets.com

I

At one time the whole neighbourhood was one property, and what is now the Segelfoss manor was the owner's seat and home-farm. Segelfoss was then, as things went in the Nordland, a considerable estate with its half-hundred head of cattle, besides a saw-pit, flour-mill, tile-works and many miles of forest. The homestead swarmed with serving-folk and farm hands and idlers; there were beasts in plenty too, not only the many cows, but horses and dogs as well, cats and pigs, and all along the back of the barn was a whole colony of fowls and geese.

"Aye, they say things were grand here then," old folk will still tell you, calling to mind what their parents used to tell about the days of their childhood.

The proprietor was Herr Willatz Holmsen, a fat and grasping landowner who had been a body-servant. He bought farm after farm round about at a low price until finally he had got together a great estate. In the end, too, he became a merchant and coastwise trader in a great way; he set up the tile-works, the flour-mill and the saw-pit—all most useful things.

The said Herr Willatz Holmsen was a Norseman as we are Norsemen, but he had a uniform and spoke Danish. At the spring and autumn Sessions he wore gold braid and a sword; he could read and write, he was a judge; his judgments were according to Norse law. His lady might have been from anywhere, from Holland or Holstein, from Skaane, from a fairy-tale. She too had likely been in service with great folk at one time and learned fine ways; a broad road was laid down from Segelfoss that she might drive by coach to church. Yes, they were rich folk and grew richer as time went on; there was no doubt that Herr Willatz Holmsen buried money, for, as every one knows, long after his death his ghost still haunted the tile-works.

But it is his son, Willatz Holmsen Number II, of whom old folk think when they recall old stories of the estate. He was a real gentleman, if you like. He dropped the fisheries and the coasting-trade as something he did not understand or did not care to carry on, but he built a new manorhouse on his estate with pillars and a tower, he set up the hot-house, and laid out the swan-pond in the park and the playing-ground for those in his employ. The pond is filled in now and the playing-ground broken up for fodder crops. It was he who made Segelfoss into such a splendid place; he set apart one room for a picture gallery and another room for nothing but books from floor to ceiling. He had flowers and heavy silver standing upon his dinner-table and figures of marble and bronze in his rooms. When his wife, the stately lady of the house, passed, it was the custom that the servants should stand still until she had gone by; she had her own estates in Sweden, she spoke French and had a lady's maid. When folk were grand in those days they were grand and no mistake; master and mistress had each a footman, each a coachman, and each a suite of rooms at Segelfoss. They could not dress themselves of a morning, and for the matter of that did not need to: "Put on my waistcoat!" said Herr Willatz Holmsen to his man. "Do my hair!" said the lady to her maid.

They were grand folk. A somewhat legendary pair, with the nimbus of that age about their heads.

In the first years they were much away from Segelfoss; in the autumn they would pack ten trunks and travel in foreign lands with the children, and there they collected many more boxes and things, and so filled their house bit by bit with all the treasures they gathered. In later years they lived more at home on the estate; the squire by no means allowed that this was for economy's sake; he gave out, on the contrary, that he and his wife had seen the whole world now and no longer cared to travel. Governess and tutor were kept for the three children, two girls and one boy, who were taught all manner of things; and there was the same large staff of servants at the house.

Oddly enough, about this time the squire sold some good farms and forest lands belonging to the property. He did not in the least allow that he needed the money—those few coppers; he merely admitted that as he grew old he found the estate too big for him to manage. And if he said so, then it was so; the squire did not lie and did not need to either. Spiteful tongues whispered in later years that he had begun to search for his father's buried treasure; oh! but that was to misjudge Squire Willatz Holmsen, that great gentleman. He met his end on the mountains, good gentleman; it was very sad, far away from all his family, lying on a couch of heather with only the eight men around him who had gone on this inspection tour with him to arrange about a big new mill-dam. The eight men carried him home on a litter and his wife got such a shock that she shrieked something in French to her maid and fell down, and the maid came running with a smelling-bottle. The gracious mistress of the house was alone now in her old age, her daughters were married and settled in big towns in Sweden, and her son, the third Willatz Holmsen, had been for some years at the cadet-school; his course was to finish in spring and he was to come home for a while.

❧

The winter went by, spring drew on, and the third Willatz Holmsen came home. Elderly folk remember the man well, though it is many years now since he died. His sisters inherited the property in Sweden, he himself got the Segelfoss estate as it stood. He made no very deep mark in his country-side, he was proud and sparing of speech, and though he married and kept up the same large establishment as his parents—yes, and even did some notable things in the course of his life—there was nothing on the surface very splendid about him. What, indeed, was a man so crippled in his means to do? His career was at an end, his father had left him a solid debt to the bank, his mother flitted over to Sweden to her daughters, they all turned Swedes and never came home again. So he was alone. Whatever esteem he could gain he must win for himself, and he did indeed win not a little. He was not popular, but he compelled immense respect; he was only called "Lieutenant," for that was all he was, but he was greeted like a general.

It is with this man and sundry other people that this book deals.

Willatz Holmsen the Third—perhaps he was not a really big man, perhaps he was bigger than any other master of Segelfoss. There was no doubt something ridiculous about a lieutenant out of service, as there also was about a lord of the manor going jauntily downhill; add to this, he was in his younger years hot of temper and stubborn beyond measure. But this same lieutenant had some valuable qualities too; little legends about them still live in the countryside; his abilities kept pace with his peculiarities all the time—yes, and even outstripped them. How has Pastor C. P.

Windfeld described him? As a foolish and crazy being, and here his description stops. That was the petty official's conception of an odd character. The Lieutenant was a well-read man, and when, as the years went on, he learned to control his temper like a philosopher, it was not because he had grown old and stupid, but solely because he had reached mature manhood. Did he need a defence? Because he was brought to his knees, perhaps? It was the law of nature. He came in the last of three generatiens of riches and luxury; the succession ended with him. Besides, he was not brought to his knees. A man of his stiffness remains standing.

His wife came from Hanover, a lady who had passed her childhood in Denmark, where her mother had relations. She was a colonel's daughter and of rather unusual appearance; her face was not at all handsome, but her body was supple and beautifully formed, and this, with her hands, her voice, and to some extent her smile, gave her a great charm. As she had known Danish from her childhood, the language caused her no difficulty. It was but rarely that she was a little at a loss—she could say all that she wanted. In fact, she had a good ear for languages and knew many of them.

She was fond of riding and was a fearless horsewoman, was the good lady; and since rumour had it that she was of noble birth too, she won great respect in the romance-loving country-side, so that the lady came to feel quite at home. It was by no means disagreeable to her that the women should stand dumb in her presence and make their requests and wants known through the housekeeper, Jomfru Salvesen.

People found it hard to understand why she had married the Lieutenant; could it be that there was some slip in the background? Impossible. The Lieutenant, this prim and particular little Willatz Holmsen, would surely have steered clear of anything of that sort,

No, there was a better reason near at hand. The lady had come from home with a brown saddle-horse—with that and nothing else, no boxes or cases, no shipload of goods; she was probably poor, she had come empty-handed—did she take the Lieutenant on that account? This was a good explanation.

All the same it would not have done any harm if she had brought a little money with her to Segelfoss. For now things began to go downhill. The Lieutenant could be tenacious enough, but things went slowly and steadily to the bad with him and the property; he managed the estate and the tile-works as before—yes, better than before—but the times had changed, they no longer paid. He let the mill come to a standstill altogether; the dam which his late father had wanted to repair and enlarge had at last collapsed, and the Lieutenant was unable to build it up again. His own flour he got from Bergen.

In the parish he was looked upon as a strange man for not rebuilding his mill-dam. His late father would never have thought twice about it.

In other ways he had the good qualities of his forbears, the great folk who had been lavish and fatherly to their servants and cottagers; this third Willatz Holmsen, too, was all for living well himself, and he was far from being unhelpful to others. When timber went up in price and he began to sell, he even developed a taste for benevolence.

"I have set all our cottagers and fishermen to work in the forest," he said to his wife. "I am giving them good wages."

Thus he too helped and was lavish and fatherly like his forbears. These were winter days and there was nothing to be earned before the Lofoten fishery began; it was a great boon to the people to get work in the forest.

"The men say that your father sold some of Segelfoss?" asked his wife.

The Lieutenant retorted:

"Indeed?"

"That he sold five of the Segelfoss farms? And that much forest was sold with them?"

"My father did rightly," answered the Lieutenant. "He rounded off the estate; it grew too big for him in his old age. We have enough left."

The husband and wife could never agree on this point; for several years they continued to hold different opinions on the subject. The lady had even written to her father the Colonel in Hanover and laid the matter before him, and the Colonel had answered that in view of the present prices for timber it was a mistake to have disposed of forest lands from the property.

"It was *not* a mistake!" answered the Lieutenant. And his little hand, grasping a button of his uniform, grew white over the knuckles. So positive was the Lieutenant, so self-willed was he.

Ah, but his wife, Fru Adelheid, was no fool—bless her for it! Though she too was passionate and quarrelsome, she was German-born and bred, with sound common sense. She showed that many a time in her consultations with the housekeeper.

❧

The Lieutenant was also a constant rider; not a day passed, indeed, without his mounting his horse. But while his wife dashed all over the country with the skirt of her habit falling over her stirrup, and at times with Halflapp Petter at her heels as groom, the Lieutenant rode mostly at a walking pace and without attendant—

there was little show about him. He rode in his uniform without epaulettes or sword and looked quite shabby, with his head a little bent, deep in thought or sunk in apathy. That his mouth was shut so firmly might also point to obstinacy.

One day in summer-time his wife set herself to sketch the débris of the ruined mill-dam. The Lieutenant came up just then with a number of men; his lips were oddly compressed, but that was from embarrassment. He greeted his wife and asked how long it would take her to finish the picture.

"As if I could tell before I have begun!" answered the lady, annoyed. "What are all these people here for?" she asked.

"To rebuild the dam."

"Indeed! Then—hm—they must have had some idea that I had just come here to-day to sketch it!"

The Lieutenant's face changed a little, and he answered that he really had had no idea of it.

The lady in her impetuousness had already packed up her sketching things. Suddenly she stood still, her anger passed, and a penitent smile crossed her face. It had just occurred to her that her husband had only the day before found the means for this outlay.

"Willatz!" she said meekly. And she began to intimate that she was not so stupid, not so unreasonable; of course be must start repairing the dam, now he had the money—

The Lieutenant flushed red with anger.

"Money?" said he. "You are too sharp-sighted, you deceive yourself. Money? To tell the truth—I did know you had come here.

His wife let her head droop:

"Then your first denial was incorrect?"

"Yes, I—yes—have it so!"

Ah, it looked as if all was not just as it should be between husband and wife, but no one heard of any serious disagreements between them, and for the scene at the mill-dam circumstances were to blame.

The Lieutenant lived for some weeks in a constant struggle with himself. He would try and give his wife a pleasure, something big; he went to her room, looked out of the window, and said casually:

"The church roof is falling in, I see."

"Is that anything to be pleased about?" she answered. Oh, she had become so wretchedly irritable the last few months, she herself did not understand why.

"The west wind has damaged it badly during the night. You might set some of our men to put it to rights."

"—might?"

"You and I, if you like. In this case, you. In short, men and money are at your disposal."

He probably thought at one stroke to put an end to her degrading suspicions about his money matters and to show his power; what else could he mean?

"That would be a good deed on your part," said she.

"On my part?"' he protested at once. "I tell you—"

"Well, then, on mine," she parried.

Truth to tell, the lady had many a time been in fear of her life in the little rickety church. The Lieutenant, of course, never went; it would never enter his head. A little reading here and there in the works of the humanists and the encyclopaedists in his father's library—that was his divine service. As long as his mother was at home at Segelfoss, the old lady and the young mistress drove together to church every Sunday, but after the old lady went to her daughters and never came back to Segelfoss again, the young mistress drove to church alone. Oh, but the church was a dangerous place to be in during storms from the west. She sang when she sat there—she sang with her great, sweet voice so that the others fell silent. She sang, partly to harden her heart against the fear of the tumble-down church, partly because the church service had come to be her one and only theatre, now that she lived so far out of the world. It was a fine spectacle when the congregation stood and watched her coming, saw her coachman doff his hat and help her out of her carriage; saw her step through the doorway and up the aisle, right up to the Segelfoss pew. This performance took place every Sunday.

She felt grateful to her husband for the sympathetic thought he had bestowed upon the wretched house of God; perhaps this brought her to a communicative mood; she began to tell him something, to hint at a possibility—indeed, as a matter of fact it was a certainty, she could speak of it now—

He turns abruptly towards her and looks at her, just looks. His eyes light up; his body trembles. It is with amazement; surely his ears deceive him, it is unbelievable.

What—after so many years of married life—does he hear aright?

His wife nods and answers yes, it is true, and it was that which made her so irritable at the mill-dam the other day.

"Irritable? You? How dare you—?"

"Oh, well, I only mean— But what do you say to it, since so it is? I could not say for certain before, but I can now."

"God bless you—that is to say—hm—the greatest event of my life. Adelheid, you must unuerstand that I was not pleased that the church roof is falling in."

"No, I beg your pardon—"

"Stop! You still dare, at such a moment as this, a situation—in short—"

He could have sunk through the floor. His confusion drove him to the door; he opened it and went out. He was away a long time; his wife heard him go up to the library and wander round there. Then he came back.

"Forgive me, but I cannot get the church out of my mind. It is a question whether the whole building will not—I mean in the next storm—it is dangerous. And besides, it is a disgrace to us, to the whole estate. If you will leave it to me—I understand a little about draughtsmanship—I might design a new church and you could have it carried out. You have timber enough, you have plenty of builders, Severin, Bertel of Sagvika, Ole Johan. Mark my words, in the next westerly gales—besides, the thing is not creditable; we are no longer only two, there will soon be more of us. What do you think? Of course I will bear in mind the acoustics for your singing, a free passage for your voice from your seat through the whole church. If you would allow me to send to the south for the necessary technical help for our people—"

"Yes, thank you, Willatz, if you can manage it."

"Manage? Costs me only a word. And now let *me* thank *you* for—for everything!"

Opposition made this man cold, but there was no opposition now. This was something new, a piece of good fortune, a blessing. With the event he linked a strange notion of wealth, of actual profit—what was the connection? And his sisters whom he had not seen since they had become so Swedish—and his mother who could not live in straitened circumstances, but had gone away, what would she say now! Truly she had left the ship like a rat; and the ship was not sinking.

The Lieutenant took off his ring and put it back on to his right hand, where it belonged; he had been wearing it for some time on the left. This change of his ring to a different hand was meant to show that he was thinking deeply, and wished to remind himself of something or other of importance. It was always done so quietly as not to be noticed; no one knew why he did it, but perhaps he knew himself.

II

The Lieutenant falls into a strange habit; he takes off his boots and puts on slippers when he has an errand upstairs on the second floor. But then you see there were no longer only two of them; they were as good as three already; could he allow himself to walk about among the humanists in his boots with his wife's rooms just below? There were two great flights of stone steps at Segelfoss; the master and mistress had from the earliest days had each an entrance. The Lieutenant now took occasion to examine his wife's flight thoroughly, and to cement anew the joints where the stones were loose. When the frost came, too, he saw to it that the steps were kept clear of ice.

But he irritated the lady inside so much that she writhed with impatience: "You might find something more useful to do," she said. "You have many people at work at the mill-dam."

"They are working," he replied. "They are carting stones and building walls. They will very soon be done. That reminds me that one of your carriage-horses was used one day."

"Why was that?"

"Against orders, without my knowledge. And the horse has gone lame."

"Naturally."

"So you cannot use it for going to church."

She was on the point of bursting out, but restrained herself. "What a pity!" was all she said. "Then I will go on foot."

This way out of the difficulty he had not bargained for. He had hoped to get his wife to give up her church-going, at any rate until all was over, until after the event: the church seemed to him more tumble-down than ever now.

"You could take another horse," he said unwillingly.

"No, no other horse. No, thank you, I shall walk."

"But at any rate;" he persisted, "at any rate you should be careful. The church will collapse one of these days. Each new storm makes it more unsafe. A bad accident might happen."

His wife laughed, putting him to shame with her boldness:

"You are so timid, Willatz, always so timid."

The fact was the lady had come to the conclusion, from some of her husband's little ways, that he was none too courageous, that, not to mince matters, he was a bit of a coward, and for the last few months she had not always taken the trouble to conceal this suspicion. Why did he nearly always ride at a walking pace? Why, in the summer-time, did he avoid the crazy bridge over the millstream whenever he could cross by the ford? There must be some reason for it.

He had gradually grown used to being suspected; probably his feelings had become blunted; it did not seem to embitter his life. Now of course the reason might be that the Lieutenant could think undisturbed when he rode at a walking pace and that when he went round by the ford his idea was to give his horse a bath. But the reason might also be that the man was a poltroon.

❧

The Lieutenant changed his clothes and rode off to the pastor's. He rode on a good errand—to tell him of the new church that was to be built. His men had already felled the timber and carted stone to the spot, overseers had arrived from the south, the work could now begin.

It was this same pastor, C. P. Windfeld, who later wrote the story of the new Segelfoss church. He describes the appearance of the Lieutenant at that time, when he was about forty: lean, but of well-knit frame, with bent head, a long, clean-shaven face with grey eyes, eagle nose and bluish chin. His hair, sprinkled with grey, was very carefully parted on the right side and combed forward at the ears. His hands were long and thin, and he wore untanned leather gloves. His costume was a blue coat and yellow riding-breeches, and over all a heavy military cape suitable to the time of year. Except for the ring on his right hand and the hair watch-chain, with a gold running-band, lie had no ornaments.

The Lieutenant knocked and stepped without more ado into the pastor's study. He brushed the dust off the chair with his yellow cambric handkerchief before he seated himself. What contempt there is in his arrogant heart for this man of God!

"My wife has decided," he said, "—I mean—our church will collapse one of these days."

The pastor answers something to the effect that it is unfortunately true, the church shows itself to be—like all earthly things—subject to decay—

"Rubbish!" said the Lieutenant. "My wife has therefore decided to use up some of her timber in building a new church."

"Truly, a—"

"Let me finish—and she has asked me to inform you of this. That is my errand."

"An act of the greatest beneficence both on your part and—"

"On mine? If you should ever permit yourself to suppose that I have anything whatever to do with this—this project, your days here would be numbered. Understand that!"

The pastor knows well enough that he is quite secure in his living, but at the sight of this man in such a towering, trampling passion, he shrinks from him in terror. The Lieutenant had become quite unlike himself, he had half risen from his chair and stood leaning forward, pale as death.

After he had sunk down into his seat again and panted for a time, he threw a roll of paper on to the table and said:

"And there is the design, if you wish to see it."

The pastor unrolls the paper and gives an exclamation of involuntary delight at the beautiful little church.

"Only think! Tower and spire!"

"My wife has approved it," says the Lieutenant for all answer, and takes back the drawing. He unrolls another. "Here is the groundplan, if you wish to see it."

The pastor does not understand this so well, and he would gladly ask a few questions, go into details a little. Putting his trust in God, he says:

"But the whole will have to be approved, of course?"

"No."

"The authorities, the department—?"

"No."

The Lieutenant rolls up the drawings and returns them to his pocket. Then he says:

"If you write, you can mention that the new church will now be erected to the north of the churchyard, where there is no clay and the rock is near the surface. My wife gives the new site."

The pastor could see that this was a good idea, and he nodded.

The Lieutenant rises:

"My wife has engaged expert workmen. The work is to begin at once."

"May I not," says the pastor, "on behalf of the parishioners, come and thank your wife for this most generous gift?"

"If," says the Lieutenant, looking back over his shoulder at the pastor's boots, "if you come to thank my wife, she has her own entrance, the south stairs. I wish you good day."

He mounted his horse and rode away at a walking pace.

And so little thought did he give to what had just passed that he turned off the road all at once, and rode away on another errand, rode over the home-fields and through the forest up to the dam.

The work here was almost at an end; an entirely new dam with a greater fall than before, and also a branch leading over from the river to the old dam down which to float the timber from the forests on the estate. This was a well thought-out scheme of the Lieutenant's. Hitherto the timber had had to be dragged over the snow during the winter all the long way to the sea, but, now the old dam had burst and smoothed out the fall, the timber could float down without breaking itself to pieces.

The Lieutenant sat and surveyed the work from the back of his horse.

"We finish here in two days," he said to his men.

"In two days? Ay, ay!" said the men and nodded assent to the order.

❧

At the time the child was born the mistress of Segelfoss was eight-and-twenty years of age, quite a young woman therefore, and of such fine physique that she seemed as if made to be a mother. But the Lieutenant, nervous as usual, was so afraid that something might go amiss that he took special precautions.

A couple of days before Christmas he said to his man Martin:

"You will harness the pair of horses, the greys."

"Yes."

"And drive them without a sledge to Ura—to Ura farm, to the sheriff's. You will stable them there till I come for them."

"Yes."

"When that is done you will come back on foot."

"Yes."

"That is all. . . ."

From early morning on Christmas Eve there was great suspense and expectancy at Segelfoss. A woman wearing a black cap had arrived a few days before. The housekeeper had spoken with her; there was a rumour that the mistress was very ill.

Later in the day the Lieutenant was standing bare-headed down in the passage between his own and his wife's apartments, speaking for a moment with the black-capped woman

"But there is no immediate danger, I hope?"

"No, but— No, with God's help, but— I have not attended the lady before and the responsibility—"

"The doctor?" asks the Lieutenant.

"Yes, if only the doctor is at home."

"He has been warned. I can have him here by to-night."

The Lieutenant called his man and gave him orders to harness the brown pair at once, while he himself put on his travelling-dress. When all is ready he seats himself in the sleigh and drives round behind the outhouses that his wife may not hear the sleigh-bells and be made uneasy.

Yes, he is going himself for the doctor.

He drives quickly, he drives very hard, arrives at Ura, puts the grey pair into the sleigh and drives off again. He reaches the doctor's house.

Now if it had not been the Lieutenant from Segelfoss the district-doctor would rather have been left in peace for the night.

He offers brandy, offers refreshments, the housekeeper comes and offers coffee and cakes; the Lieutenant thanks them and replies to all offers: "I have come only for the doctor to-night."

Now they are in the sleigh. They do not talk much on the way; they hardly know each other. The doctor is the young District-physician Ole Riis. At Ura the Lieutenant puts in again the brown pair, which have had some hours' rest, and they are off once more.

They reached Segelfoss at two o'clock. The child was already born.

The child, the fourth Willatz Holmsen, was born just at Christmas, on the very Christmas night. It was almost like a miracle But the mother was very ill, there must have been complications, and the young doctor got a chance to show what he could do. He stayed at Segelfoss until the Christmas week was over; at last he was recalled to his head-quarters, or he would perhaps have stayed longer. The lady came to value him greatly once she had got over her aversion to his hairy hands.

❧

The winter drew to an end, the mother grew strong again, and the child grew older month by month; all went well. To be sure, the lady had grown a little thin and her nose seemed larger, but she was too much occupied to think much about her personal appearance now. She had the child, and that was enough; a splendid boy with a roar like a nature-force, passionate, headstrong, and oh, so sweet. And now his teeth were coming.

"He ought by rights to be baptized in the new church, but—What do you think, Adelheid?"

The lady answers that the idea pleases her.

Ah, how much gentler and more reasonable his wife had become now—quite an amiable being. When could the church be ready?

That could not be said exactly: sometime next winter. The stone-work for foundations was finished already; the tiles had come from the tile-works.

Yes, but the stone-work was a small matter. The Lieutenant had been right in calculating that as the church was to stand to the north of the churchyard, scarcely any stonework would be needed to make the site level. The stone-work was finished in the autumn; that was a small matter. And the tiles, they were a small matter too. Now for the building!

With the very first of the spring the work began, and week after week went by. The building grew higher and higher; they were above the windows already. One weekday the pastor drove up; he had had a letter, he said, informing him that the authorities wished to see the plans.

"Do they?" said the Lieutenant. "They are in use."

"They wish the work stopped until the plans are approved," said the pastor in his mildest tones.

"Indeed," said the Lieutenant.

He held the authorities in all due respect: both his education and his training had imbued him with obedience to his superiors. But here he showed himself self-willed; he would not give up the drawings.

When the church had been roofed in and the tower was half finished, the pastor came again and asked for the plans on behalf of the authorities.

The Lieutenant called his master-builder and asked:

"Do you need the ground-plan any more?"

"No."

"Give it to the pastor."

This was of course a mere farce—the ground-plan of a church already finished! And the pastor being C. P. Windfeld and no lamb, he tells us himself that this angered him. It is true that he was dealing with the man whose wife had presented the community with the new church, but Lieutenant Willatz Holmsen's high-handedness went too far.

"Am I to have the ground-plan only?" he asked.

"We cannot spare the other drawing," answered the Lieutenant. "I have some calculations on it."

Then the pastor unfolded a large letter he held in his hand and said:

"It is my duty to inform you that the authorities demand that the work be stopped at once."

"Indeed," said the Lieutenant.

From, the church and tower the strokes of hammer and ax sounded on uninterruptedly; not for a moment did they stop, and the pastor had to go off with the ground-plan.

The church was finished and stood there like a little beauty on the edge of the wood; but before the fittings also were completed most of the winter had gone. With the first spring sunshine after Easter the Lieutenant had the new church prettily decorated inside and outside with painting, and placed his wife's name upon a gilt scroll in the choir

The work was done.

And now the Lieutenant sent Halflapp Petter with a letter to the pastor to say that the church was finished: "His wife had had a church built with her own materials and by her own people upon her own ground; the authorities had nothing to do with Fru Holmsen's private property. She now presented the church and ground to the community. The authorities might decide whether the gift should be accepted or not. Design herewith enclosed."

He waited for weeks; no answer came. He sent a second letter to the pastor to the effect that if the church were not accepted and consecrated within four—4—weeks from date the Lieutenant and his wife would travel to Trondhjem to have the boy baptized. And at the same time the Segelfoss estate's contribution to the upkeep of the chapel-of-ease would be reduced to the amount fixed by law.

This settled the matter. Bishop Krogh came in person to the parish from his diocesan visitation and formally accepted the church, consecrated it, and baptized the big boy. He received the names of Willatz Wilhelm Moritz von Platz Holmsen.

III

But why conceal the truth?—things were far from what they should be between the husband and wife at Segelfoss. Their differences had merely died down for a short time at the child's birth; as time went on they revived, and now they were in full bloom again. Should not the Lieutenant as a grown man have put up with the little things that rubbed him so terribly the wrong way, instead of making the worst of them? So unhappy, so ill-humoured as they were in each other's company, this husband and wife, it was enough to make one laugh or cry. "*My* son," said she; and that vexed him. "My little *Moritz*," she would say, feeling her way; that vexed him again, and he answered:

"He is called Willatz, like his forefathers."

"Yes, but his name is Moritz too."

"No. Hardly at all."

Then his wife laughed and said:

"Yes, but when he gets bigger and I call 'Willatz,' might not the wrong Willatz come?"

"When," answered her husband tartly, "when you call Willatz, my namesake and I will certainly understand from the tone of your voice which of us you mean."

His wife laughed again and said:

"Yes, that is not unlikely— While I think of it: you have been so good as to get the housekeeper a new girl to help her. She is from one of the hill cottages, I think; she is young and pretty, her name is Marcilie. But she seems to be a little crazy."

"Is she a little crazy?"

"Would you believe it—she goes up and down your stairs at night."

Pause.

"She goes up late in the evening and comes down some time after. A good while after."

Pause.

"You evidently do not think it as strange as I do, or else you would say something."

"I am silent," answers her husband, "because you wish me to be, or you would not overwhelm me so. You strike me dumb."

His wife gives a loud laugh.

"Do I strike you dumb?"

"Almost dumb. I am overwhelmed by the fact that I have been so clumsy in the choice of a kitchen-maid for the housekeeper. Does the girl not do her work, then?"

His wife does not answer; she is thinking. Both are thinking, both are getting ready for another bout. The lady withdraws from the contest and asks:

"Is there anything else you wish to say to me?"

"No—I knocked at your door a week ago."

"I was engaged, I asked you to excuse me."

"I knocked at your door three weeks ago. I knocked this year, last year. I begged to speak with you for a few minutes."

"I asked you to excuse me each time."

The man bows and stands still.

"And I beg you to excuse me *now*," says his wife to clinch matters, and looks at him.

He had misunderstood her. Why did he stand there? He was making his wife uneasy. Perhaps she feared something, she wished to forestall him, and that was why she said: "I beg you to excuse me!"

The man laughs then. "Ha, ha," he says. It is a shallow sound, his mouth opens, his throat contracts, a laugh is produced. Then he goes—goes out of the house, across the courtyard to the stable, gets his horse, and mounts. That is what the gentleman does.

How they both flounder in the net! The lady flounders too. She can feel no great affection for the man who has just gone out, no excessive tenderness any more, so it would seem. It is incomprehensible; is he not her husband, and should one not be fond of one's husband? There is a good point of view at the window; she stands there and looks out till he has ridden away—then she seems to feel safe. There is a key in her door, she would perhaps not exchange it for a key of gold; she is in the habit of using it, of turning it on the inside of the door.

It is all so unaccountable. What had he done to her? Was it married life itself that was repellent to her, the intimacy, the immodesty of it? Perhaps his long hands, his breath?

She goes to her desk and writes; these are reflections, notes—it is a diary. She turns the pages and handles the pen tenderly. Here and there Norse words have slipped in among the German by mistake; this annoys her, but she will not spoil her book with corrections. It is no doubt everyday things she enters, trifles such as would occur to the Colonel's daughter that she is; but it interests her, perhaps, to turn over the leaves at times, to reread them and reawaken an old echo within herself.

After a time she goes back to her place at the window again, to see if some one is coming down the hill, if some one should have turned back—and then she goes humming to her little Mozart piano and settles down to it.

Settles down to happiness.

Was it not she who had left an aristocratic home in the great city of Hanover and buried herself alive here at Segelfoss? It was to her the luckless, blind king once said in her girlhood: "I can hear by your voice how beautiful you are, my child!" Her voice, yes indeed, strong and sweet, luxuriant; she sings the songs of her home-land, she sits with swelling breast. Of a certainty there is resonance in this voice, the accompaniment blends softly with it, she throws back her head, she rocks to and fro—

Suddenly she breaks off, and hastens through two rooms to the nursery, to the boy.

This scene repeated itself often as time went on. The servants in the kitchen listened to her singing, they alone; they used to open a couple of doors that they might hear the better. There was no one else in the whole house who opened doors and listened, that the lady was sure of. She met her husband only at meal-times, and she had no intercourse with neighbours either. Old Squire Coldevin and his wife still remembered Segelfoss as it was in the time of the former master. They came sailing from their big island once a year and stayed a week; that was about all. That was almost all the society she had. And then Fru Adelheid took in her German papers and received her German letters—but there was no living voice in them.

❧

And day by day the Lieutenant went on his sedate ride, his long daily round. He had cotters and tenants from hilltop to sea-strand and rode right down to the fishermen's huts by the sea. There he sat on horseback and watched their work and their home-life and looked at their girls. The Lieutenant was by no means heartless; now and again he would help a girl to service on the manor, now and again he would send potatoes and pork to a needy family.

He leans over sidewise from the saddle and knocks on a window with his riding-whip. This is where the fisherman Lars Manuelsen lives. The man comes out and greets him; the doorway behind is full of faces; farthest back is the housewife, who lays her hand upon her breast as if to hide behind it.

"Are you fishing these days?" asks the Lieutenant.

The man shakes his head humbly:

"There's not a thing to be got, your Honour, believe me."

"I need some men at the river. You can bring a couple of others with you and keep the dam clear."

"Ay. So you are going to clear the timber-booms already, sir? There's a heavy flood in the river?"

"Well, we begin next Monday, then— What long lad is that standing there?"

"That? That's my son. Why don't you show your manners, Lars? —He's called Lars. He was confirmed last year and was number two, so it isn't brains he lacks. But what's the good of them?"

"Is that your daughter there? What use have you for a grown girl at home? Why in the world have you so many grown children at home?"

"They can't get out in the world. Where are they to go?" And where are they to get clothes fit to show themselves in?"

"Rubbish!" says the Lieutenant. "Is Lars his name, did you say?"

"The boy? Yes! He's a curse to me, he will do nothing but read.

God has given him good big bands, but he does nothing with them and earns nothing."

"Are you fond of books?" asks the Lieutenant.

"Why don't you answer, Lars?" cried his father threateningly.

Lars twisted himself and grinned sheepishly, and could not get out an intelligible word.

The Lieutenant asks:

"Are all these your children? The little one too?"

"Yes, to be sure," answers Lars the elder. "Five years old last autumn as ever was. His name is Julius."

Suddenly the Lieutenant says:

"That girl over there can have service at the house. What's her name?"

"Daverdana."

"Daverdana?"

"Go and tidy yourself, Daverdana, and don't stand like that right in front of people."

"Let me see your hands," says the Lieutenant abruptly.

Daverdana has begun to blush right up to the roots of her red hair, but she holds out her hands confidingly.

"Can you read?"

"Can't you open your mouth, girl?" bursts out her father. "She gallops through a book with the speed of a reindeer," he answers for her. "Was number three at confirmation."

"No, number fourteen," says the boy Lars, who has at last found his tongue.

"Number three," says his father. "Sure you know you were yourself, Daverdana."

The Lieutenant nods:

"Get some clothes made for yourself, and come up to the house. I will pay for the clothes. Come Sunday week. Let me see your hands again. Good, wash them well. Daverdana?"

"Yes, Daverdana," says her father.

The Lieutenant turns his horse and says:

"Well, then, we pole the timber next Monday."

Then he rode off, a little bent, a little shabby, in his threadbare uniform, but firm and spare and Arab-like, as though he would ride clean over any obstacle that came his way.

Yes, to be sure, he was selling timber, it fetched a good price now; he was cutting planks and boards at his own saw-mill and was flush of money. Why shouldn't things go right? The land did not bring in anything; no, indeed; a great estate only beggared one unless one had plenty of capital. But if one had— And the tile-works—upon them he lost less and less since they were at a standstill. The mill made money, a little thin stream of money; the mill paid its way, more than paid its way when he reckoned what it ground for the freeholders, for which he got nothing. Things would go all right yet!

If only there hadn't been that rebuilding of the church that had been a costly affair. Year after year had gone by since it was built, but the Lieutenant still had more than one unpleasant reminder of it. But the timber and the forest, these were an immense godsend.

❧

The Lieutenant comes home. There is a tinkling, tinkling. What is it? Ting-a-ling! His wife is playing at horses with her son in the courtyard, driving him with reins. It is tremendous fun; both are laughing and running, ha, ha, ha! When the Lieutenant comes the game stops and the boy begins to whimper. These tears cut his father to the heart, but when his mother says: "Don't cry, little Moritz!" the Lieutenant's lips are at once compressed and he sits motionless on his horse, saying nothing. No doubt his wife was using this name, *Moritz*, to show that she was above him in rank, of noble blood, Moritz von Platz.

"Hm!" says the Lieutenant. "Those bells—take them off him!"

"It is only a game," answers his wife.

"One does not hang bells upon a Willatz Holmsen, even in a game."

"What a fuss you do make!" says his wife. "If I allow it, surely you can— Come, little Moritz, we will go in now."

Yes, a little bickering had broken out again, a little lively friction. What a number of pin-pricks they dealt each other—far too many! Some scenes would be quite ludicrous, every sentence bristling with pins.

There—they had begun already to play the piano in the house. The lady was teaching her son to read and to play and be a constant joy to her; sometimes, too, they would draw with coloured chalks, and sometimes they sang little songs—everything came easy to the boy. Well, take it all in all, he was a godsend to the house, little Willatz in his blue velvet jacket with the broad embroidered collar.

So when the Lieutenant came to table, an easy friendliness and careful politeness ruled once more.

No more quarrelling, no more pin-pricks; the quarrelling had stopped for want of fuel. But during these peaceful times at table little Willatz was no longer Moritz, no indeed. His mother either avoided using his name at all or called him just Willatz, as she should. And in gratitude for this concession, the Lieutenant on his part did not persist in calling out "Willatz," "Willatz," all the time. He said instead, "my dear," "my boy," avoiding his name.

But this did not mean that the Lieutenant gave in in any way. He made short work of the name Moritz whenever by a rare chance he heard it from the maids or the housekeeper.

"Excuse me, Jomfru Salvesen," he would say; "of whom are you speaking? Who is called Moritz in this house? Is it my son Willatz Holmsen you mean?"

"I beg your pardon," she answered. "The mistress has—the mistress sometimes says Moritz."

"Only a slip of the tongue. Neither of us wishes the boy to have a nickname."

Whereupon the Lieutenant nods and goes.

"By the by, Jomfru," he says, turning back, "Lars of Sagvika has a houseful of grown children who are doing nothing. One of his daughters will come and ask if you can employ her in Marcilie's place."

"Is Marcilie to go?"

"So I understand."

"Oh, indeed, and so a new one is coming?"

"Her father has too many children to feed," says the Lieutenant.

He is perhaps afraid the housekeeper may have her own thoughts about this story, so he adds, at once:

"He has a grown son too, who will do nothing but read. I am sending him to Tromsö."

Well, anyhow, the good Lars Manuelsen will have his burden sensibly lightened! The same idea had occurred to the Lieutenant for an instant down at Sagvika, but he had said nothing there; now he has said it, the boy Lars must go to the seminary at Tromsö. Nothing but outlay on all sides. What was the girl's name? Daverdana? After the beauty in the fairy-tale. Red hair, long hands.

As the Lieutenant crosses the courtyard he notices something at his feet. He always walks with his head bent, looking on the ground, and so he sees all that lies on his way.

"What stranger has been here?" he asks one of the men.

"A stranger? None."

"There's a half-smoked cigar lying over there."

"It must have been the doctor who threw it there," says another of the men.

"Yes, that must be it," says the first.

The Lieutenant goes his way. So the doctor had been there in the forenoon? How forgetful his wife was sometimes; she had never mentioned the doctor's visit during the whole dinnertime. He was on the point of going in to say to his wife: "Has the doctor been here? What did he want?" Suddenly it occurs to him: how curious it sounded; a stranger had not been here, but the doctor had been. Was the doctor, then, not a stranger at Segelfoss?

At the supper-table little Willatz happened to tell how the doctor had lifted him up to the ceiling, higher than the chandelier.

"The doctor?" asks his father.

His wife answers at once:

"The doctor was in the neighbourhood, so we sent for him this morning."

"Who is ill?"

"Marcilie."

"I knew nothing of it."

"She has caught cold. The doctor said it was serious."

The Lieutenant merely repeats: "I knew nothing of it."

"I did not wish to mention it. It was not anything to tell you of."

The Lieutenant smiles:

"You wished to spare me?"

But as he takes the matter in this way, ignoring the delicacy of her behaviour, his wife is hurt and says:

"Yes, I wished to spare you. The girl Marcilie's trips up and down the stairs at night have evidently not agreed with her."

Pause.

"I fancy the girl Marcilie would have got over it without the doctor," says the Lieutenant. "But then of course you would have had no chance to make a scene."

"A scene—I? If you only knew how utterly indifferent everything is to me but my little Moritz. Are you finished?"

The lady rose from the table.

IV

A boat came rowing, a white eight-oared boat, with a cabin aft, rowed by four men. As it was a fine warm spring day, the four men were rowing in their shirt-sleeves, but their passenger must have been inside the cabin, for he was not to be seen. The boat laid to a little way up the river, near the tile-works.

Out of the cabin of the boat crept a big, fat man in furs and heavy clothing. It was not the doctor nor yet old Coldevin, nor was the boat known, so it must have come from some distance. The man got out of the boat, said a few words to the crew, and began to walk up along the river bank. Two of the men went with him.

People stood in front of all the houses on the way up and gazed at this unwonted sight. It seemed to get too warm for the big man; he pulled off his fur coat and gave it to one of his men to carry. He had such a broad back, his coat-tails flew out sideways at each step he took, and he did not walk quickly either; he often stood still and pressed his hand to his breast. And so they went on and on; perhaps they were bound for the waterfall. At last they disappeared up in the woods.

And now people strolled down to the eight-oar to find out all about it; idle people went down, Lars Manuelsen went down, and many of the children from the cottages followed at a short distance. The boatmen knew well what these visitors wanted and took up the proper attitude; they understood to the full the importance it gave them to be in possession of a secret.

"Peace!" says Lars Manuelsen, though by rights the others should have given the first greeting, since they were the visitors.

"Peace!" is all they answer.

"It's grand weather we're having."

"It's warm rowing."

They talk about this for some time: wasn't there a breeze outside and wasn't it easterly? The boatmen are sparing of their answers.

"That's a thumping eight-oar," says Lars, "Is she yours?"

The men spit and look big.

"No such luck," they answer.

"Where are you from?"

A pause, a telling pause. The children are all ears.

"We are from Ytterleia!"

"Thought so," nods Lars.

He goes nearer to the boat and looks at it, but finds he does not know it; on the oars and bailer are only a letter or two.

But now the men probably think that things are moving too slowly, that perhaps their attitude is frightening this native into going away and leaving them to consume inwardly with their untold secret; they open out a little, and one of them says:

"No, the boat's not ours."

"No, worse luck," says the other.

And from now on the two boatmen do most of the talking, so Lars does not need to ask many more questions. They venture forward step by step, one watches the other, one outstrips the other in daring, but pulls himself up in time:

"For we've only got the job to row this boat."

"Ay? Then who is it you are rowing?" asks Lars.

Pause. Hm. Now he is going too fast!

"The owner of the boat," answers one.

The other, who has stood fidgeting as if on thorns, adds:

"Yes, he bought the boat just for this trip."

"Took out the money and paid on the nail for it, just for this trip."

'The men looked at Lars Manuelsen. The children stood and looked at the men, and listened, listened.

But Lars only remarks:

"It would be an extra important trip then, I suppose?"

He has already asked once who the stranger is and received no answer; now he lets that alone, no doubt it will come in time.

"As to the trip, I can't say anything about it," answers one of the men.

"He is up the river now," remarks the other.

Pause. It was wonderful how impressive and pregnant with matter this pause managed to be.

Lars examines the boat long and closely, talks with the strangers of indifferent matters, of the spring, of the herring at Langö, of a galliot from Ytterleia which was driven in here by bad weather one year. It belonged, by the way, to Henriksen, the general dealer at Utvaer.

The men show by nods that they know Henriksen and his business.

"It's not him you are rowing, I suppose," asks Lars.

"No."

Lars seems to have grown tired. He spits, puts his hands behind his back, and stands still awhile. All at once he says, making as if to go:

"Yes, it's a thumping eight-oar: I wouldn't mind if it were mine!

But here I am standing wasting your time."

The men become wide-awake.

"You're not wasting our time," answers one.

"No, far from it," answers the other too.

And now the men reckon with much probability that if they do not reveal the secret themselves, the other two fellows who are up the river may soon come and do it; might not one of them, for example, easily make an excuse for going to one of the cottages, beg for a drink of water and then tell whom he was carrying the fur coat for!

So one of the strangers asks:

"Then maybe the man we are rowing is not known here in your parts?"

"No," answers Lars and stares.

The children stare too.

"No, I saw that," says the other stranger, breaking in. He looked as though he were standing on hot bricks. "But it will surprise you to hear," he adds.

By this time Lars was consumed by curiosity. Besides, the annoying thing was that his neighbour, Bertel of Sagvika, had grown tired of waiting, and he too was coming now sauntering down over the fields.

"Well, then, it's not the County Magistrate?" asked Lars.

"No," answered the men.

"But I am sure he's some sort of bigwig, since he is so fat?"

"Yes," answered the men, "he's something like a man."

Lars waited a little, then at last he thought he might go. For there came Bertel, and he had no mind to share the secret with him.

"Good day to you!" says Lars.

"And yet he's no more nor less than a man from our own parish,

I might almost say," continues one of the strangers.

The other stranger joins in again:

"A boyhood's comrade of ours, I may call him."

"Well, well," says Lars.

"Yes, we can say that without lying. To be sure, he's not exactly from our district, but— There are a couple of parishes between us, but— But we know many of his people. He has been away these thirty years."

The other stranger feels himself outdistanced; determined to make up his leeway, he makes a bold bid:

"He went away from home when he was only a child. He was in all manner of foreign lands, and he came to Australia and he came to America. Then he married and made himself a big business. Then he found gold."

From now on the boatmen run neck and neck watching jealously each other's every word.

"How now, you're in such a tearing hurry, Jon," says one of them, annoyed, correcting his comrade; "he was in China too, though!"

"Yes, where hasn't he been?" replies the other. "Why, he was hanging to the bottom of a boat for several days—I don't remember what country he was in then."

"That was when he went to sea, that was when he was a boy. But I'm speaking now of later years."

"You needn't bother to tell me anything about that; I know it just as well as you do. He was on the bottom of a boat for days; ask him and you'll hear. Queer that I can't remember where it was."

"It was in an unknown land. But he got his wife in Mexico."

"Well, do you think I don't know that?"

"What's his name?" asks Lars Manuelsen.

"He calls himself—"

"Holmengraa!"* strikes in the other in a flash.

"He is that Tobias that left his home," the first one hurries to explain. "Haven't you heard of a boy who went out into the world and made himself a king?"

Now it was out!

Lars Manuelsen gasps for breath and stares. As if he hadn't heard of Tobias, the fisherboy from a little grey holm in Ytterleia, the boy who had left the country ages ago, had become a great king somewhere, had been exalted by God and men, and never came back again! And now he was here!

The children had heard the legend too. They stood there listening to the men, with mouths wide open.

"What! Him, Tobias!" says Lars Manuelsen. "And his father's name was Tobias too, so I've heard?"

"No, his father's dead," answers Jon. "His mother is dead too now, but they say he has a sister who lives in Bergen."

"Yes, his father's name was Tobias," says the other boatman emphatically, correcting his comrade again. "But anyhow he calls himself Holmengraa now and nothing else."

"Mercy on us!" says Lars.

He glances up towards Bertel, who has come uncomfortably near now. Lars still has time to put the most important questions, and the boatmen answer alternately.

"So he's married? Has he his wife with him?"

"No, she's not with him. She is left behind in a foreign land."

"Yes, she has been left in distant foreign parts."

"I suppose she's a fine lady, then? What's her name?"

*Translator's note: Holmengraa = the grey holm. The pronunciation of graa (grey) *approximately* = English "grow."

"That's what I can't say, but she is—"

"She's dead," says the other man, and puts an end to the matter.

"Good gracious, is she dead? Has he no children?"

"He has two children, quite small, a boy and a girl."

"You needn't talk about them being so small, Jon, for the girl is a good many years old."

"Yes, well! but the boy is little. That's what I'm telling you."

Here comes Bertel. Lars manages to ask at the last moment:

"Where has he got his children? What are their names? What's he doing up the river?"

"He told me that he only wanted to have a look round."

"He told me that too."

The boatmen repeated this once or twice in different words, agreeing, each time.

"It was grand, the way he was dressed?" says Lars.

The men shake their heads in awe:

"Yes, he has furs and velvets too, a plenty."

"He says he freezes in our cold country and can't keep warm."

Bertel does not offer any greeting, but just listens. And he has the longest of ears.

"Who is it you're talking about?" he asks.

The boatmen do not answer, but continue to address Lars and to tell about the wealth of the king, of the bank-notes with which he paid for the boat, of his pocket-book. "Mercy on us!" says Lars Manuelsen.

"Are you rowing some one?" asks Bertel.

The boatmen look him up and down, spit, and answer yes, they have a fare. Whereupon they turn again to Lars and talk and shake their heads and think and hold forth about the rich gentleman.

"Ay, a man might almost say, I and Jon here are nothing but bits of trash to what he is. And yet we grew up by the same sea."

"Yes, that's how things go in the world," agrees Jon.

Bertel turns to Lars now, and asks:

"Who are they talking about?"

But Lars has no time, not a moment; he seems not to hear Bertel's question, and says suddenly:

"Well, I'm sure I've hindered you long enough now."

And with that he goes.

And now it is Bertel's turn to worm out the secret. How he burns with curiosity, and how the two boatmen torment him!

At first Lars walked at his usual pace up over the fields, he felt ashamed to run. But little by little his speed increased, and about half-way he turned off to Ole Johan's cottage; that was the quickest way. Lars is bursting, he is big with mystery, he knows more than any of the folk in the cottages up above; if he husbands the secret he may be an important personage well on into the day. He already sees a couple of women up at Ole Johan's cottage waiting for him.

But when Lars arrives it turns out that the children have forestalled him, the brats from his own and his neighbours' houses, the long-eared, ragged pack, and his own Lars, the big, ugly lout, along with them. And now these same children were going from house to house and spoiling the whole thing, led by his own son. A pretty business!

Ole Johan met Lars and asked:

"Who was it they had on board?" And when Lars was just beginning to put on airs of mystery, Ole Johan demanded straight out: "Is it true that it's Tobias, the one who went off and made himself a king?"

❧

A couple of hours later there was a crowd of people down by the white eight-oar; they were intent upon getting a glimpse of the fairy-tale king when he went on board again. The women had even tidied themselves and put shawls on; among them Daverdana, so wild and red-headed, so big and young, even a king might look at her.

Ah! but they were all nicely sold!

When the three wanderers came back from the waterfall, the two boatmen went down to the boat with the fur coat right enough, but the gentleman himself turned off the main road and made for the manor-house, for Segelfoss, for the Lieutenant's. And you could not tell from his looks that he had no business there.

He was no light and nimble walker, so it took time; he carried his hat in his hand. The man was far from romantic to look at; he wore new clothes, and had a thick gold chain round his neck. He was like any ordinary man otherwise; had a pale face and sharp features, with full beard, straight nose, and a quantity of wrinkles round his eyes. He might be pretty well on in the forties. Upon his right hand he wore a small, plain gold ring. His hair was thick. His stoutness was confined to his stomach, which was unhealthily fat; his thighs and calves were thin.

When he got to the manor he looked round and chose the back way, the way by the kitchen, though there were two great flights of stone steps in the front of the house. He greeted a girl he met, asked if Herr Holmsen was at home, and handed her his card.

The Lieutenant came out and stood still a moment. The stranger bowed and said:

"I do not know whether I may be allowed to pay my respects. I should quite understand if you said no."

This was modesty indeed; the man had chosen, too, to take up

"Was that when l was with you?" asked little Willatz.

"Yes. We do not go there any more, unfortunately."

The Lieutenant fumbles and fumbles with something, with his hands in his lap; he is changing his ring on to his left hand.

"I don't even remember whether it was fun there," says Willatz.

"Hush! No dear, you were little then. Don't you remember they let you play with grandfather's sword of honour?"

"No."

"Fru Holmsen's father is an officer?" asks Holmengraa.

"A colonel. His promotion stopped at colonel. Everything is stopped at home now, of course."

"I have heard of the great changes in Hanover," said Holmengraa. "I have never been there. It is a rich and beautiful country!"

"Yes, a rich and beautiful country."

"And Fru Holmsen's father resigned?"

"Well, Colonel Moritz von Platz was not old and had distinguished himself. But he was one of those who felt themselves too old to enter—what shall I say?—alien service."

The Lieutenant asked:

"But does what you have now seen of Norway give you the impression of things having gone forward or back, Herr Holmengraa?"

"Forward. Distinctly forward. All countries are advancing. People live in bigger houses, they have more livestock, they live better. And as we know, the population has increased too. However, I have not seen much of the country yet; I got an English steamer to call in at Trondhjem with me. And I took the chance of a passage north from Trondhjem in a coasting vessel. Yes, the statistics show the country is going ahead."

"The statistics?"

"I mean, judging by the returns of quantities and weights, the increase of population has enforced a little more cultivation, a little more care. Whether it has made the people much more efficient in themselves, I do not know."

"It would be a bad lookout if it had not."

"Here in the north, it seems to me the progress is least. New people have grown up, but they are remarkably like the old ones; they go about with their hands in their pockets; they are true Nordlanders."

"Yes, they go about with their hands in their pockets," repeats Fru Holmsen.

Holmengraa began to smile at a thought, at a recollection, and went on:

"When I wanted to hire a boat for my little excursions I could not get one. I was referred to Henriksen, the general trader at Utvaer. He had an eight-oar boat with a cabin, which was never used, but he would not hire it out. 'Will you sell the boat?' I asked. He thought I was joking, and answered yes, if he got two hundred dollars for it. So I bought the boat."

Fru Holmsen smiled, the Lieutenant smiled. Holmengraa continued:

"When I wanted boatmen, I could not get any. They lounged there in Henriksen's store and loitered about on his wharf with their hands in their pockets. They were ready enough to sail, but there was no wind, and they were not going to row. I knew my fellow-countrymen again."

"Had you not made yourself known?" asks the Lieutenant.

"I had thrown out hints, even more than enough, as I thought; but they evidently did not believe me. Then I said straight out that they would surely be willing to row an old acquaintance from the island, that my name was Tobias; didn't they remember me? But they looked me up and down and did not quite take my word for it. I knew my men again and I went home, rolled a whole lot of scarves round my waist to make myself stout, put other clothes on and hung this chain round my neck. I knew that if there is anything that will impress the Nordlanders, it is fatness and grand clothes and finery. The weather was so warm that I did not see how I was going to stand it, but all the same I put my fur coat on as well. When I burst upon them rigged out like that, they looked at me with very different eyes and I got my boatmen."

Here the whole table laughed. A wily trick, to be sure!

"And you really believe that it was the change in your dress that got you the boatmen?"

"I am certain of it, Madam. As you know, these people had heard a lot of wonderful tales about me for years past—that I had grown so powerful, that I had grown so rich, that I was next-door to a king, and must I not look fat and rich then? When I came in furs and gold chain, I was Tobias from the Holm, I was acknowledged at once. In much the same way a Negro king, alone of all his tribe, wears a cooking-pot upon his head, though the rest of him is naked. One has to do with children; the Nordlanders are children."

"I suppose there was a great to-do when the people at last realized who you were?"

"It was anything but pleasant for me. People came from all quarters; they wanted to see me; they came with tin pails and with sacks; they begged for money and souvenirs; all wanted something. Some remembered me when I was a child, all knew my sister who was the last of us to live on the island, most of them were related to her and consequently to me. One woman wanted help for a burial, a man wanted timber for a cowhouse; a boy came with his father, the lad had been caught thieving, and I was to get him off—"

"Well, I never heard—!"

"Yes, Madam, you may believe those were busy days for me. However, I managed to damp down the madness at last; it got abroad that I was not giving so tremendously much away, that I had not provided myself with more than a million in my pocket-book, and consequently must limit myself somewhat until my proper supply of money arrived; that was on the way, in fifty cases, and each case with four locks. In short, I was in the old land—not the land of work and industry, but of romance. I felt I was at home again."

The Lieutenant had listened attentively and politely; latterly he had glanced several times at Holmengraa's thick chain. Had he not noticed it before? Or had a doubt occurred to him as to whether it was gold? It would be just like this pernickety little man to harbour such a suspicion and perhaps feel a little disapproval in consequence.

"Well, have we finished—?" he said and rose.

The lady was in a good humour, and accompanied the gentlemen into the garden-room. Coffee was served, old and valuable silver shone again in the stranger's eyes, and the liqueur was of the best. The windows looked out on the same view.

Little Willatz cried out at the sight of all the people down by the sea: "Come and look!"

His mother joined him.

"What a crowd of people!" she said. "What can be the matter?" And she did not take warning from the tone of her husband's reply: "They are standing gaping at Herr Holmengraa's eight-oar!" His wife was amused, she laughed: "Good gracious, they are standing looking at your boat, Herr Holmengraa, they are waiting for you! You will have a great reception down there!"

Holmengraa joined the lady and looked out too, smiling and shaking his head. But he said not a word about the crowd and not a word of the reception; he admired the view again, the river foaming on its downward course, the landscape. He turned to the Lieutenant and expressed the dizzy ambition to acquire a little land hereabouts.

The Lieutenant had no objection to his wife's hearing talk of the glories of Segelfoss, but he was careful not to overstress the note.

"Do you think it such a fine place?" said he.

"Yes!—oh, yes! I took a walk up to the fall," said Holmengraa, "a beautiful fall, a most refreshing walk. My sickness seemed to leave me."

"You must live here!" cried the lady. "You must certainly build yourself a house and live here! Then you will get well again!"

Holmengraa said:

"If Lieutenant Holmsen will sell me a plot of ground."

They all looked at the Lieutenant, a shade of surprise passed across his Arabian features, he bent his head and thought.

"I am sure that can easily be arranged," said the lady.

The Lieutenant remarked with a smile:

"My wife makes an exception of you, Herr Holmengraa. She is usually so averse to parting with any of Segelfoss."

"Yes, with any of the forest. That's another matter," interposed his wife. "My father says the same."

Oh, this lady, singer and player though she was, was not a German housewife for nothing. She had sound common sense, she had brains, she had knowledge of the world.

"And I suppose you are the only one who does not now regret that your father—that farms and forest-lands were sold in his time," she added.

She had overstepped the limit.

"I do *not* regret those sales!" answered the Lieutenant.

Pause. The lady smoothed little Willatz's hair and chatted with him.

"Ah! forest, I did not mean that."—Holmengraa shook his head as if overcome by the idea—"I would never think of that. But a plot of ground anywhere you liked, a little bit of land up above by the river—"

That did not sound so bad. Here was a sick man with a reasonable wish; maybe there was some money to be made out of it too, and that would not come amiss. Why was his wife there just then? Why did she not leave them? Did she think he sold bits of land because he needed to?

"Naturally I would not oppose your attempt to regain your health here," said the Lieutenant. "If that is your idea?"

"I must admit that it occurred to me as I was coming down by the river a while ago," said Holmengraa. "The scent of the pines was so strong and good, one seemed to breathe more easily. It might be worth a trial, I thought. And of course there's something tempting to a man from the little grey holm in the idea of a cottage on Segelfoss," he added, smiling modestly.

You may be sure the Lieutenant sat there taking note of both words and expression; he asked:

"Are there no pine-forests in Mexico?"

And Herr Holmengraa answered without hesitation:

"Yes. But not where I live."

Nothing more was said on the subject. When Herr Holmengraa had drunk his coffee and sat awhile, he took his leave with the most cordial thanks for his kind reception. "Come again soon!" said his hostess.

The Lieutenant had his horse saddled, and accompanied his guest down the road; he was going to take a ride.

But now something happened. The crowd of people down by the sea had waited patiently for King Tobias up till now; but at the moment when he at length appeared, first one, then several, and at last all of them stole away over the fields to their homes. It was so unreasonable, when you came to think of it, so senseless: the whole, long time of waiting thrown away! What could be the reason of it? The good cottagers and tenants had not reckoned on the Lieutenant coming with him, the Lieutenant himself; but there he was, on horseback as usual, while King Tobias was on foot, and moreover his fur coat had been sent in advance. At this time Lieutenant Willatz Holmsen was a man it was as well not to offend in any way; he was a gentleman born and bred, and one did not stand in the middle of his path and take no notice when he came.

"I could fancy somewhere up there, on the other side of the river," said Holmengraa pointing.

"What do you mean? Oh, the site. Yes, we can no doubt arrange about that, in case—"

"I thank you. It is worth a trial. And as regards price, I will leave that entirely to your discretion."

They went on together a little further, till Holmengraa had to turn off towards the sea. He took off his hat and thanked the Lieutenant heartily for a pleasant day. The gentlemen parted.

But as the Lieutenant rode on he thought: Was that all, was that the whole fairy-tale? A sick man who wanted a bit of ground for a cottage, perhaps a hut, or whatever it might turn out to be. Just an ordinary and a modest man; he made no unpleasant impression. His table manners were remarkably good.

V

It would seem that the Lieutenant was right after all; the girl Marcilie had no need of a doctor. It was merely the others who had made a great ado about her being out of sorts, and had put her to bed. She was about again the next day, set the master's rooms in order, helped with the washing up, put candles in the chandeliers and candlesticks all through the house, beat carpets, saw to the stoves—Marcilie slipped about upstairs and down over the whole of the north wing. And in the evening what must she do but go up the master's stairs again?

The Lieutenant is lying on a sofa smoking.

Marcilie curtsies—this her master had probably taught her. It was prettily done, and so he gives her a friendly nod in return. Marcilie knows beforehand what she has to do here; she goes up to her master and stands in front of him. This is prettily done too. A young girl is a young girl; when she touches a thing she does it gently and prettily. She looks at one, and not in vain; the look tells. A young girl's glance always tells.

Marcilie takes the book from the table. Her hands were of the kind which can bend back a little, but they were large and swollen with doing much washing; no veins were to be seen on the backs of her hands.

"Perhaps you are not well enough to read this evening," says the

Lieutenant, raising himself so as to face her.

"Oh, yes, indeed," answers Marcilie with plenty of spirit.

She finds her seat under a special sconce with two candles and sits down. Then she begins to read, blushing and a little bashful at first, but gradually reading better and better. At difficult words she wrinkles her brow and looks troubled; when a fairly long piece goes easily and smoothly her face clears and becomes calm again. Her master has stretched himself out at length again, perhaps fancying that this makes him seem quite the pasha. He lies so that he can follow the girl's changing expression, and this seems to please him; when Marcilie wrinkles her brow, he sometimes wrinkles his own in sympathy. He has not instituted this short hour's reading aloud every other evening in order to teach Marcilie to read; he does not correct her once; no doubt he thinks it not worth while. But he does not fail to notice that her reading improves steadily, so she probably practises by herself between times. He has instituted the reading-hour for his own enjoyment, simply and solely. What a pasha, what an egoist!

No doubt he is past the age when he might count upon amiability from a woman for his own sake; and, as he cannot get it in the house in any other way and he cannot do without it altogether, does he buy it every other evening from his maid, from a menial? It must be so. One does the best one can for oneself.

"The customs of the Trausians resemble in other respects those of the rest of the Thracians," reads Marcilie from a translation of Herodotus, "except in what concerns newborn babes and the dead. Thus, when a child is born, the relations, who are assembled on such an occasion, enumerate all the ills to which human nature is subject and lament the sad fate which of necessity awaits the child in this life. When, on the other hand, any one dies, they give vent to their joy as they commit him to the earth and rejoice that he has been so fortunate as to be released from so many tribulations."

She reads further that "the other Thracians have a custom of selling their children on condition that they must not remain in the country. Over their daughters they do not watch, but with their wives they are, on the contrary, very strict, look after them carefully, and buy them at great cost from their parents. They have themselves marked with signs or brands, and with them this is a proof of noble birth; whoever is not so distinguished, they look upon as of low descent. In their eyes there is nothing so admirable as idleness, nothing so honourable as war and rapine, and nothing so despicable as agriculture. These are their most remarkable customs—"

The time passes, Marcilie reads on, the Lieutenant is enjoying himself. Now and again he glances out into the room; a great mirror hangs on the opposite wall, and perhaps this attracts his eyes, perhaps it is the back of the girl's head he wishes to see, perhaps it pleases the pasha. Or is it, perhaps, something else? Has it dawned upon him that the whole situation, this girl reading, and reading Herodotus, is comical and makes himself ridiculous? Not at all. Nothing that *he* has hit upon can be ridiculous. Such a thing has not occurred to him. He is enjoying himself, his eyes wander hither and thither, and he blinks in a peaceful and friendly way.

Here, in this room, he has collected many of the trifles that little Willatz has grown too big for; here are his very first tiny pair of shoes of green morocco leather, a rag-doll, rattles, balls, reels, pine-cones. A cardboard alphabet has its place upon the wall as if it were a costly painting. With all this before his eyes and with a young girl to read aloud for him, a man of his age should surely rest satisfied.

Or should he not?

The pasha rises and Marcilie closes the book; he wants a change, no doubt. Marcilie puts back the book in its place and brings out a parlour game, no more nor less than a draught-board and men. What a pastime for a Willatz Holmsen! Then they sit down to play.

But now the girl Marcilie becomes still more bashful. The Lieutenant is such a master at the game, he makes his moves with hardly a moment's thought, and when he is waiting for hers, he sits and looks at her. Now and again of an evening when they have been playing and she has happened to raise her eyes, she has met his. Now, was that worthy of a Willatz Holmsen?

They play a few games and he lets her win. What a strange, narrow field for his mental life, an occupation like this! "If you make that move I shall win!" he says. She starts and is about to take it back, their hands touch, their breath mingles; they play the game out, but he is certainly not quite himself, he breathes hard. A couple of his men fall to the floor in front of him and she stoops to get them, now—now, with that strangely Arab-like look on his face, what if the table were to upset?

"Thank you, that will do!" he says, getting up.

She clears the things away, and puts them back in their places; she goes to the door and curtsies.

"Oh, yes!" he says. "Hm! When Daverdana comes to-morrow tell her what she has to do."

"Yes."

"Bring her here and show her what to do."

"Yes."

"That is all."

This was the last evening with Marcilie.

But many a time had the girls down in the kitchen discussed among themselves these evening readings in the Lieutenant's study.

"What in the world do they do in there?" says the housekeeper.

"Isn't it a queer notion of them!"

Oh, that housekeeper—she is full of queer notions herself, and when she makes an audacious remark she has to twist her mouth to keep in her laughter. She is from the West-country, and is "over" twenty, and her name is Jomfru Kristine Salvesen. But God help her if the Lieutenant should some day hear one of her audacities!

"Do you think they sit and look at each other?" she says. "Marcilie says that she reads aloud from a book, answers one of the parlour-maids.

"Reads?"

"So she says."

The housekeeper's mouth twists as she says:

"To be sure, they read. They spell and lay their heads together."

"Ho, ho, ho!" all the girls double up with laughter, holding their hands to their mouths.

❧

As it is a summer evening and the sun is still shining, the Lieutenant goes out again, wanders about, looking at things. Since he is the soul of order, he looks up, not only at his own windows, but also at his wife's—they are open, voices can just be heard from within, his wife is talking to some one. Since he is the soul of order, it would be better if his wife did not speak quite so loud to the doctor.

"But the girl is up again?" she says.

And the doctor replies:

"Up again? Then I must have exaggerated the danger a little, Madam—in order that I might come again to-day."

The Lieutenant goes down the garden. There is a fountain there which his father set up; the jet of water rises into the air and flashes in the sunshine like a bowed steel blade. He gazes across the big garden, down across the fields, out over the sea. A strange boat with its crew lies at the jetty; no doubt it is the doctor's boat. There is a shimmer of light on the smooth and leaden fiord, all is quiet as before a thunderstorm, far away against the mountains lies a dark cloud, violet, with a broad edge of gold. It seems trying to turn a golden lining outwards.

The Lieutenant goes over to the garden wall; he hears steps behind him, but does not turn. Since he is the soul of order, he locks the garden gate and takes the key from the lock.

"Heigh!" some one calls behind him. "Don't lock it, sir. One moment—"

One does not shout "Heigh!" to a Willatz Holmsen. The Lieutenant turns slowly.

"Excuse me, Lieutenant. I have been to see the patient, the servant girl," says the doctor. As the Lieutenant only stares at him he takes his hat off, and says: "Good evening. The girl made a quick recovery," he says.

"Yes, she is up again. She is well," answers the Lieutenant.

"Yes."

"Yes."

They look at each other. The Lieutenant begins to smile.

"Excuse me," says the doctor; "would you kindly let me out?" As the Lieutenant makes no motion towards opening, he asks half in joke and half in apprehension: "Or shall I get over the wall?"

"Only if it is quite convenient for you," answers the Lieutenant.

"Convenient—?"

"For if it is not, I will throw you over!"

The Lieutenant was clearly beside himself. He clutched the great door-key till his knuckles stood out white. The doctor looked up and down the wall, cast one last uncertain look at the Lieutenant, and made a few hasty bounds. Such a calm evening, such capital weather for climbing a wall!

When a little later the Lieutenant has calmed down and goes up to the house, his wife meets him in the doorway, his wife, Adelheid, is there standing at the door. He had nothing against her standing there, he greeted her. So be it, here she might see the man who had nodded to the girl Marcilie for the last time! He wore a friendly and superior air.

But she took it up wrongly, and said:

"I have been waiting for you, but you were out. You have been out walking about."

He answered:

"You are not in the habit of waiting for me of an evening; it is a very strange thing for you to do. Were you really waiting for me at so late an hour? Will you not come in?"

They went in.

"I have been waiting for you to ask you what sort of a fool this doctor is that you have brought here."

"Doctor? I do not know him. He is the District-doctor; he has been your doctor for ten years."

"For ten years. But not any more."

"Why so? I do not know him, but you surely do? Ole Riis—there is not much to say about him perhaps, but his sister Charlotte Helene, who was married to the Hungarian magnate Rodvanyi, had, I believe, an extraordinary fate. Has he not told you about her?"

"You are just putting me off with talk."

"I am merely saying what I know. I have not troubled my head further about the little ignorant self-satisfied person."

"Yes, you are just putting me off with talk, Willatz. I wanted to ask something of you, but now that I think of it—"

What had come over Fru Adelheid? She was so agitated; she suddenly threw her arms round her husband and said:

"Oh, why are you like this? I beg for your forgiveness!"

To her great surprise he did not respond to her tenderness any more. He stood there stiff and turned away his head.

Then she released him and, wavering to one side, sank into a chair.

Most likely she did not understand what all this meant, did not realize that she had worked mischief between them past repair, that his patience had at last broken down, and his stubborn will had taken its place.

She only felt her humiliation.

"Why did you come in then?" she said.

"To hear what you had to say," he replied. "For that reason only."

Ah, now it was he who had the upper hand; and he was using it. She felt this and answered:

"I have nothing more to say."

"You cannot mean that?"

"Would you like to know what I wanted to say?" she asked, rising abruptly. "The doctor—I wanted to ask you to tell that boor that we have no further use for his services. Now you know."

"Hm!" said the Lieutenant.

"But, I suppose, you do not care to do that."

"I cannot," replied her husband with insufferable superiority, "I cannot imagine a more agreeable task."

But, irritated by his tone, she cried:

"You will not do it though. I am sure you will not."

"You are speaking wildly."

"I know you," she continued excitedly. "You always ride at a walking pace, you won't expose yourself to any risk. It is a characteristic of yours. But as you will. Good night!"

He carried his malicious self-command so far as to say, as she reached the door:

"At dinner a day or two ago you mentioned that you would be glad to pay a visit to the home of your childhood again. There is no objection to this on my part—in any case the money will be forthcoming—now as before."

Pause.

"Very well. Thank you."

But this proposal of her husband's filled her with confusion, and she left the room with head bent, and with long quick steps, that she might be alone before she burst out sobbing.

But the Lieutenant changed his ring on to his right hand again.

VI

Little Willatz has grown tall and sturdy—quite a big boy; he is good at singing and piano-playing, but wild and headstrong; it is no longer easy to manage him; he does as he likes, and shirks his mother's lessons.

His father had long been exercised about him; the idea of a teacher such as he himself had in his boyhood, a private tutor with some book-learning and nothing more, was a horror to him. This teacher from some country parish or other would be always about the rooms at Segelfoss; he would eat at their table and be one of the family; a teacher during the day, he would spend his nights grinding at his continuation studies in divinity or law. The Lieutenant knew the kind of man; he could not talk with such people, their whole cast of thought was different, they had an inherited culture—only acquired book-learning.

The Lieutenant thought of England; that was the country for his son, the right training-ground, the land of wealth. If only he could afford to send him there! Afford? Had he not already been at the expense of sending Lars Manuelsen's long lout to Tromsö and of keeping him there, and was his own son to rust at home! And, moreover, was he, the Lieutenant, to be so far outdone by old Coldevin who in his time had sent his son Fredrik to school at Saint-Cyr?

The Lieutenant broods and broods over the question.

But little Willatz does not brood. For a year past he has been used to play with his neighbour Julius, Lars Manuelsen's second son, and these two have blissful days together. Little Willatz has even dragged Julius up the backstairs to his own room and shown him all sorts of things, and painted in water-colours with him. Julius was new and wonderful to him in no end of ways; and besides, Julius compelled a vast deal of respect by reason of having much bigger hands and feet—they had of course at once measured. In front of Willatz's bed lay a strip of carpet—"Take care! you are treading on the cloth!" said Julius. "What?" said Willatz in surprise. But when Willatz happened to tread on the carpet again, Julius took it up, shook it, and laid it on the bed. "What are you doing that for?" said Willatz. "You know you oughtn't to be bad and step on it," said Julius.

The two comrades had bedaubed themselves well with paints, and when Willatz washed both face and hands in cold water, Julius stood and looked at him pityingly. "Are you not going to wash yourself?" said Willatz. "No, we must hurry now," said Julius, "for the tide is coming in."

Julius was nervous and begged Willatz to go down the stairs quietly; if they met no one else they might meet Daverdana, and the truth is Daverdana had slapped her brother more than once at home. At Julius' suggestion, Willatz is to go down first, and if all is safe he is to cough in the passage down below. Willatz goes. Julius returns to the room and takes an india-rubber ball which he has seen among the other things in there, thinking, no doubt, they will have a use for the ball outside. Then Willatz coughs and Julius steals down.

Then they went down to the sea and found starfish and shells and bladderworts. And after that they built a stone house and a cowshed on the beach and drove cattle into the cowshed; the cattle were all kinds of shells. The cows were painted, some with spots, others with stripes; the paint was crushed brick and spittle. Dear me! how keen they were over all this, though both were big boys now.

Then Julius felt hungry and wanted to go home. But were they to part now just when they were having most fun? Willatz remembered with a start that he had forgotten his dinner at home; how should he have remembered it when he hadn't felt a bit hungry? It was in for a penny, in for a pound, now; he went home with Julius.

"Such a visitor as you've got with you!" says his mother to Julius; "You must come in and try to find a seat, Willatz. Come and get something to eat, Julius. Where have you two been?"

"I've been home with Willatz," answers Julius.

"Home with Willatz? But you weren't in the house, I am sure."

"Wasn't I? We sat and painted drawings. Just you ask Willatz himself!"

"Good gracious!" says his mother and is as proud as any lady. Her daughter, Daverdana, was servant girl at Segelfoss already and now Julius has been inside the house too.

Julius manipulates herring and potato with great dexterity without knife or fork. His plate is square and wooden. Everything is most remarkable. Willatz begins all at once to feel frightfully hungry.

"You seem to have very good herring and potatoes," he says.

"Well, it is nothing to complain about; if we could only always have enough of it!" answers the woman. "Now, if we only had something to give Willatz! Could you eat a slice of rye-bread, do you think? No! I don't suppose you could."

"Oh, yes, I could, thanks," answers Willatz. For his hunger had become something unheard of.

The woman butters a thick slice of bread. Then she crushes some brown sugar-candy with a bottle and sprinkles it on the bread.

"There now, you must see if you can manage to get that down, such as it is."

Willatz ate. Willatz had never had a better piece of bread and butter in his life. Bread with caraway seeds in it and crushed candy on it was a hitherto unknown delicacy for him. He would ask his mother to introduce it at home.

Then the boys were off outside again, and they hit upon all sorts of jolly games. This Julius was a grand fellow, a real find for Willatz; he was very bright and was great at inventing all sorts of schemes, and besides he swore horribly and knew such a lot. They had climbed up on to the roof of the tile-works, and now the question was how to get down again. It was a case of going backwards and feeling their way with their feet; they tried many times in vain, till at last Willatz got tired of it, and jumped down. He landed unhurt and now gallantly offered to catch his comrade when he came. But Julius would not jump, he was just going to several times, but always gave it up. "It isn't because I'm afraid," said Julius, "but I might kill myself!" At last he tried the first way again, crawling down backwards; and when he had come a little way he asked: "Is it far yet?" "No," answered Willatz, "it is hardly any distance, let yourself go!" There Julius hung a long time, but he did not let go; then he began to crawl upwards on the roof again, but gave that up too; he seemed to lose all hope, began to cry, and said he could not hang any longer. "Just let go!" shouted Willatz. Then Julius shut his eyes and let go.

"There, you see it was nothing much!" said Willatz. But Julius had hit himself some nasty knocks, and now that he was out of the wood he grew angry and swore big oaths. "Just you see how I have hurt myself," said Julius, and showed his bruises and bumps. "I can tell you that was a tremendous height to tumble from!"

But what was this? The ball had fallen out of Julius' pocket and lay there between them.

"Have you got a ball like that too?" asks Willatz.

"Ball? It must have been lying here before," answers Julius. But suddenly he thinks better of it and admits that he brought the ball so that they might have something to play with.

Then they play at ball, then they catch pollacks, and then they caper about like young colts. The common is wide and the skies are high above them; their laughter and shouts are shrill as the cries of the sea-gulls. Then the ball gets lost, in the grass, among the stones, quite unaccountably lost. They search and search; no, no ball is to be seen. So there is nothing to be done but to give it up.

And now from one of the neighbouring houses little Gottfred comes on to the common. He had no doubt heard of the grand society Julius was in and came quietly and bashfully to take his share of it. "There's that Gottfred!" whispered Julius jumping up; "let's run away." So they ran. And Gottfred was so taken aback by this that he came no nearer, but began to pluck some grass, and at last he sat down on the ground and went on plucking at the grass.

"Why should we run away?" asks Willatz.

"Well, I'll tell you," answered Julius. "If there's any one I don't want to have anything to do with, it's that fellow Gottfred. That's all I say."

Willatz had no idea what this meant, but Gottfred became all the more interesting for it.

"His mother steals sea birds' eggs from the nesting-ground."

But even this did not make Gottfred any the less interesting; there was a mystic attraction about a boy with such a mother. To divert attention from Gottfred, Julius says:

"What do you think happens in their mothers' bodies to all the lambs that don't get born?"

This puzzles Willatz completely. He had never sat so open-mouthed before.

Whereupon Julius says:

"Well, when a sheep does not have lambs, the lambs rot inside her."

"Really," says Willatz; "do they rot?"

"Yes. We had a sheep that it happened to.—There now, just look at Gottfred; he has sat down on the ground. What the devil is the little beast sitting there for?"

But now he catches sight of something else, a horseman up on the road, the Lieutenant.

"There's your father coming!" he whispers. And, without a moment's hesitation, he slinks off.

Willatz found himself left standing alone, even Gottfred, away yonder on the common, had seen the Lieutenant and seemed to shrink together and grow even smaller than he was before. So Willatz has no choice—he must go and meet his father.

"Is that you?" says his father and reins in his horse. "You forgot your dinner to-day. Whom were you with?"

"With Julius."

"What Julius?"

"Julius. I don't know. He is from that cottage there," says Willatz, pointing.

"Go home and beg your mother's pardon," says his father and rides on.

VII

A week later comes Coldevin with his wife and son; they are grand people and have a warm reception at Segelfoss. Young Coldevin, Fredrik, was at this time a man of over forty, married and settled in one of the towns on the west coast; he was a merchant and French vice-consul. Fredrik Coldevin was well spoken of, he was so amiable and elegant; he parted his hair at the back and wore rings. The year before he had been particularly lucky. A French vessel had been brought into his port damaged and, apart from his having bought the cargo and having made a great profit on it, he had made quite a name for himself with the entertainments he had given in honour of the Frenchmen. The guests came masked, and there were blue grottos and fireworks; the serving-girls were dressed in short skirts and the town-band played outside the windows. When the officers' entertainment was over, the crew had theirs; the Consul made no distinctions: even a Negro from Algiers, who was among the crew, was included.

Fredrik Coldevin was quite willing to tell all about the happenings of the year before; yes, they had had great times, and the strangers were lively fellows. His schooling at Saint-Cyr had repaid itself.

"Strangely enough," says Fredrik Coldevin, "one of the waitresses married a joiner a few days after. It has just occurred to me."

"Was that so remarkable?"

"Oh, no. But this year she presented her husband with a boy, a mulatto."

Pause.

"I don't understand," says Fru Holmsen. "No, no one understands it," answers Fredrik Coldevin. "Our doctor does not understand it either."

"We too have had a visitor," interjects the Lieutenant. "Won't you tell them about him, Adelheid? Excuse me a moment."

With that the Lieutenant leaves the room.

He goes out into the courtyard; the girl Daverdana is standing there, and he says to her:

"You did not come yesterday evening; did you forget?"

"No, the mistress sent me on an errand," answered Daverdana.

"Where were you?"

"At the shoemaker's."

"Quite right, now I remember. I said myself that you were to go to the shoemaker. The boots needed mending."

"No, the mistress said they were only to be polished."

"Yes, and to be polished. Also to be polished."

And with this the Lieutenant went on. Perhaps he had no special errand to take him out of the room, but he went out all the same, he had so much to think about. The Lieutenant is in his best uniform to-day to do honour to his guests, so he does not go into the cowhouse or the stable, but he finds his way into the barn where he seeks a dark corner and stands still there for a time. He is not at all annoyed, quite the contrary; as he stands there he gives a nod of satisfaction. "Also to be polished!" he repeats and rubs his lean hands together. Before he goes back again he changes his ring on to his left hand, that he may remember something.

The girl Daverdana is still standing in the courtyard, and the Lieutenant says to her as he passes:

"Did you bring the boots back with you?"

"No," answers Daverdana, "I only left them there."

And the Lieutenant nods anew and seems still more pleased.

When he came into the parlour again the company was sitting occupied each with his own thoughts; the Consul had been the last to speak, and now he speaks again:

"I hear you have given audience to King Tobias and that he wants to buy land. That's right, sell him land."

The Lieutenant's answer was brief; he merely said:

"We thought—Adelheid and I—besides, he is a sick man. But you have probably heard about him too?"

Old Mrs. Coldevin wags her head, quite overcome, and answers: "Yes, I should think so."

"We have split into two camps," says the Consul: "father and mother on the one side and Fru Adelheid and I upon the other; and I'm sure little Willatz is on our side too, aren't you, Willatz? Yes, I knew you were. Well, then, we will sell the land!"

Old Coldevin sat deep in thought; he was a slow-moving old man and did not like changes of any kind. When Fru Holmsen had told about the King, about this Tobias Holmengraa who wanted to settle here side by side with the lord of the manor, he had looked hard in front of him and cautioned them, warned them against the sale: "No, don't do it!" said he. "Don't do it on any account!"

He repeated his warning now:

"If you go on selling and selling, what will be left of Segelfoss? Of course there will be plenty left, any amount of Segelfoss left," he hastened to add; "but in the end—the last Willatz Holmsen is not yet born, I take it."

"These are modern times, father," says the Consul. "These big properties do not pay, they only waste the owner's means. It is all right for those who have an accumulation of capital from past years upon which they can draw."

"I had no large accumulation of capital," answers his father. "What I should have had took wings and departed during the bad years and the war. But just for that reason—"

"Oh, yes, father, oh, yes, you had a lot. And since then you have inherited—"

Old Fru Coldevin gives her son a look and stops him.

"But just for that reason I will not part with an acre of my modest property; no, I will not."

"But, father, you are not making anything out of it."

"No, maybe not. Oh, no, I am not making anything out of it. Must one make a profit on everything?" asks the old man. "But if we drew in our boundaries now, your mother and I, if we were to sell and sell and got money and means in exchange, well, we would have nothing to look at but a few coins—no broad lands. And who would the people have to go to when anything happened, if they had not your mother and me any longer? Why, this spring Henrik—you know him—lost his cow. A good cow, in calf. Henrik, whom you rechristened, don't you remember?"

"I remember him. What about it?"

"No—that is all," says old Coldevin. "He came to your mother—"

Pause. As he says nothing more, Fru Coldevin says:

"Yes, and I went to your father."

Pause.

"But," objects the Consul laughing, "it would have been all the same whether you had given him money or a new cow."

"No, no," answer both the old people, shaking their heads, "he would have frittered the money away."

To smooth matters over, the Lieutenant says:

"There is no question in this case of any very large transaction; we promised to think about a plot of ground, enough for a cottage; and possibly nothing will come of it. Adelheid and I talked with the man about it; he was a sensible and modest fellow."

"I must say I took a liking to him," says his wife. "And then, he was sick and wished to try the air in the pine-forests."

With that the conversation dropped, and each sat and thought. But little Willatz, who loved change better than anything, had gone off into the drawing-room and was playing on the old-fashioned piano.

"Boom, boomboom, boombo," the Consul took up the air. "By the way, the said Henrik had no father, but his mother's name was Lisbet and the son was called Lisbet-Henrik. So I rechristened him Henri l'Isbet."

❧

Daily life at Segelfoss was quiet and monotonous. Fredrik Coldevin knew it through and through; it was not to his liking; but he made the best of it, and managed to have quite a good time. He and the Lieutenant had been friends from boyhood, and as the years passed the lady of the house had become his friend too. He talked and whistled and sang about the house and cracked a bottle or two with the Lieutenant in the evenings; even with the housekeeper, Jomfru Salvesen, he would chat sometimes through the open pantry window.

"Jomfru Salvesen, it is true that I have said How-do-you-do to you since I came, but I have never had the chance of speaking a serious word with you."

"A serious word, this year again?" asks Jomfru Salvesen laughing.

The Consul shakes his head:

"It is really serious with me this year. And I have come to make an end of it."

"You did that last year too, ha ha!"

"I write verses to her eyebrows and to her eyes. 'Her eyes are all my wealth,' I say—no, how did it go? If you only knew what I say of her eyes! Jomfru Salvesen, it is true then, that you have engaged yourself to some one else since I was here last year?"

"Well, what was I to do?" says Jomfru Salvesen, playing up to him, and screwing up her mouth. "You threw me over, Consul."

"I? How can you have the heart to be so faithless? That's why I say: 'Her eyes are her riches, she bribes all men with them.'"

"Fie! Consul."

"Can you wonder if I have gone clean out of my mind? Three years on the rack, and then I come and learn that you have given your promise to some one else. Oh, I ought never to have seen you —or what is it that Shakespeare says? You have much to answer for."

"Yes, you look thin and worn!"

"But that's the way with you women. I met a man on my way north—God knows if he wasn't a pastor somewhere or other. He had been sitting by his wife's deathbed, he said, and had had his three sons with him. He owned to two of them, they were like him, he thought, but the youngest, the small and puny one, he could not bear. Then his wife said: 'He is your son!' and the man dropped as though he had been shot. After a time he pulls himself together and asks: 'And not the others?' His wife does not answer. 'And not the others—not the others? Do you hear?' he repeats. His wife was dead."

The Consul and Jomfru Salvesen look at each other.

"Ugh!" she said and shuddered.

"Put yourself in this man's place, Jomfru Salvesen: all his life long he will go about asking: 'Not the others?' he will never get an answer."

Pause.

"Bring the man here and I'll answer him!" suddenly said Jomfru Salvesen full of animation. "The mother was naturally afraid for the last child and so she says—she was just about to die and she wished to help the smallest—you must remember that he was the smallest, poor little fellow, and besides he was under suspicion already—I have never heard anything so wicked! And so she says—"

The Consul waits.

"She only did it to help the smallest one a little," cries Jomfru Salvesen. "Don't you understand that?"

The Consul nods. He yields to this good-hearted faith:

"Just what I told the man: 'Hold your tongue,' I said to him—"

"Ha, ha, ha! Yes, you might well say that. He had his answer that time!" Jomfru Salvesen grows downright good-looking and flushed from sheer good-hearted faith.

The Consul retreats still further. He had perhaps gone a little too far just now, and now he makes up for it:

"Just what I said to the man, partly in your very words. Almost exactly word for word. And that makes me think of how well we could have got on together, Jomfru Salvesen, if only you had not been so faithless. So now I shall have to go about all alone, asking: 'What is life, then? what, in Satan's name, is life?'"

"I do believe you are going crazy!" cries the housekeeper, shrieking with laughter. "Ugh, I am laughing so that my hairnet is falling off," she says, putting the net straight and preening herself a little.

"Is that straight now?"

"Oh, yes, quite," answers the Consul. "Oh, when you stretch your arms up like that and give me such a good chance—"

"Now, my dear Consul, *can't* you be serious?"

"What a waist you have! I really ought to come in and lift you in my arms."

And goodness knows if he did not come near to going in, for the housekeeper only said:

"Yes, that would be a fine sight! What 1f the mistress were to come!"

But he stayed outside after all and brought their talk to a close with a few well-turned phrases. Jomfru Salvesen asked after his wife and children: were they never coming to Segelfoss again?

But the Consul talked mostly with Fru Adelheid. He told her droll stories, and experiences he had had since he had been here last; he was courteous and entertaining. The lady's spirits rose and she dressed more and more becomingly as the days passed—Fredrik Coldevin himself was so gay and elegant. And it was not as if his talk was mere chit-chat and flummery; not at all: he gave vent to opinions and advanced a philosophy of life—a philosophy which consisted in the view that one must go with the times.

Fru Adelheid liked to sit and listen to him. She was ultra-German in those days, and Consul Fredrik was French, but all the same—

"Why do you always speak of the Franco-German war?" she would ask. "It is the Germans who are winning, so it is the German-French war."

"Yes," answers the Consul, "it is the Prussians who are winning."

"The Teutons. Are we not all Teutons?"

"With the exception of the French, yes. But, dear Fru Adelheid, don't let us talk of that now. Yesterday I heard the wild swans trumpeting, far away; at times there were a number of swans trumpeting together so that it was like a chorus. It sounded so soft and yet so wild, I could not help thinking of you."

"Could you not?" says Fru Adelheid.

You see, she was not by any means a cold woman, as was clear when she played and sang for any one she cared for; for then she would throw back her head and let the hidden warmth find a vent in her song. Consul Fredrik had seen a good deal of her, and no doubt her singing echoed in his ears; he begged her to sing again.

"Yes, later," she said; "this evening, if you like."

"If you like!"

"But you must not thank me as you always do. It is I who have to thank you."

Fru Adelheid sat very quiet after these words, and made no attempt at concealment as the flush that had dyed her face slowly spread.

A silence followed. It was as though an *Ave* had sounded in their ears. Consul Fredrik was silent; this madcap, this jester sat still, gazing at the floor. And he had none of the air of a conqueror, not a smile, only a look of the deepest compassion.

Then the lady rose and left him.

Each of us has his destiny, and doubtless Fru Adelheid had hers. That was why she had a key to her door, that was why she had an indiscreet doctor turned out of her house, that was why she kept a diary.

VIII

When Consul Fredrik sat drinking and chatting with the Lieutenant far into the night, discussions were not to be avoided. Had not the Consul a philosophy of life? He had; but when he sat in an old, stately, luxurious apartment full of precious heirlooms, smoking cigars and drinking wine from Venetian glasses, enjoying, with a good friend he had known from childhood, an interchange of thought such as he sometimes had to do without for a year at a time in his fishing-town—then he would relapse into a different life from that which he usually lived. And in these circumstances, you see, he found it very hard to stand or fall by his philosophy. But what was he to do? Why, exaggerate, take revenge for all he had to swallow during the course of the year, come out with the most narrow-minded views, repeat with emphasis the same middle-class opinions he heard at home night and day—what else was there to do! His parents had at one time proposed to make a diplomat of him; it was for that reason that they had made him so proficient in French—he would take his oath that his own son Anton Bernhard Coldevin should not go into diplomacy either! What was this about hereditary instinct, a tinge of blue in the blood? Frippery, dreams—the devil take them all!

A cow for Henri l'Isbet? No, thank you, Monsieur, here is the money, hard cash, but you shall work it off on my wharf and you shall give me security on your cottage! The landowner is all right, the war did not take his land from him, nor his sofas and mirrors. Even his stoves are still there; some have silver ornaments, others have broad friezes with gilding on them. The war did not take the two hundred hill sheep, the boat-sheds with the boats and gear; there is much on a great estate which is left behind even if a war sweeps over it. And at the worst one can outlive it. Wait a little, stay a while, there are reserves, latent resources—in a few years we are on our feet again, we stand erect. Then father-in-law dies; God bless his soul, he was of the same caste, old and full of pride of race; he too was brought low, but got on his feet again. What then? The landowner inherits his property—inherits. Poor old father-in-law, God bless his soul once more. It is all right. The others, the working-men, businessmen, the day-labourers, go about showing their teeth at one another and fighting. That is life. They are really fighting over the old landowner, they are fighting over him who has something, they are fighting over his possessions.

The old landowner is the bone, the others are the dogs. But what does the bone do? When dogs fight for a bone, the bone just lies there, does not join in, does not mix itself in the fight. Oh, he is all right. But all the others must go with the times.

As to Consul Fredrik—oh, he very likely had troublesome reminders of his hereditary instincts often enough: but to the devil with dreams, here he stood or fell by his philosophy of life! At times he grows more vehement than need be; why? has he difficulty in keeping these dreams in leash? It is certainly not that his friend, the Lieutenant, does much to excite him; he is sparing of words, though so firmly of the opposite opinion that nothing moves him. Why, then, take the trouble to argue with him year after year, and get so worked up? Fredrik Coldevin had perhaps taken the wrong turning in this life, and now he was doing all he could not to be left alone, doing all he could to carry others with him? God only knows.

"I go so far that I will let my daughters marry whomever they like," said he. "Thea is eighteen years old, and was half engaged to the mate of a ship; what do you think of that? But that, I said, was going a little too far. Indeed, she understood that herself—'Willatz Holmsen and Fru Adelheid are among your godparents,' said I; 'you must have *some* consideration.' She saw that. 'But any one else you like,' said I. 'Fire away! I won't interfere!' Gerda has time enough before her; she is only fifteen years old. God bless me, we mix with the best people in our town, you know; it would be a pretty business if we didn't. All the officials, for example. The district-judge's family are people of culture, and my wife has a cousin who is a solicitor. Then there is the pastor's family, and my colleagues in the business-world. When one gets accustomed to the life it is surprising how much satisfaction one gets out of it; I wouldn't change with—with any one."

The Lieutenant had listened with bent head, as was his habit; now he looked up and said:

"Rather the mate!"

"What do you mean?"

"Tell Margaret—whom you call Thea—tell her from me: 'Rather the mate!'"

The Consul smiles a little uneasily:

"You mean in order to hasten the extinction of the Coldevins."

"My dear Fredrik, to delay it. Perhaps to prevent it altogether. A seaman has many opportunities, he sails here and there and sees the world, he may become a captain. So also with a soldier; if war breaks out he may make his mark. A seaman and a soldier are not quite lost in the common herd, as officials are."

Now was the time for the Consul to stand or fall by his philosophy of life:

"Excuse me; sitting here at Segelfoss you get wrong ideas," said he. "If you were abreast of your time you would know that opinion has changed since the days of our boyhood. With us nowadays the officials have become the nobility. We have no other."

"The government officials—believe me, they are a miserable tribe. Son after father, generation after generation, copyists and clerks. Recruited from peasant lads who 'work their way up.' Work their way down rather, from good fishermen and cultivators to scriveners and priests. But enough of that. It seems to be a law that officials must breed officials—why? Do but look at them—nothing but mediocre abilities and stunted energies; the triumph of the commonplace. Average honesty and efficiency in their own departments, yes! But outstanding ability, greatness? No! Son after father, generation after generation the same. The law in that world is: the sons shall be officials, the daughters shall marry an official, even if he be no more than doctor or priest. This law excludes all irregularities, it is very rigid, and it plays havoc with the official species. No room is left for the play of chance, no thunderbolt ever falls; the father has begun by clerking, the son must do the same; and this they call acquiring culture. I, for my part, have more satisfaction in conversing with my workmen than with our officials. But, for the matter of that," added the Lieutenant, "I converse with no one."

"No, you are so proud," said the Consul with annoyance. "We others may buy and sell, talk and bargain!"

"Proud?" cried the Lieutenant with a sudden burst of his old temper. "I hope I am proud. But what I feel is disgust—do you understand?—disgust. They make me deadly sick with their talk, the judge and the doctor and the bishop. Living here in solitude, I have gone ahead of them, have left them behind. They bask in their own nothingness, they thrust themselves forward and think they can take part in conversation—I let them be. They are not ashamed to carry their heads in the air; I bow mine, I am never done with gazing at the earth, at the grass and the stones; no, I am never done with the grass and the stones. Here come these sons of clerks and know that after rain comes sunshine; they stand with heads erect and proclaim it, shout it into my ears. Perhaps you have never had to put up with that? They can read and write, things that used to be the work only of inferiors in days gone by, and should be the same now. One can live upon culture, one cannot live upon mere ability to read and write; one cannot live on school-learning—though some can make a living out of it. In order to live upon culture you must, in the first instance, be born to riches and luxury handed down for many generations; to pass from common circumstances and unbroken poverty into an official residence is of no avail. Riches and luxury for several generations are required to lay the foundations of that character which gives a man individuality. Let such a one live upon culture. Officials—God bless you! my friend, can't you see with your own eyes how stupid they are, however useful and adaptable? Look at the way they are promoted—is there any inevitability, any irregularity about it? Did you ever see promotion given on account of great qualities? How could it be on account of something that does not exist? It is given on account of age, length of service, and school-learning. Those do exist. Nor could promotion be given them in any other way—I do not say it could—they have to be plucked out of a garden of the commonplace and put to common uses. It is so in all countries, it is so with us. Therefore I say: 'Rather the mate.'"

"Excuse me," answers the Consul; "I say, not the mate."

"Yes, for the reason—"

"I say, 'not the mate,' for the reason that I do not wish to fling Thea headlong into a misalliance."

Oh, how delightfully banal the man was!

Pause. The Lieutenant sits with open mouth:

"Is what I have said so incomprehensible? I say: 'Rather the mate.' Haven't I explained to you that the other is worse?"

"He is not even from a home; his father is a raftsman. So that, in fact, he is nothing more than a common sailor."

"A man can live upon nature too. The official cannot live upon culture which he has not and cannot have, since culture is not a branch of school-learning; the mate can live upon nature. You may object that the mate is no longer unspoiled nature; but of the two he is the one who is nearest to nature, so he will be the more bearable of them. Tell Margaret that, with my love."

"You must excuse me, that I cannot do. And it would be the death of her mother. My wife's family belong to those who have worked their way up."

"To officialdom? Then they have worked their way down. She has a cousin who is a solicitor, and it is impressed on you daily that that *is* something;—you know in your heart of hearts that it is not. You have said some fine things this evening! He is not even from a home? And if he came of a solicitor's family, he would be from a home! Are you all mad? Where is the thunderbolt, the wild flash from something far back in the race which would make him of any account whatever to-day? The official caste knows of one irregularity and one only, that of marrying 'beneath' them. That is their thunderbolt. They have not even qualifications for anything else, they are born in the commonplace, for the commonplace. Listen:

there was a doctor here; he had to be brought to the house, there was sickness; he was skilled in medicine. He came in, into this very room; he understood nothing, but he pretended that nothing astonished him. He looked at the chair yonder, he thought it was for sitting upon, and he sat upon it. He ought to have sat down on the floor and taken the chair on to his lap. He looked round the walls. He had heard from his fellow-doctors that paintings were things to look at; he looked at the Aphrodite there, at that group, at the Seasons, at the chandeliers with glass pendants, he looked at everything—he did not drop his eyes, he did not fold his hands—his name is Ole Riis, I believe."

"His sister is a Countess in Hungary—what are you thinking of!"

"That fact may possibly not be entirely without importance—for her offspring some day, As far as her brother is concerned, it can at most produce snobbery."

The Consul drinks off his glass and prepares to take up the cudgels against his friend, to finish him off. Oh, how he would overwhelm him with all the banalities he had learnt by heart in his own home and his own town!

"This evening *you* have said some fine things! You go about here at Segelfoss and are a law to yourself and others, you are contradicted once in an age—that is when I come. But now *you* shall have your answer. I will deal with you quite logically and first ask you whether you know my excellent town? No, then neither do you know Bommen. Bommen is a houseowner and has a son who is studying; that is, he is a father who wishes to see his children rise in the world. I will make use of some of this man's sound and just observations. Bommen would have said to you: 'According to your view, then, it is best to induce irregularities in races?' And then

Bommen would look at you."

The Lieutenant smiles:

"Bommen does not believe that. Artificially induced irregularities? No, Herr Bommen, for the individual will remain the same as before. An avalanche of wealth and tradition must have swept over your ancestors before your student son can become anything but an official. That is one condition, the first. And you must have gone on being rich. You must, on that foundation, have evolved characteristics such as make you differ from the clerk with the ordinary equipment—"

Here the housekeeper comes in with a card and says:

"He begs a word with the Lieutenant."

"At this hour?" He reads the card, frowns, considers a little, and says: "Excuse me a moment, Fredrik, I had something more to say, but—"

"Yes, see you don't forget it. I, too, shall have a little more to say when you come in again, you may depend upon that."

The Lieutenant goes out and comes back in a couple of minutes, just as though he has got rid of the man outside.

"A strange proceeding!" he says looking at the clock. "Did you get the impression that Adelheid might be willing to sell that plot of ground?"

"Yes," answers the Consul surprised. "Well?"

"The man is here now, is waiting outside, seems anxious to settle the matter this evening."

"Yes, I got that impression. So he wishes to settle it this evening?"

The Lieutenant paced the floor a little perturbed.

"I am not in the habit of disturbing Adelheid so late—that is to say, I—not without good reason. She can hardly have gone to bed, her window was open, so if you would knock and ask—"

"Shall I speak to Fru Adelheid?"

"If you will be so kind. You are more cheerful than I; she has not much to cheer her, and I am not cheerful. Listen, before you go: you won't put any difficulties in her way if she should perhaps think, as I do, that we may sell the ground."

The Consul goes.

The Lieutenant remains standing where he is, he looks vexed. No doubt it is this Herr Holmengraa who has displeased him. What a time to come to Segelfoss too! Did he think the lord of Segelfoss manor was so hard up for cash? He was anything but that.

The Consul returns and reports: "Yes, Fru Adelheid—she wishes it."

"Well, then, will you do me another great service and speak to the man? Excuse my asking you."

"With the greatest pleasure. Shall I just act for you?"

"Yes, thanks—to-morrow. Point out to the man that it is night now."

"I have no objection to meet the King and go out to the plot with him at once. We business folk recognize no night. It won't trouble you in any way."

"Do as you like. All the same, I should be very sorry to offend your parents by this transaction."

"I'll take the responsibility. I have had to go against their wishes all my life; they would have had me go into diplomacy among other things, but—"

❧

Later on in the night the Consul disturbs Fru Adelheid again.

The King wanted the plot on the other side of the river. He wanted a few roods of ground up from the sea; he would pay well.

Once again the Consul rouses Fru Adelheid, but this time it is morning: the King wants half of the river, right up to the mountains, and also half of the mountain lake. What he wanted with so much fluid was a mystery!

❧

At the breakfast table Fredrik Coldevin is missing; he has not come down yet. Fredrik Coldevin has been wandering up and down the west bank of the river the whole night long with Herr Holmengraa and his men. They have been right up to the lake. They are now seated quietly in the Consul's room at Segelfoss writing out the contract. But old Coldevin and his wife are to be spared as long as possible: "Fredrik will be here immediately. Let us have our breakfast."

And after breakfast the old folks are taken out of the house for a little walk over the fields and meadows, so that the two business men may have breakfast in peace.

"Look, Willatz—what are they doing down there?" says old Coldevin as they go.

The Lieutenant has seen already that there are people down there on the roof of the old church; but though he has been given the clue to this mystery, he has not wanted to say anything. "They are pulling the place down, I suppose," he replies.

"Who is pulling it down? Is it sold? Let us go and find out."

"It is too far for you, my dear friend."

"Not at all. Let us go and find out."

So they went to the church and old Coldevin heard that the King, this Tobias Holmengraa from Ytterleia, had bought the church as it stood and was now pulling it down. There were ten men at the work. And a little later Coldevin finds out that Herr Holmengraa intends to build himself a house out of this old church. They are in full swing already digging the foundations up there, on the west side of the river. "See yonder what crowds of people—!"

When old Coldevin was going back to the house, he walked more slowly than when they came out. "You were right after all, Willatz, it was further than I thought," he said, and took the Lieutenant's arm. "Yes, it was indeed. They are fine broad fields, these Segelfoss fields."

They met Herr Holmengraa half-way up the slope. He greeted them respectfully and offered his thanks for the hospitality and kindness he had enjoyed. He again made apologies for coming so late the day before; Consul Coldevin had been so extremely kind as to remain out helping him the whole night.

The Lieutenant was surprised to see that when he was not stuffed out round the waist with a lot of scarves this Holmengraa was a thin and wiry man. He could not avoid introducing the gentlemen, but he got it over quickly.

"Ay, indeed, so it is; the Segelfoss fields are broad fields," said old Coldevin, taking breath. "And you have a very fine stretch of young forest yonder; little Willatz will be a rich and powerful man. Well, let me thank you for your company; I will go and read a little in my room now; I make a habit of reading a little of a morning."

❧

"In the first place," announced the Consul, "I have to convey to you his thanks for your hospitality."

"He has done that himself," answered the Lieutenant. "Did he also apologize about last night? Did he say why he came so late? An exceptionally sharp fellow, that Holmengraa, a genius! He has a couple of score men with him, he gives them from a few shillings to a dollar a day each; that runs into money, thinks Holmengraa; let us make the most of it! So he uses the night to arrange the business and pick out the plot, and at six o'clock this morning he sets the gang to work. What do you think of that? Not an hour wasted."

"Such thoroughgoing parsimony is beyond me, I am sorry to say," answers the Lieutenant. "Perhaps I had better—like my late father—begin to search for my grandfather's treasure," he adds, smiling.

"Well, I am not quite sure that this parsimony is so thoroughgoing," says the Consul; "of that you may judge for yourself. Here is the contract."

The Lieutenant does not read; he just sits and holds it.

"The chief thing is that Adelheid does not disapprove of the affair."

"Fru Adelheid is quite satisfied."

"By the by, I have just spoken with your father. I am sure he guesses what is going on; he went to his room in deep dejection."

"Will you not read the contract?"

"Yes. Presently. Many thanks for the great service you have done me."

Fredrik Coldevin sits still a little, then he says:

"This is a fine way to take it!"

"What? My dear Fredrik, excuse me if I have said any thing—"

"This is a fine way to take it; is the only thing that matters, then, that Fru Adelheid should not disapprove of the bargain? I should like to give you a few simple answers to what you have said both yesterday and to-day. It is all very well for you and my father to talk like this, for you to adopt this attitude to a bargain; I have had to do things in a different way during my life. You don't need money, you have never been at a loss for it, you could simply spend, spend; I have had to earn it. Do you understand, Willatz—earn it?"

"I have often been in need of money," says the Lieutenant uneasily.

"You? Never, I am sure."

"I have had heavy expenses."

"But have you not, as well, hidden sources to draw upon, have you not inexhaustible treasure under the earth?"

"I wish I had!"

"My father has."

"Indeed. Well, I have not. So your father has? Strange. But indeed, I have wondered many a time where he got it all from."

"I will tell you now, as an answer to some of the questions we have been discussing: he gets it from me."

The Lieutenant probably thinks he has not heard aright, hence his vacant look.

"He has had it from me for a score of years back. But for that he would have been bankrupt."

Pause. The two men sit for several minutes, thinking, thinking.

"Pray do not misunderstand my frankness," says the Consul. "I have mentioned this as a slight justification for myself. I am not at all blind to the greatness of being a great landowner like my father, but it is a greatness that is dead. Great, but dead and gone. The new age has left it behind."

"Yes, the new age has left us behind," says the Lieutenant thoughtfully.

"Of course I am not speaking of you. You have very different resources here."

"They are exhausted."

"They are not exhausted. As I took the liberty of saying yesterday evening, there is still much left behind on a great estate even if a war sweeps over it. Exhausted—!" The Consul laughs, either to hearten his friend, or for some other reason.—"Suppose, for example, I wanted to buy your river?"

"The river?"

"Half the river, half the fall and half the lake—suppose I were a half-crazy lord who bought liquids and could never get enough liquids—what would you take for them?"

The Lieutenant smiles.

"I am in earnest. Half the river together with the fall and the lake?"

"Take the river if you like. You can have it."

"I sold it last night."

"Indeed? Well, I wish you joy of all you got for it!"

"Well, well! I should like to know your price so that I may see what sort of a bargain I have made. Also the price of the ground. It is not a small piece, he didn't want anything cut fine, he said. The whole stretch from the sea along the west bank of the river up to the site for the house, four hundred yards deep, and double that on the sea-front, on account of the lie of the land."

Pause.

"It is not that I wish to undervalue your great services," said the Lieutenant, "but to speak plainly, you seem to have sold the ground and the—liquid away from Segelfoss without any great advantage to me. The price? He may have the river. My saw-mill, my flour-mill and my tile-works can stand idle or work just the same on my side, I suppose?"

"Yes."

"Then he may have the river with pleasure. But that strip of ground four hundred yards deep is land. Not valuable land, not forest; along the river-bank there are only willow thickets and pasture or stony ground. But it is land. So I must have something for that."

"How much?"

"How much? My dear Fredrik, in any case it would not be enough to do much good. A great sum is needed. Everything here is going downhill; little Willatz has to be sent abroad, there are heavy daily expenses, the fields are neglected. Two thousand dollars is probably too much? One thousand dollars? I don't quite know."

"Will you read the paper?"

"Yes, thank you. Presently."

"To indicate the character of the transaction, I will tell you how I sold the river. Holmengraa says he has a small flour-mill in another part of the world. If he is to live here he must have something of the same kind here too to potter about with, he must have half of the river. I am a business man: I answer: 'That will come expensive.' 'How much?' he says. I think it over; I have sold many things, but never rivers. 'My friend the Lieutenant is not the man to care about selling his river,' say I; '—if any one were to come and offer him three or four thousand dollars for it, he would simply smile,' say I."

"Are you out of your senses? Three or four thousand!"

"Just you listen. Herr Holmengraa is a wonderful man. He merely replies that of course he does not know the value of rivers hereabouts, but he has a fancy for this fine, big river, and fall, and lake, and he has gone over the matter, too, and figured it out at a reasonable estimate, on the basis of international prices, and he thinks he can give six thousand dollars for the river, if he gets the ground as well."

Dead silence.

"He was making a fool of you," says the Lieutenant.

"Anyhow it is down in the contract now."

Golden possibilities rise up before Willatz Holmsen, he is strangely powerless to resist, he feels things slipping; he opens the contract, closes it again, then all at once he smiles, and asks with trembling lips:

"But perhaps—this is only the contract, not the money—?"

"I must again express my respect for that remarkable man Tobias Holmengraa," says the Consul. "He paid for his purchase on the spot."

"He paid for it?"

Now Fredrik Coldevin is lofty indeed? He opens his coat and takes from his pockets the money, the immense sum of money.

"That is for the river," he says; that, for the ground along the river, altogether eight thousand dollars. Herr Holmengraa was willing to give so much, he said, on account of the glorious view. Count it over; I have already checked it; it is correct. Phew, it's a great relief to my pockets to get that out of them!"

Yes, indeed, Fredrik Coldevin might well bear himself loftily!

As for the Lieutenant, he was quite unmanned; he was overwhelmed; he moved his lips without uttering a word. Then suddenly this strange man broke the tension on his nerves by a curious action: he put his arms behind his back and slipped his ring on to his right hand; he had worn it on his left for a whole week.

"By the by," he said, straightening himself, "you have been up all night; go to bed now."

IX

Holmengraa sets to work with strong forccs; he has his foreman of carpenters and his foreman of masons; he hires horses wherever they can be had and pays well; but he does not pay by the day, he pays by the load. It turns out that the old church is built of splendid timber inside the weather-boarding.

There was a great stir throughout the country-side, both for the better and the worse. Segelfoss became a centre of industry; there was movement everywhere; blasting on the ridges, much coming and going on the roads. Coasting-yawls landed timber and provisions, stoves, wall-paper, furniture, sacks and cases, big cases; Swedes came and asked for work.

Holmengraa lived at the manor. "That is a matter of course," said the Lieutenant. "It is one more example of your great kindness," said Holmengraa. The foremen lived at the manor too; each of them had his room in the servants' quarters. Round about, in houses and cottages, people grew rich by lodging labourers at twopence a night.

As long as the Coldevins were at Segelfoss, not a day passed but the old gentleman and lady took a walk eastwards—eastwards across the Segelfoss lands, gazing at the meadows, the corn-fields and the forest. "Segelfoss covers a great stretch of country!" says the old man each day, and his wife never remembers that he has said this before, but answers every time: "Yes, it seems so indeed; I did not know the place was so large."

Holmengraa kept up his character as a straightforward and considerate man. When Consul Fredrik told him that the old couple were grieved at the sale of the land, he tried to propitiate them and to give them a good impression of himself; he rose when they came in and remained standing until they had taken their seats; he did not force himself upon them, but awaited the best opportunity of speaking to them. One day he sat down by them and told them something of his family: that his wife had died in Mexico, that he was waiting to bring his children over until the spring, when he would go and fetch them himself. Holmengraa made many apologies for all the disturbance he had brought in his train to Segelfoss; he hoped they would soon be over the worst of it, as he had many people at work. "And then you will be able to enjoy peace and quiet at Segelfoss again," he concluded.

"As far as we are concerned," answers old Coldevin, "it is no great matter; we are leaving soon. But I must say," he adds with a smile, "I do not envy those who are left behind."

His wife tries to smooth this over, saying:

"To think of all you have set going in so short a time! Gangs of day-labourers at work and shiploads of material coming in. And all manner of things."

"That is another thing for which I have to thank the Lieutenant and his lady," answered Holmengraa. "Trusting to their first half-promise of some weeks ago, I was able to prepare everything in advance."

"Thank God, then the whole business was not Fredrik's fault, after all!" the old folk no doubt thought; their minds were relieved, they had one care the less. Old Coldevin asked:

"We see from our windows on the first floor that you have pulled down the church that stood there. I suppose you have bought it? Oh, don't misunderstand me—" he adds in some confusion.

"I quite understand. Yes, I bought the church," answers Herr Holmengraa. "It turns out there is splendid timber in it, more solid than ordinary timber It is my intention to make a house of it this time."

Coldevin recollected stories of the old church: it was built in his father's childhood; there *was* big timber in the Nordland then. "Oh, logs it took two men's span to go round! And, thank goodness, there is still big timber here on Segelfoss."

"Without doubt."

"A vast extent of timber, leagues of it, perhaps. Don't you think there are leagues of it, Charlotte?"

"Yes, I have always heard so," says his wife.

"And the finest of young forest; little Willatz will be a wealthy man. As I was going to say, Herr Holmengraa, we see from our windows that there is work going on down by the sea too; it is your men who are working there, I suppose?"

"Yes, they are masons. I am building a quay right out to deep water."

"So that the smacks can lie alongside, I suppose?"

"Yes, and larger vessels too—ships, cargo boats. I had meant among other things to put up a flour-mill on a fairly large scale. It depends upon whether I see a chance of support."

"Indeed. And then you would grind the grain? Yes, but the people have their hand-mills, they grind with hand-mills. We have a mill at our place. It is working; we could grind more than we do."

"But you no doubt buy the rye elsewhere, sir?"

"Yes, in Bergen. I bring it home by coasting-smack. And then we grind it. But we buy the fine flour. Our mill cannot bolt the flour."

"My idea was to bring the rye here from the rye-growing countries."

"Indeed! Well, we have never done that. My parents did not do that. How about your parents, Charlotte?"

"We got the rye by coasters. And the fine flour and the groats and the wheat-flour came by smacks, too."

"There you see!" says the old Coldevin, nodding his head.

"It is quite possible that was the best way."

"Yes, indeed! Now you are going to grind flour, but what are the people to do with their hand-mills? They will fall to pieces."

"But it is not every one who has a hand-mill. And flour they must all have."

"In that case we grind for them. Those who have not hand-mills, grind with the mills of those who have. That's the way we do it. That's the way our fathers did it."

"My idea is that if I bring the grain home direct from the corn-growing countries, it need not pass through the hands of middlemen in Bergen, which makes it dearer."

"Won't it come to the same thing? Whether you bring it home direct, or the Bergen people bring it home direct, will surely make no difference."

"I will compete with them. I will do it cheaper. If necessary, I will undersell the Bergen people."

"Oh, indeed," said Coldevin.

"The transport from Bergen costs something, of course; people save that by getting the flour here."

"They save that anyhow. We bring the grain home by smacks."

"But it is not every one who has smacks?"

"No. But we who have bring enough for all. That's how we do it;

that's how our fathers did it."

"Yes, but excuse me," says Holmengraa laughing, "it costs *you* something, at any rate, to bring the grain home for every one?"

"Oh, if nothing cost more than that!" answers Coldevin. "Would you have the smacks come home in ballast? They have been to Bergen with fish, and have to come home again; are they to sail in ballast, and not bring any cargo? No, no, you must excuse me, the smacks can't do that, they can't sail home in ballast."

Fru Coldevin sits gazing at her husband. It was wonderful to see her admiration, the worship in her old eyes. Neither she nor her husband saw that this bringing of food-supplies home on the landowners' coasting-smacks was a relic of a dying age.

❧

Then the Coldevins went home again.

But before that happened the Lieutenant had taken counsel with his friend the Consul about a school for Willatz. "A school for human beings," the Lieutenant had said, "a school offering its pupils knowledge, of course, but good breeding too, wide culture, and refining intercourse—a school fit for a Holmsen." What did Fredrik think of England? "Good; the school you want is Harrow," the Consul had answered. He knew it through his business connections. Xavier Moore could keep an eye on Willatz. The Consul wrote at once to Xavier Moore and prepared him.

Nor did Fredrik Coldevin forget to have a last boisterous exchange with the housekeeper, Jomfru Salvesen, before he left.

"Dear me! How you frightened me, Consul! Is that you standing there?" says the Jomfru, speaking from the pantry window.

"I have been standing here looking at you; show me the man

who could have helped doing so."

"Ha, ha! now you're at it again!"

"I have to go, my last hour will soon strike. I have come to make an end of it."

"Ha, ha!"

"Don't laugh. It shows contempt for my feelings such as I do not deserve. But I have nothing more to say. When you became engaged to another man some years ago, it was the end of me. Now I mean to do the deed; I only wish to consult you as to the form. Chloroform is a good form, isn't it?"

"I do believe you are crazy, Consul! Ha, ha, ha! you make me laugh till I don't know what I look like," says Jomfru Salvesen, bridling.

"To laugh at such a moment may mean one of two things: either you are simply laughing, which would be unworthy of you, or you laugh so as not to cry."

"Yes," says Jomfru Salvesen, "yes, I laugh so as not to cry."

"Thanks!" bursts out the Consul. "That was what I meant by making an end of it. It is not the best end, not the most glorious, but, in all the circumstances, the most fitting end. So some feeling stirs in you at this fateful hour; I thank your kind heart for that; my bitterness has passed away; I can sit down and brood upon my memories."

"Oh, dear; but poor man, what a future!"

"My one hope is that a happier life may be mine in the hereafter."

"Ha, ha!" laughs Jomfru Salvesen, in spite of herself. Really you *mustn't* stand there and joke about such things."

"When I am lying on the last of my thousand and three beds in this world, I will think of you. Do you doubt that I shall remember?"

"Oh, no!"

"What will you do in return?"

"I will sit down in the pantry here and howl at the top of my voice that day—or will it be at night?"

"It will be at night—at dead of night."

"That is a pity. For then I shall be afraid of awakening people."

"Woman, woman, do you trifle with a soul nearing its end? Jomfru Salvesen, give me your hand."

"Dear me, I don't know if—well, just wait a moment!"

The housekeeper dries her hands energetically.

"Thank you. And now, Jomfru Salvesen, farewell; may you fare well! That is my wish."

"Farewell, Consul, and again thanks for your kindness this year."

The Consul walks away, but turns round.

"By the way, I met a man on board the boat when I was coming up north—"

"The parson? You told me that."

"Was he a parson? Surely not."

"You told a story about a parson."

"Surely he couldn't have been a parson? Did I tell you a story? I don't remember."

"About a parson with three sons."

"Oh, no! I didn't tell you that story. You must have heard that from the man to whom you are betrothed; I feel sure it is a perfectly horrible story. Three sons—illegitimate, of course."

"Oh, dear! Consul, you *really* must not make me laugh so!" screams Jomfru Salvesen.

"How you women play with us men!" says the Consul. "I met a man on board the steamer who had something to say on that subject too. He had the most pathetic, the most sorrowful face I have seen, and so you may know at once what was the matter. A woman had ruined him. How did it happen? 'Well,' said he, 'she filled me up with lies, she said I was the only one. But afterwards I found out that I was another's successor,' said he. I, Fredrik Coldevin, answered as delicately as I could: 'Then you suffered much?' 'Oh, yes,' said he, 'I suffered terribly. But it was some comfort to me when I found that I was the predecessor of a third.' 'Good heavens,' said I, Fredrik Coldevin, clasping my hands, 'was she a regular hotel for lovers?' 'Hotel?' said he, and thought a little. 'Refuge is the word I would use,' he said. 'We all loved her and she opened a refuge for us.'"

With this the Consul prepares to go.

"It is just as well you are going," says Jomfru Salvesen. "Otherwise I do not know what I would have done. Ha, ha, ha! That is a perfectly awful one," she said.

"What!"

"Yes, I tell you so frankly. But the fact is, one is always a little afraid of what you may say, Consul."

"More than of what your sweetheart says?"

"My sweetheart?"

"Remember the parson with the three natural children."

"Ha, ha, ha! No, really! I won't speak to you any more."

"Good-bye, Jomfru Salvesen."

"Good-bye. I hope we'll see you again next year."

❧

Is the daily life of Segelfoss quiet and monotonous? Not now: that is a thing of the past. Holmengraa had changed all that. All these people, all these horses, the songs of the masons, the reports of the blasting, the chanteys from the smacks—all had a disturbing and vulgarizing effect on the dignified Holmsen manor. But the Lieutenant may have consoled himself by thinking, in towns one can keep one's dignity even in the midst of noise. Yes, but even there one can best keep one's dignity in peaceful surroundings. See! numbers of his own men and horses are working all over the fields, toiling at reaping and harvesting; in other years, under the leadership of his head man, Martin, they had been an army to be proud of—now they were lost in the crowd of strangers.

But you can't get anything for nothing!

The day after the Coldevins had left, the Lieutenant meets the girl Daverdana and says to her:

"We will discontinue these evenings. We will not read any more."

Daverdana grows pale and frightened and says:

"I did not forget yesterday evening; but the mistress sent me for the shoes."

A look of satisfaction passes over the Lieutenant's face and he answers:

"It was I who sent you. We will not read any more for the present."

As the Lieutenant is about to go. Daverdana says:

"Am I to—to leave?"

"No," he replies. "Leave? You are a handy girl; the housekeeper needs you."

A good word from the Lieutenant was highly prized; Daverdana blushes with pleasure and submits to his decision.

The Lieutenant went on. Things were now comparatively bearable with him; he had money at his back, a large sum invested at

Trondhjem; he was more of a free agent; he no longer changed his ring to his left hand as often as before. Adelheid might visit the home of her childhood now; what was she waiting for?

To tell the truth, he was not at all anxious that Adelheid should go; for some reason or other she always returned from her home in Hanover a little less amiable and more haughty; he, for his part, had broken off all relations with that same home. There was some excuse for Adelheid. Was not her father a Hanoverian general whom fate had retired at the rank of colonel for want of a Hanover? And was not she his daughter, who had buried herself alive in Norway, in the Nordland, in a dead world?

"I have been thinking," says the Lieutenant to her, "Willatz is running wild here at home, he has begun to learn bad words and to swear; I suppose he ought to be sent away?"

"I should not be surprised if he learnt these new words from Daverdana and her brother," answers his wife. "As to his going away, I don't know."

"Daverdana?" says the Lieutenant, looking pleased again. "By the by, Daverdana can be entirely at the disposal of the housekeeper after this."

"Is she not to wait on you?"

"No. She displaced the alphabet."

"What alphabet?"

"The boy's. Perhaps you don't remember it, but I have kept it since Willatz was little. I have it hanging on the wall where I can see it. A big alphabet on cardboard. She displaced it."

At this point a little smile broke over his wife's face, and the Lieutenant himself smiled, he was so pleased at the moment.

"A whim of mine," he said; "when Willatz leaves home I want to have some few small things to remind me of him. I have been thinking that if you were to pay your visit to Hanover at the same time, you could take the boy with you."

"Where is Willatz to go?"

"You are German, of course," answers the Lieutenant, feeling his way, "but—to England, don't you think? To Harrow; Fredrik has acquaintances there. To England, naturally."

"And I am to go to Hanover?"

"To go by Harrow will unfortunately be rather a roundabout way. But if you had good weather such a journey ought not to be an unwelcome change; it might do you good. You might take your maids with you."

All at once a suspicion seemed to awaken in her. She moved across to the window and stood there looking out. As she stood there she smiled once more, but this time it was an empty smile.

"What do you think of it?"

"Yes, perhaps," she answered.

"It seems to displease you."

"Is it absolutely necessary that Willatz should go away?"

"You know that he spends nearly all his time in the labourers' cottages and when he comes home he does nothing but play the piano."

"Could you not bring yourself to have a tutor?" she asked.

"If there were no other alternative."

"I am not going to Hanover."

A pause.

"No?" he replied.

She turned towards him and said:

"So that's how it is. I begin to understand!"

What was it now? He was irritated by her scornful attitude; for had he not shown himself conciliatory to the last degree? He was tempted to give her a lesson for her foolishness, but he knew well enough that it would not be of the least use, and so he remained silent.

"You reckoned without your host," said she. "But I think it odious and crafty of you."

"What a way to talk!"

"Well, that's what I think."

"And so I am odious and crafty now as well? Yet you will never make me better by forever counting up my faults. My faults—I must admit I have lost interest in them."

"And I must admit," she answers, "that once, long ago, I at least, would not have believed this of you."

"You should not say that; at least it is not wise of you. Do you not see that you cast a slur upon your own judgment?"

"Oh, nonsense, I was a child."

"A child? Is your memory quite correct?"

"I was a child."

Yes, now it was open war, and she had no thought of sparing him, but only of firing hard, of firing hotly. With eyebrows lifted high, with eyes half closed, she looked at him askance—with oh! what incredible scorn.

"You wanted to set my mind at ease by dismissing her from waiting on you. And then I was to go away. I thank you."

He had heard many an unreasonable speech from her in his time, but he appeared never to have heard anything which gave him more gratification, not to say pleasure. He seemed on the point of going to her and saying something, assuring her of something, God knows what; but she did not expect it from him, and did not give him time.

"I thank you!" she repeated, and left him.

He might, indeed, still have made her listen to him. He could have said: "I was so far from wishing to set your mind at ease that I never thought of your requiring reassurance in that direction!" He looked for a chance throughout the day; but she was utterly implacable, she avoided him; and at last she wandered out to Holmengraa's workmen and watched them. At their evening meal he could not say anything, as Herr Holmengraa was present, and when she retired to her own room for the night it was too late. He should have been a little readier of speech at the moment; that was it.

Late in the evening he goes out. Her window stands open as usual, he hears her step within, a sudden impulse seizes him and he asks in a whisper:

"Is your door locked, Adelheid? I just wanted to—"

"Yes, I am in bed," she answered.

❧

The Lieutenant rode out again next morning. His rides had been interrupted during the Coldevins' visit; it was a pleasure to him to sway in the saddle once more and to look far over land and sea. "Now then! Blackie, you have stood idle so long, you are above yourself!"

The Lieutenant rides down the main road; the horse is full of spirit and prances along. He hears a shout not far off: "Look out there!" The Lieutenant rides on; he is not the man to be stopped on his road; in fact to shout at him at all is not the thing.

A blast goes off with a loud report.

The next moment is laden with catastrophe; a convulsion goes through the horse, he gives a leap, gives a great sidelong bound, throwing the rider off his balance, so that he hangs over to one side. Away they go down the road, the ground thundering under the horse's hoofs; away they go further and further, past cottages and farms, till they are out of sight. The rider is hanging lower and lower on the horse's side, the saddle is slipping round, it is a matter of seconds now—now!

It is a critical moment. The rider has one leg over the horse's back, the other under its belly; he is stiff as a rod, his body stands straight out from the horse's side as it tears along—then he grabs at the horse's neck, at his mane; it was as if a steel grappling-iron flew up and got a grip. At the same moment the saddle slipped right round and the horse was entangled in the gear; his next convulsive bound ended in a fall.

What! has he not done enough! he struggles up on to his fore legs and falls again, rises and falls once more, snorts, trembles, tosses his head. The Lieutenant has at last dragged his leg from under the horse and can reach its head; then he loosens and takes off the saddle and gets his steed upon its legs.

On the way home he sits his horse again and rides as usual at a walk. He meets people coming running towards him: his own man, Martin, unknown labourers and foremen, Holmengraa himself, all very anxious. Holmengraa is full of regret and self-reproach. "These explosions, this horrible blasting! Are you really not hurt? And the horse?"

The Lieutenant sees his wife coming hurrying down from the house, and wishing to meet her, to save her coming far, he does not stop with the anxious enquirers, but answers them shortly.

"Did he bolt? How—did you fall off?" she asked hurriedly. "Have you hurt yourself?"

"I did not fall off," he answers.

"Didn't you really? How did it happen? Just think if there had been a bad accident! And you are not hurt?"

"I am not hurt," he replies.

He seemed to hear by the tone of her voice that, while she was really glad that he was still alive, she thought perhaps he had not ridden carefully enough, had not been careful to ride at a walk as he was used to do!

"And the horse?" she asked. "I hear it took fright at a blast? I don't understand it; were you not holding the reins firmly? A blast is such an ordinary thing."

"Yes, quite an ordinary thing."

"Yes, indeed, a blast is nothing at all! But of course one must be able to sit a horse. And you are an old cavalryman too."

"By the by," he says, as though he had thought of something quite different from what they had been speaking about, "when you go riding you ought to take care of the blasting for a while now. There are some very loud explosions at times. The rock blastings, I mean."

"I am not at all afraid of the blasting," she replied. "What an idea!" She patted his horse and said to it: "How foolish of you! Suppose you were in a battle and could not stand firing!"

"While I think of it," says the Lieutenant, "this day week Willatz and I leave for England. You will perhaps be so good as to see that his things are in order."

What need was there for him to stand on ceremony with Adelheid? None! and he had no mind to do so any longer.

In the evening he sat down in his own room and amused himself with playing patience like an old lady. Daverdana no longer came to read to him; he had to have something to take her place, something to keep him occupied; why not a patience, an innocent lady-like pastime? In the morning he rode out again, expecting to hear a blast or two. All was still; he heard the masons singing as they worked at the new quay; that was the only sound. This was not what he wanted. When the same thing had continued for a couple of days he determined to have a change. There were plenty of blasts all day long, but when the Lieutenant went for a ride, all was quiet. There must be some one keeping watch. The extraordinary thing was that all became quiet from the moment he gave orders to saddle his horse, not just when he came riding down the hill. What was the meaning of that?

One morning as he is standing at his open window he notices that the miners are beginning to bore. He sees them drill deeper and deeper, using longer and longer drills, till at last they are ready. He has loitered at home on purpose that he may have the full benefit of this great blast; now he gives orders to saddle his horse. During the further work of drying out and charging the bore the men are constantly watching the manor-house; at length one makes a sign to the others with his arm. There must have been a signal from somewhere; the Lieutenant leans out of the window and looks his house up and down. What was that? A cloth, a white towel is hanging from one of Adelheid's windows. It is hanging in the sun, no doubt to dry; the wind blows it out gently.

The Lieutenant goes out, examines the saddle and bridle with care, tightens the saddle-girth by one hole and mounts. As he rides down the road he glances up at the towel; it is hanging there still. Had Adelheid settled with Holmengraa that her husband Willatz Holmsen could not sit a horse and must be spared the reports of the blasting? That he was nervous of anything that went beyond a walking pace?

He rides down the road, he notices that all is in readiness for firing down below there, but that the people are now busy about other things. He rides straight up to them and gives an order:

"Fire!"

Now the Lieutenant was a man that it was by no means easy to disobey! The workmen went off to the mine. The foreman came up and asked:

"Are they to fire?"

"Yes."

"We thought—you see, the horse will not stand fire."

"It must be taught to stand it."

Stiff and stubborn, there sits the Lieutenant, knowing well that this is a stupid way of teaching a horse to stand fire; but there he sits.

"Look out there!" shout the workmen.

"At any rate you should not stand here, sir," says the foreman.

"You are standing here yourself, are you not?"

"It is a different matter for me. I can jump aside out of the way."

"We will get out of the way too, never fear," replies the Lieutenant, smiling. The match begins to smoke and the workmen take cover.

The horse sniffs at the smoke and grows restless, it suspects that something is going to happen; the Lieutenant strokes it with his whip and talks to it. As there are many onlookers he shows himself, perhaps, more self-possessed than he really is, but it is noticed that he presses the stirrups close into the horse's belly, as though this might save him if need arose. He keeps on stroking his horse and talking to it.

He was still so engaged when the blast went off. The next moment was a crowded one: the horse leapt from the ground, flung itself about, and set off with a series of tremendous bounds over the rocky ground. But this time a rider was on its back who would not come off, whom it was wasted effort to try and unseat. Soon the wild flight turned into a hard, but regular, controlled gallop uphill towards the road, as they neared the turn of the highway the horse slackened of itself more and more, and they came up on to the road safe and sound. Then they swung round to the right towards the back country and disappeared in a cloud of dust.

❧

It is Sunday.

Little Willatz is going round the cottages saying good-bye to his comrades, and amassing both honour and renown in the process; is he not going to *Engelland*, into the great world, and not coming back again? Poor little Gottfred, it is true, had not enjoyed his daily companionship, but even him he does not forget; nay, he even makes him a present of two trifles which may be a comfort to poor Gottfred through the coming years: a whistle in the shape of a cock and one of Fru Adelheid's combs which has lost a few teeth.

Then Willatz went to Lars Manuelsen's house. He had brought with him for Julius a horse on wheels and a whole boxful of miscellaneous rarities. Julius looked into the box and said:

"The cock's not here?"

"Gottfred has got the cock."

"Has he! Then he has got the paint-box as well, I suppose?"

"What do you mean by sitting there asking questions?" says Julius' mother. "You don't even say thank you for what you have got! I've said it before and I say it again: you are just as bad as ever, you troll!"

So Julius thanks Willatz for his gifts and Willatz feels quite ashamed that they are so poor.

Then Julius' mother takes down from above the rafter a letter which she asks Willatz to read; it is from Lars, from the seminary. Old Lars Manuelsen is lying asleep on the bed, it being Sunday, and his wife awakens him and tells him now they can get the letter read at last.

"Dear parents!" began Willatz.

"When was it written?" asked Lars.

Willatz reads the date.

"Why! it has been a month on the road."

"It has been a whole week up on the rafter," says his wife.

The letter told about the journey to Tromsö and the town and the life there; all the houses, all the ships down at the sea, thousands and thousands of people in the streets. It was a long letter in a plain schoolboy hand. And as to food, there was first-rate food every day, but not enough pieces of rye bread, and the way the other seminary boys did him out of things was a sin and a shame; but he, their son, put his trust in the Lord.

"If only I had been there!" says Lars from the bed.

"What do you think you would have done?" asks his wife.

"Don't you hear that they are starving him to death?"

Then the letter told about what they learnt, that there were a tremendous number of books of all kinds, and a schoolroom bigger than the Segelfoss church, besides a house for nothing else but hopping and jumping about in for the sake of exercise. "But all goes well, your son is firm in the faith which no one can take from him. To finish with, a hearty greeting to every one at home and to Daverdana at the Lieutenant's house."

When Willatz was going Julius followed him out; they two had so much to talk of; but Willatz was depressed and down-hearted.

"Well, you must be sure and write," says Julius.

"Yes, but you can't read it."

"Oh, yes! if you print it."

Willatz promised to write printed letters.

"Yes, you must be sure and do that."

"What broken ball is that lying there?" asks Willatz.

"Ball? Oh, that's the one we lost. I went down again and looked till I found it, but it was rotten. Just you look how rotten it was—"

X

The autumn passes.

Holmengraa has hurried his workmen on with might and main and has got the roof on to his house. Only carpenters and painters are at work now in the big building. In the same way he has had the sea-wall of the quay completed and has begun the clearing of a large space for a warehouse; boring and blasting went on constantly—every day saw the end of some great boulder.

But it was difficult for his big gangs of workmen to obtain a steady supply of provisions, and one day after the Lieutenant had come home from England, Holmengraa went to him and asked, in a polite and friendly way, if he had any objection to a trader setting up a store down by the sea. It was important for him that a store should be established on the spot: his half-hundred men had to make a long journey every week to fetch food, tobacco, coffee, and clothes; it took up a lot of their time, and some of them came back drunk from their trip.

What the Lieutenant would have preferred would probably have been to see all these strangers leave Segelfoss, but Holmengraa had a singularly courteous way with him in putting forward a proposal, and the Lieutenant had made it a rule to agree to all his requests.

"Well, but," he replied, "when your masonry and building work is finished and your workmen are gone, what is the trader to live on?"

"It is true," said Holmengraa, "that there will be less demand for provisions then; I have thought of that. But in the first place, I shall be working with my present strength of masons and builders for a long time yet—"

"What is the next thing you mean to build?"

"There is the mill I mentioned to you, sir."

"And then?"

"Then I must make a road up to the mill."

"Well, so much for the immediate future. And afterwards?"

"Afterwards I shall need a number of permanent hands for my business. They may be people with families; it is possible there may be more than we at present foresee."

"It looks as if it would end in your making a town here," said the Lieutenant.

"It's quite true that I've made your place much more noisy than it was, but I will not bring a whole town upon you. Yet, has it not struck you, sir, how well this place is suited for extensive trade and industry? It has a clear coast, deep water close inshore, timber in the forests, a river, a waterfall, a thickly settled upland, fields and meadows, an enormous extent of grazing country on the outskirts—"

"My grandfather should have heard all you say; he was so energetic. But, as regards the store, where is it to stand?"

"By the sea, on my little bit of ground down there."

The Lieutenant looks up:

"Are you asking me for leave to build on your own ground?"

Holmengraa bows politely and answers:

"I must admit I did not care to do so without asking. And besides, I knew that if you had any objection, it would be so well grounded that I would feel bound to drop the idea."

"I have no objection to make."

"I thank you."

"And—it occurs to me—as you intend building a big warehouse down there and may need all the space you have, the store might as well be built alongside of it, on my ground. There is nothing but stones down there anyhow."

"I owe you many thanks for settling the matter in this way, sir. A yearly rent will be paid for the ground. Moreover, I have no doubt that you show your foresight in permitting building on the outskirts of your property—"

"Do you feel well here? Has your health improved?"

"A thousand thanks; this summer has been a real blessing to me!"

"I am very glad of that," says the Lieutenant. . . .

Holmengraa lost no time in putting the whole thing through; he went to work with judgment and no lack of money and erected buildings of stone and wood. You will observe he no longer needed a fur coat or an enormous paunch to impress people; and even his gold chain seemed only to make him uncomfortable when he took a meal at the Holmsens' table, so that he would often button his coat over it. No, what impressed people about him now was his full money-safe on Saturday evenings when he paid out the wages. And no doubt some of his work-people perceived his great business capacity too, and respected it.

Time went on; the wharf and store were built and the storekeeper arrived with his wares. He was a peasant from along the coast; his name was Per and he signed himself P. Jensen when he could get any one to write it for him—he could not write himself. He was an ignorant, common fellow, but in one thing he was conspicuous: in close-fistedness, and in the ability to scrape together halfpence and hoard them up. He met the needs of the place; he traded cautiously and kept only those goods which the workmen needed; he took care not to jump so high as not to be able to land on his feet again. People called him Per of Bua;* he was a stout, florid gentleman with a common peasant-face and eyes that nothing escaped. He was homely in dress and plain in his ways, and yet he made every one keep their distance, even his wife, even his children; he was interested in two things only in life, his halfpence and his business. These were his philosophy and his religion, they were never out of his thoughts; and even when he used the yard-measure or the weighing-scales he might often be detected using his fingers to make a little extra profit on his transactions. People did not like sending children to his store, but when now and again it could not be helped, the little ones were told to keep their eyes open.

Holmengraa had brought this man with him from Ytteröya because he was distantly connected with his wife. But Holmengraa had only shown him where he might erect his store, and had nothing to do with it or the way it was managed—store-keeping was not his business.

"I hear," said Holmengraa, "that people don't trust you overmuch, Per."

"Don't they?" said Per.

"No. They say they have great trouble in getting their correct change and they complain of your yard-measure."

"Here's the yard-measure!" said Per.

Holmengraa examined it, laid it down again, and said:

"People complain to my foreman. Bertel of Sagvika bas a little

*Per of Bua = Per of the booth, or shop or store. Translator.

boy called Gottfred."

"He comes idling about here every day."

"Bertel sent him here for coffee. He got the coffee in his handkerchief and went home. Is that so?"

"Yes, quarter of a pound of coffee."

"But Bertel had to come here himself to have it weighed over again."

"That's just what I always say," said Per; "why don't they buy half a pound and not a quarter?"

"But even a quarter of a pound should not be less than quarter of a pound."

"But how much is there in a quarter of a pound of coffee, can you tell me that?" asks Per. "A quarter of a pound is nothing when it's put into a handkerchief. I could put it in my eye."

"He got too little coffee; you had given short weight."

"It is just as likely that he had a hole in his handkerchief. How can I tell?"

"But you had to weigh it again for Bertel."

"I gave him very little more. I did it out of kindness."

Holmengraa said:

"Don't let people have cause to complain of you, Per."

He had to take the dealer to task again later, but it was of little use; the good Per of Bua could not cure himself and people never got to trust him. However, he was the only one to go to, and if you kept a good look-out and had your eyes open you could deal with him right enough. Odd, stupid, Per of Bua! He believed, no doubt, that he would live for ever and a day, and that was why he was so grasping and could never get enough!

"I have received an application from one P. Jensen who is said to keep a shop here down by the sea," says the Lieutenant to Holmengraa. What a gulf between him and a P. Jensen! How absolutely by his tone he could make a mere nothing of a P. Jensen! That could do no harm; on the contrary it was just the right tone with Adelheid sitting there listening.

"That is Per of Bua," answers Holmengraa. "Has he applied—?" Holmengraa was much surprised.

"Written. He wishes to put up a dancing-room, a dancing-booth, or whatever it may be."

"Well, well! Per of Bua!" exclaims Herr Holmengraa, shaking his head.

"It might add a little to his takings while there are so many labourers here, he writes."

"Hm. You, sir, have, of course, not—?"

"No. I have not answered him," says the Lieutenant smiling as indifferently as though a P. Jensen were of less consequence than a fly.

"Of course not. I will, if you will allow me, have a little talk with the good Per of Bua. I very much fear I made a mistake when I brought that man here. The truth is he is married to a relation of mine, a distant relation, a second cousin or something of that sort, or I would not have thought of him. Now I must really see about getting rid of him again."

The Lieutenant listened quite unconcernedly to all this, perhaps he did not even hear it; he just sat there at the supper-table and, having finished his meal, pondered and blinked. His wife asked out of politeness:

"Has he any family?"

"Yes, quite a large family, sons and daughters."

"And perhaps he is not well off?"

"Oh, yes! quite; he is quite well-to-do."

After supper the Lieutenant went to his own room. Ah, little Willatz, the madcap, is gone; no one asks quaint, childish questions now, no one sings; the piano stands silent in the parlour. But Willatz is getting on well in England; he is acquiring the accomplishments of a gentlemen; he writes that he has learnt to swim and box, he plays upon a grand piano, too, and goes to school besides. Those letters from Willatz were his father's delight—he had never watched for the post as he did now. As arranged with Willatz before he went, the letters were always addressed to his mother, that she might read them first; and she was always so good as to open them at once and read them aloud to her husband, a thing he was most grateful to her for. That she might not feel bound always to do this, he once made the housekeeper take his wife's many letters in to her, but Adelheid at once sent word to him:

"You did not notice that there was a letter from Willatz to-day."

"Oh, indeed! from Willatz! Thank you."

The letter said that he was learning to speak the language a little, and could already read just a little in spite of the foreign words and the Roman type. Sometimes he longed for you, dear Mamma, for there were forty thousand words in English and he was afraid he would never learn them. There was no snow here in England, but all the same it was cold and bleak, and his window was kept open at night to make him hardy. He had a new dancing-master, for the old one said he had sprained his ankle; but Mr. Xavier Moore said he was not quite *proper*. In conclusion, Mamma must give his love to Papa and remind him what fun they had on the journey to England.

"Very many thanks. Hm."

As he was going she detained him, saying:

"That's the second time he reminds you of the journey to

England."

"Yes. He saw so much that was new and strange to him."

"A journey that I refused to take."

"Do you regret it?" he asked with surprise.

"Yes," she answered, moving to the window.

Pause. She continued:

"If I were to ask you again, to ask you now—I can't bear it; he is with strangers, alone; who is Mr. Moore?" she enquired, turning round.

"As far as that goes, I am sure you may be quite at ease, but—"

"His window open at night— They are muddling his brains too. There is no sense in his learning forty thousand words; one thousand is enough."

"I believe you are right."

"I did not want to go to Hanover at all, but to him; I have regretted it each day since he went. I did not want to go home, far from it—"

"If it were not winter—" he began.

"You would let me go?"

"With the greatest pleasure. That is to say—don't misunderstand me—but of course, if you wish it—"

"Thank you, Willatz. Then I will go. I am so glad."

Now he could have twisted her around his finger, could have taken her into his arms and carried her out of the room and back again, and she would only have clung to him, and never noticed if he had knocked her against the door-post. Perhaps he expected an outburst on her part, and stood on his guard.

"Well—here I am keeping you from reading your other letters," he said and made a bow as if to go.

"Willatz!"

"I must go out and arrange about your journey. You will go at once?"

"Yes, thank you. But, Willatz—" she said, and drew near to him; she was surely humble enough and her head was bent. Then, as she raised her eyes, and saw his expression she knew it was useless, that it was too late; unshakable determination was written upon that obstinate Arab face.

Then he struck home. At last he had the upper hand completely, just as in former days she had had it for years—now he struck home:

"No, there is nothing else—of that sort."

But was he not taking advantage of his triumph a little too soon? He should have known Adelheid better; she did not fall down and hit her head upon the floor. On the contrary, she drew herself up at once and said with great self-possession:

"That sort? I was only thinking of asking you for a fur coat—a small fur coat for Willatz—whether I might get him one."

Pause.

"Certainly," he answered. "Thank you for reminding me of it. If it is usual for children to wear furs in England."

"No, perhaps not. I don't know. It does not matter."

"I have no objection. Make enquiries. In any case, it does your mother's heart credit."

It almost seemed as if she had lost interest in the whole trip now, in the preparations, the mode of travel and everything; perhaps it had only been an experiment, an expedient to soften her husband, to give him a chance to deal indulgently with her changeable moods. It is not impossible that, at the last moment, she might have given up this journey to England which had taken shape so suddenly, but, as it turned out, it was Holmengraa who revived her courage and inclination for it. Holmengraa said at the dinner-table:

"I am off too. My children are expecting me already."

"But you, I fancy, have much further to go?"

"To Mexico. Up into the Cordilleras."

"Just think if I could have had your company to England!"

"That would be a great honour for me."

Both Fru Adelheid and the Lieutenant look at him.

"Do I understand you aright? when can you start?" asks the lady.

"Whenever you command, Madam," answers Holmengraa with a bow.

"Why, I never—!" exclaims the lady in surprise. "Can you start at once?"

"In a couple of hours, with pleasure."

"What wonderful good fortune!"

"I shall do my best to be of service to you, Madam."

The Lieutenant asks:

"Can you go away and leave all your people?"

"I shall have to do that sooner or later in any case. And, then, I have foremen who will remain in charge."

"But I understood you to say your children could not come before the spring?"

"I will not bring them away before spring. But I have much to wind up and arrange in Mexico. Well, not so very much, of course, but a little, some few things; I need all the time I shall have to spare. I have some factories to dispose of, a couple of factories, and a little property. There is not much altogether, but of course it takes time to get everything put in order."

"Well, if I can have your company to England without any sacrifice on your part, I shall really be most grateful," says Fru Holmsen frankly.

The Lieutenant nods in agreement:

"If only you are not hastening your journey out of consideration for my wife?"

"By no means."

"Perhaps you would not otherwise have started for a couple of months yet?"

"That was indeed my first intention. But now my children write that they are expecting me already."

"It looks, Adelheid," said the Lieutenant, "as if you really should take advantage on your trip of Herr Holmengraa's company and exceptional experience of travel. And then there will be no difficulty about it."

"No, there will be no difficulty about it."

All the time Fru Adelheid was away the Lieutenant did not seem to miss her; on the contrary, he became more alert in mind and body and was more active than before. "It is extraordinary!" said the housekeeper, Jomfru Salvesen. He was to be seen on the roads on horseback or on foot, he had business to transact with the tenants and the neighbours, he gave personal directions as to where the wood for winter fuel should be felled in the forest this year—a thing he had not done for several years—and he had all the vehicles on the place put in order ready for the spring. What did he mean, too, by going about with his uniform coat unbuttoned, with his thumbs in his waistcoat pockets and humming? Perhaps he wondered a little himself at his own energy, and, in order not to draw attention to the fact that he was more cheerful than before, gave his orders in a low voice, which, however, did not prevent their being obeyed at once. Had a weight been taken off him? That subdued air, what had become of it? Apart from the outward signs of well-being, due to his now having money in his pocket, the Lieutenant seemed in every way a freer man—he did not go about so much with bent head, pondering over the dust of the road.

And of an evening there was no more lying on the sofa like a pasha letting Daverdana, from the other side of the room, send surges of emotion through his heart, no—not a wave, not a ripple. It was by mistake that, one evening, he met the red-haired girl in the passage, and she stood against the wall, just where his cloak hung, and he thought she was the cloak: "What—is that you, child? It is so dark here. . . ." He went back into his own room again and with trembling hand filled and drained a quieting glass of water. Then, after pacing the floor a few times, he began his everlasting game of patience.

But did he fall back into his old, brooding depression when, late in the spring, his wife came home? No such thing; he had begun to hum and sing to himself and probably could not stop all at once. So he continued to hum for months, just as if nothing had happened to upset him: indeed, he went on doing it quite as much after his wife's return as before—the man did nothing by halves. Did he do this in order to throw dust in the Segelfoss people's eyes?

"I sometimes hear you humming?" said his wife.

"Do you? I am sorry," he replied. "A bad habit. I shall try and break myself of it."

"Why should you do that?"

"Because it is more fitting that you who can hum properly should do it, and that I should hold my peace."

"You don't hum badly."

"I hum so entirely for my own private pleasure that I am horrified at the idea of your having overheard me."

"It is a good thing that some one should hum in this house," said she.

"Since Willatz went," he answered, "you are the only one left to sing, Adelheid. But you don't do it."

What was there to be said? After a pause she began again: "On my journey I saw some married couples who struck me as very peculiar, indeed quit extraordinary."

"You did?"

"Yes. It was dreadful."

"You excite my curiosity."

"Do I? They were married couples. And yet one day they would smile and nod to each other; they were happy together, they even kissed each other, talked to each other, and wished each other good night."

"And the next day?"

"They did the same."

"Remarkable. What sort of married people were they?"

"They were all the same."

Pause. The Lieutenant was taken unawares; he felt as if he were again hanging on the side of a horse. His wife went on:

"I saw them while I was on my journey; I have to thank you so much, Willatz, for giving me the opportunity of seeing them."

The Lieutenant bowed and said:

"What else?"

"There is nothing else," she replied. "They were married people, they loved one another, they were happy."

"Hm. If I understand you correctly, Adelheid, you think I might take a lesson from these married people?"

"Both you and I; I thought that we might both learn a little from them. I don't know—"

"You will excuse me if I take this small chair for a moment," said the Lieutenant, sitting down. "I do not propose to enter into details, but it really seems as if you wished things to be a little different between us?"

"I have wished that before to-day; do you not remember? But I was rebuffed."

"That was sad."

"It could not well have been sadder," said his wife with tears in her eyes. "And I could not help being deeply hurt by it. But it can't be helped."

Evidently this self-willed man had to restrain his impulse to show himself ungovernably perverse again, for his smile was a wry one and cold sweat stood out upon his brow. But he merely asked her to reconsider what she had said.

"Were you rebuffed?"

"What a question—! Was I not? Did you not twice refuse to listen to me? Did you not say there was to be an end of it?"

Pause.

"Hm. I do not wish to cross-examine you, but was it I who locked my door year after year?"

"My God! no! it was I who did it. Did I not ask you each time to forgive me? You agreed to do so, too, each time, but I see that you have not forgiven me. And now I don't know where I stand."

It seemed that the Lieutenant must all at once have become completely bewildered; he bent forward and stared at her, he seemed not to understand a word. Was it stupidity or cunning that made her talk like this; did she wish to drive him mad?

"I know very well that I went too far then," she continued, "I should not have punished you for so long. Oh, I see it now and I am sorry."

"In the first place, do you not misunderstand the position when you speak of punishing me? What should you punish me for?"

"Well, you see—. And so I could not punish you, could I not? not in my own domain?"

"Have you a domain of your own?"

What hair-splitting! . . . And now she launched out on a long speech which she had probably turned over and over in her mind for years, but which now in her heat took a strangely crude shape. Her words came strong and direct—so unlike her: "How did you come to me? As if you had a right to, as if you ought not to be refused! That was the beginning. If the room was not in order, if I myself were not ready, if I were sitting looking out at the sea, if I were thinking deeply over something, if there was no seat for you because things were lying upon the chairs—it was really only once or twice that I put things on the chairs to keep you from sitting down. And I cleared them away at once, didn't I? Didn't I jump up and clear the chairs? But by that time you were already out of temper, you looked at the clock and bowed as much as to say you could not wait. That acted on me like a cold douche and I did not try to detain you—you didn't expect me to beg you to stop, surely! And so you went away. Then came the next time. You had, no doubt, expected me to think of nothing else in the interval but how to please you next time—excuse me if I say so—but in that case you should have tried to deserve it. But you came just as before, always just as before. 'Am I intruding again?' you would say; though you did not really think such a thing credible. You were angry when it turned out that you had, in fact, come at an inconvenient time. I might be busy with something, I might be sitting writing in a little book I keep, I might be sitting of a summer evening painting—was I to think of nothing else in the world but of having everything ready for you? Why? I was quite unused to putting myself out like that; I came from a great house and was not accustomed to wait on any one's convenience. And what, I'd like to know, would you have said, if I had come and disturbed you at your everlasting books whenever I chose? That's how it was! I see you sit there smiling; I suppose all I have said seems to you sheer lunacy. But that's how it was!"

"I will not smile."

"You won't smile? Then I am sure you will do something else to make me feel ashamed—it comes to the same thing. Oh, my God, we should never have—I mean it was a pity that I ever came here!"

A pause.

"You are silent? You mean something by that, I suppose."

"Do you wish me to speak?"

"No, do not speak, it will only lead to more quarrelling. No, but I thought you might say something—a few words to reassure me. Is there no human kindness in you? I don't know why we should always quarrel; the husbands and wives I saw on my journey were always good friends. And now I have offered to make it up and shake hands, surely you might meet me half-way? I have tried twice to make things a little more as they should be between us; I have entreated you, have wept—"

Whether because he had now picked up a thread or two of sense in her outpouring or because he was tired of fighting, the Lieutenant simply said:

"It is too late, Adelheid."

"Yes, you made up your mind on that point, on such and such a date. I did not know you had done so when you came last—you might have said it was the last time, you might have warned me. Why did you not warn me? If you had I would have acted differently, I would have thought better of it at once, and asked for forgiveness. But no, you said nothing. You said to yourself that it was the last time, but you did not say so to me. Oh! that was not right of you, not at all right of you!"

"You have so often said that you knew me?"

"Yes. So I have. But I did not believe that it was the last time; that took me by surprise."

The Lieutenant thought long and carefully and then said, speaking in simple and measured words:

"So as not to make this a more painful discussion than it already is, let us leave the matter here. Things will never be different between us, and therefore we may as well drop all discussion. If we were to make it up now, Adelheid, it would be the same thing over again before a week had passed—I speak from experience. You would take to punishing me again. We have thrown away many of our best years in standing on guard one against the other. You have practised your arts upon me and I have allowed myself to be exasperated by them—but now I am done. We are, both of us, getting on in years, we are past our prime; we can no longer play the young lovers. Both for your sake and for mine I think what I say is best."

"Then there is no more to be said. Then—there is no more to be said!" Fru Adelheid thinks a little and nods her head. Suddenly she says: "Getting on in years? You are the first who has said that of me; during my whole journey last winter I heard just the opposite. But, as you like; don't mind being rude if it pleases you."

The Lieutenant rose.

"Do you know what happened to me?" she asked, still irritated. "When my son and I went about together every one took us for brother and sister."

But at this an evil spirit must have possessed him, for he answered sarcastically:

"Just think of it! Is Willatz so big already? And so grown up?"

And with that the Lieutenant walked off to his own room again.

This scene was no more the last than it had been the first; as the years went on the Lieutenant and his wife had many a rousing quarrel. But his stubborn will won every time, he never gave way in the least. All the same, he certainly got no pleasure out of being so. inflexible; it cost him a struggle to keep it up; this stiff-necked and capricious Adelheid from Hanover had, once for all, taken such absolute hold of his thoughts and senses. Otherwise why should he have hung about outside her door for years? And why, in the devil's name, should he have condemned himself to be virtuous for her sake and to let all the women in the neighbourhood alone? He was many a time on the very point of making an end of his torments by seizing his wife, holding her fast, carrying her—carrying her with the strength of madness into her own room; yes, he could see himself doing it and hear his own tongue uttering fierce words: 'I'll teach you—teach you to have whims, dearest!' He would sit on his sofa and picture it all to himself; he even got the length of pulling himself together as if to make the spring and seize her—then his dreams would come to an end. Things had gone badly with him; yes, indeed; but he was not cowed yet. A man should have it in him to be a little greater than his fate. He thought of the consequences of such a first act of violence; it would lead to perpetual repetitions, for Adelheid would not give way in anything. Was he, then, to make her life a constant struggle? There was another way, and it could be followed without unseemly violence. Married life must be lived with imagination.

The Lieutenant acted in the manner that became him; he was the superior, he had it in his power to take the law into his own hands, and he did not do so. Was he not an unusual man! The point of the thing in his eyes was that he had adopted this attitude without being begged or forced to do so—that would have had an opposite effect, you may be sure. He had himself determined how far his superiority should go—it should go to the furthest limit; his wife should be left in peace. That was acting in the spirit of the humanists.

Time passed; the Lieutenant grew greyer and greyer; he amused himself with his beloved books and with playing patience in the evenings—a truly unworthy pastime for a Willatz Holmsen! Sometimes he would suddenly rise and pull the bell-cord for no apparent reason. Daverdana, his young servant-girl, would come in and curtsy. But she did not come at once—not immediately—he had himself trained her to wash her hands before she came. Why? Did he want to gain time to compose himself? When Daverdana came the Lieutenant would be standing with both hands upon the table and would stare stupidly towards her. He had a crazy look.

"You have not touched anything in here, have you?" he says by way of excuse.

"No," she answers, frightened.

Oh, no! since that old matter of the alphabet, which she had turned wrong side out, Daverdana had touched none of the forbidden things in this room.

"You see, all these things were Willatz's: I am keeping them. Do you remember Willatz?"

"Yes, how could I not remember him?"

"That's right. He is in England; he is growing fast, he is as tall as his mother. Let me see, what is your name?"

"Daverdana."

"I can never remember it. But you are a good girl. That's all."

But Daverdana continues to stand there; she is holding something in her hand, but does not dare to hold it out.

"Is there anything you wish to ask me about?"

"No—yes, please," says Daverdana. "It is a picture of our Lars, if you would care to see it, sir. Lars that's at the seminary."

The Lieutenant does not take the picture, but puts his hand on the girl's and turns it a little; standing thus, he looks at the likeness, with his cheek close to hers. Did he do this because he wished to see whether she had clean hands? Or had he taken a fancy to hold a girl's hand in his?

"Why should I look at it?" he asks.

"That's what I said," answers Daverdana; "but father asked me to bring it with me. And he told me to thank you so much, sir, on Lars' account."

There stood the boy Lars in fine town clothes and wearing a thick watch-chain; a dressed-up fisher-lad with a coarse, common face.

The Lieutenant shows by a nod that he has seen all he wants.

"He looks grand!" says the girl. "He borrowed the clothes to be photographed in."

"He borrowed the clothes?"

"Yes, and the watch. And the ring he has on his finger—he borrowed that from a comrade too, so he writes. He is coming home soon now, is Lars."

The Lieutenant nods again to indicate that now he has seen quite .enough. He releases Daverdana's hand slowly and lets her go.

A protégé of his must not borrow clothes to be photographed in; a stop must be put to that. Ah, but there was so much the Lieutenant had to put that sort of stop to! Here at home, with Willatz in England, with the servants, the boy at the seminary, the merchants in Bergen—money simply melted away. The Lieutenant had changed his ring over to his left hand again. There was no end to his troubles. Then, of course, Willatz would be coming home for his holidays some day, he was quite a man now; had been called *Master* Willatz for many years, had learned to ride; but there was no horse in the stables for him when he came, and could a horse be got for him? . . .

Strange to say, the Lieutenant began to look forward a little to Holmengraa's return; how was that? Possibly, because he put him in touch with money and showed him a way out of all difficulties. And that summer evening when Herr Holmengraa landed down at the quay with his two children and his servants, the Lieutenant felt his spirits slightly revived, and he rode down himself and brought them up to his house.

XI

Great changes had come about on Segelfoss estate and in all the country round; the flour-mill had been built and set agoing, a humming sound was to be heard wherever one went, Holmengraa ruled like the King he was. Why did they ring the bells for an hour each day at the little church? The King lay dead at Malmö—Herr Holmengraa had come in his stead. How he forged ahead and made everything forge ahead! When the quay was finished and a great pier with odd-looking cranes had been built out from it, it was not long before a huge steamer lay alongside; it came from distant lands with rye and had foreign sailors on board, who went ashore with shiny hats upon their black hair and spoke a strange tongue. It was a fairy tale worthy of King Tobias. Even for the family up at the manor it was an experience when they were invited by the English captain, with Herr Holmengraa, to a supper party and were lavishly and nobly entertained. Had Herr Holmengraa a finger in the pie in the matter of this party? He had, to be sure, a finger in every pie. Later on, the captain and officers of the ship were invited to the manor to a grand dinner party. These were gala days.

And, to be sure, these changes brought with them progress and prosperity throughout the country-side. All this rye which was being turned into flour made it well-nigh impossible to find any want or hunger in these parts; if the worst came to the worst one would always be able to go to King Tobias and borrow, but for the present one could get work from him and take his pay. It was wonderful how much brighter life had become; casual labourers could get as much tobacco as they could possibly chew and farmers with horses carted for the mill and earned money enough to pay their taxes and to buy goods at the store. There was no end to the progress and prosperity. And Herr Holmengraa himself, too, seemed to thrive and blossom forth; the air of the pine-woods and the congenial work had restored his health, and as to profit, there could be no danger of that failing—no imminent danger, one might be sure! How could there be? Did not the local traders far and near send their five-oared and eight-oared boats for loads of flour? And had not things gone so far that an office and rooms had to be fitted up for a warehouse-manager down on the wharf? A post-office was opened at Segelfoss now, and Segelfoss became a port of call on the coast route for the Vadsö-Hamburg boats which came every three weeks from the south and from the north and landed mails and goods and loaded flour from the whole of the Nordland. Truly, there was work enough for a manager on the wharf; he had to deal with the mails and the forwarding business; he kept the books of the mill, wrote all the letters, superintended the workmen on the pier, had control of weights and measures. Before very long he had to have an assistant, the work increased so much. Even Per of Bua had quite a big business now, and received cases and barrels by every ship, and after New Year he was to have a spirit license, and then still more cases and casks would come for him—who could see the end of it all?

But Herr Holmengraa himself kept his eye on every one and everything—he was the ruling spirit. He did as much as all the others together, and yet never varied from his quiet and thoughtful and considerate behaviour. He did not like to be stopped on the road and asked about things, but he would reply in passing. That answered for a time, and then he had to change his method of dealing with people. They followed him, waited for him; if he was standing speaking with the Lieutenant, they would take up a position near by and wait till he had finished, and then waylay him. He had to teach himself to deal with them curtly: "Go to the wharf-manager!" "Ask the head miller!" There were some who would not give in, but were insistent: they had been to the wharf-manager, they had asked the head miller, they showered questions, objections upon him,—and so Herr Holmengraa was compelled to adopt a third method: that of ignoring all applications and not answering a word. If only he could have learnt from the Lieutenant the correct demeanour for a superior! *He* was far from dumb, but people very seldom troubled him with applications. No one understood better how to keep people at a distance than this high and mighty squire; he might ride over in person to one of his cottagers and speak to him and give him an order, but the cottager did not come to him next day with some objection.

"What do these people want?" asks the Lieutenant, on horseback as usual.

"I suppose they want to speak to me," answers Holmengraa. "I see a man amongst them who gives me no peace. He is a baker who learned his trade in Bergen; he wants to build a bakery here. I turn him away every day, but he comes back again. It will probably end by my having to give him a corner of the ground down there."

"Have you any personal objection to his building the bakery?"

"On the contrary. Humanly speaking, it ought to be to my advantage, but—"

"You can let him have a piece of my ground," says the Lieutenant.

Pause. Herr Holmengraa reflects and says:

"I have every cause to be grateful for this fresh courtesy; but I ought not to take advantage of it. To-day it is one thing; to-morrow it is another. You will have no peace either." After a while Herr Holmengraa continues: "It would be another matter if, for a suitable sum, you would let me have all the ground as far as the point."

The Lieutenant looks round him as he sits on horseback and thinks.

"Then we would not need to trouble you constantly with this sort of question."

"If you are in want of building-ground for the complete development of your business, I will, of course, not stand in the way of such an arrangement."

"Here again, sir, I recognize your high-minded and benevolent way of looking at the matter."

"Did you mean from the quay out to the point?"

"Yes. And in depth up to the home-fields. There are many who want to build."

The Lieutenant prepares to ride on and says:

"We can think about it. Oh! by the by," he interrupts himself, "the baker is waiting. You can write out the contract."

Holmengraa bows deeply and thanks him:

"I thank you on my own and on many others' behalf. Will you accept a price for the ground at the same rate as before, Lieutenant?"

The price! . . . The Lieutenant starts a little; it seemed it had now for the first time occurred to him to connect money with the transaction, at least any considerable amount of money. At the rate received for the last he had sold, this large piece of land would bring in quite a good sum.

"I accept your price," he said.

As he was riding towards the house he suddenly pulled off both his gloves, changed his ring on to the right finger and put on his gloves again. Saved! he may have thought to himself. A helping hand in the nick of time!

Nor did Herr Holmengraa seem to be dissatisfied. Quite contrary to his custom of late, he got rid of the people who were waiting with a few pleasant words: "The head miller will let you know about that." "Look here, if you give the wharf-manager this slip of paper you will get a sack of flour." He kept back the baker from Bergen and had a talk with him.

While he is standing talking there, a boy and a girl come running towards him—they are his children—the girl is the bigger. She is dressed in a yellow dress, the boy in red clothes; both look foreign, both have brownish complexions and brown eyes. They look as if they came from overseas: something forcible, barbaric in the cut of their noses, together with their full lips, gives them an outlandish appearance. But they are clever children; they came to Segelfoss with nothing but Spanish in their heads, and in this short time they have learnt to speak a good deal of Norwegian; they are already big tall Nordlanders full of health, playing and shouting all day long. Here comes the girl Mariane, tearing on in front, wild and full of life, and the boy Felix after her, both at full speed, bareheaded, with their black hair and low foreheads.

Their father opens his arms to receive them. He may well be pleased at their health and rosy cheeks. "Let me have a look at you!" he says in Norwegian, and they understand and stand still a moment and let themselves be looked at, and then they drag him along with them. "Thank God!" thinks Herr Holmengraa; "their coming to Segelfoss has not done them any harm!" and his mind is set at ease. All was going well; he had taken a great step, had transferred himself and his children from their far-off home and settled in a new one. Why had he done this? Perhaps it was the call of the blood, perhaps a human weakness had influenced him. How could he shine in the Cordilleras? He had been left lonely and a stranger by his wife's death; he had money and power—but no one to show them off to—there was a grey holm far away, he knew of a waterfall in the Nordland—there, at home, one might shine!

He and the children go chattering up to the big house by the river; he has long ago flitted from the Lieutenant's and lives in his own house, but he gets milk from the manor. At first he had had the annoyance of being unable to get any servants because his house was built of materials from a church: there must be ghosts and spirits in it; there was certainly a smell of dead bodies from the walls! So, to begin with, he got the Lieutenant to lend him some of his numerous servants to sleep in the new house through some critical Thursday nights. All went well, no ghosts appeared, and by the time a month had passed Holmengraa had servants enough; among them was Marcilie, who had at one time been maid down at the manor and looked after the Lieutenant's apartments.

Holmengraa had got everything in good order; even a garden was being laid out. His house was large and had cost much money; it lay in the forest, and from it one heard the distant hum of the mill, grinding night and day. Fru Irgens, née Geelmuyden, widow of a solicitor of Ytterleia, kept house for him.

❧

The *Orion* is making for the quay; on board is *Master* Willatz; his father and mother are both there on horseback to meet him; they alight; he gives his reins to one groom, she hers to another, as if husband and wife had come from different places. Holmengraa, too, and his children, are coming down to the quay to greet young Willatz—a mark of attention to his parents.

"There he is waving!" says Fru Holmsen and begins to wave back.

The Lieutenant too takes out his pocket-handkerchief.

There were quite a number of people on the wharf. The warehouse-man stood there with papers in his hands and his assistant held the mail-bag; they were both giving some final orders to their men. Per of Bua had closed his store and allowed himself a diversion for once. Children of all ages stood lost in wonder, staring at the ship; in the background Lars Manuelsen was to be seen, red-bearded and ragged and inquisitive. A few steps in front of him stood his son Lars, the student, who had come home by the last south-bound steamer and wore starched linen and long hair.

Then the steamer reverses her engines and creeps in to the quay and makes fast.

Young Willatz steps ashore and greets his father first, though his mother is standing nearer and has all the time been weeping and laughing to him. "How tall you are! Welcome home!" says his father, looking proud of him, visibly proud. Then the son embraces his mother and pats her and answers her many questions. Oh, he has grown so tall, quite a man, almost as tall as his mother! Young Willatz goes to Holmengraa and greets him and his children—he is so English, so polite and grown-up in his manners! The horses suddenly begin to whinny—why is that? The Lieutenant looks over at them, but there nothing unusual seems to have happened. "I really believe my Elza knows you again, Willatz!" says his mother, laughing happily.

The seminarist has come a little nearer; he awaits his opportunity and salutes the gentlefolk, and the Lieutenant gives a slight nod in return.

"There is Lars, I see," says Willatz. "I know them all; there's Julius too—father, I think you are greyer."

"Do you, Willatz? There is so much noise here. Adelheid, do you not wish to go?"

They turn and see three saddle-horses before them. "Whose is the strange horse?" says the Lieutenant, looking round in surprise. Herr Holmengraa comes up and answers:

"I hope, *Master* Willatz, you won't take it amiss—it's only a little gift from me to celebrate his home-coming."

What a great and pleasant surprise! What a fellow this Holmengraa is, every inch a King! A glossy, brown riding-horse, fully equipped, for *Master* Willatz! The heartiest thanks are showered on Holmengraa from every side, and for once in a way he seems to be a little uncertain of himself, when Fru Holmsen draws off her glove to shake hands and thank him.

"I am glad. So you really like it, Madam? There's no reason to thank me, none at all—"

The steed is examined and patted; it is a mare, fifteen hands, broken to the saddle, slender, fine hoofs. Yes, indeed! Herr Holmengraa may be congratulated on having made such a good choice. *He* had no need to accept anything for nothing; and as he had lived for months in the Lieutenant's house without being allowed to pay, the only way out of the dilemma, he may have thought, was to show his hosts little attentions of this kind, to do trifles of this kind for them.

"But I had no idea that you were a grown man, *Master* Willatz," says he with polite exaggeration; "we must lengthen the stirrups."

Then the mother and son rode off to the manor-house, a rich and distinguished-looking pair; even from the ship people gazed after them. The Lieutenant gave his horse to Halflapp Petter and went back with Holmengraa on foot.

"Do you know anything of the young man who is following us, Lieutenant?" says Holmengraa.

The Lieutenant turns round, shakes his head, and says "No."

"He is a seminarist. He wishes me to engage him as tutor."

"Indeed? No, I don't know him."

"My little Indians, as I call them, need some teaching. I thought I had some guarantee for the man in your interest in him."

"No. I have none, beyond paying for his education at the seminary."

"Do you advise me to try him?"

"Yes. Oh, yes! he's probably just as good as any other of the same kind."

Holmengraa changes the subject.

"Do you propose to cut timber this year, Lieutenant?"

"Perhaps. I must think about it."

"I ask, because there are people here who are anxious to build, but lack materials."

"Indeed? Well, of course prices are not bad just now, I do not know whether one would gain by waiting. We might go into the matter further?"

"Yes, thank you. Perhaps in a week's time?"

"Good, in a week. I will make enquiries."

The gentlemen parted and went each his own way. The seminarist followed Holmengraa up the river.

It was just as well, perhaps, that the Lieutenant had not bound himself then and there to deliver timber this year; for he had really no large-sized logs left, though there were large tracts of small timber, such as was sent to the mines in England. No, the Lieutenant had dealt too unsparingly with his forests; if he were not compelled to sell, he would be glad to put the brake on now. Forests are things that require reasonable treatment.

❧

The Holmsen household was all the better for this short visit of the son of the house; the place was not so dreary now, there was more conversation at table; the familiar and friendly sound of piano-playing was heard in the parlour. In the daily talks that took place with Willatz, both his parents could hardly avoid joining in and even at times exchanging remarks with each other; it was inevitable, too, that mother and son should sing and play at all hours, even at midday, when the master of the house was actually in his rooms and could hear everything, Once more an experience worth living for; Adelheid had forgotten nothing; her voice was the same as ever, and what a heavenly voice it was!

"Come along, you have not looked at the animals yet," says the Lieutenant to his son.

They went to look at them and stayed there a short time. Ay, the latest improvements in the cowstalls were splendid, and the new arrangements for bringing the fodder in trolleys; the pigs, the huge sows which waddled about like antediluvian monsters among their young; fowls of all kinds, guinea-fowls, yellow game-cocks with spurs like scimitars—yes, indeed, it was all very fine.

But the Lieutenant came out again at once; this inspection of the cowsheds was, it seems, only a colourable pretext. He took his son down into the garden, to the queer little hothouse which he had patched up and rescued from years of decay.

"Look here," says he, "there are still a few small flowers here; take some of them and give them to any one you like. Take this one; And this. Yes, certainly, the one you are holding—that is the best of all. You have come home, and you can have them. Look here! here's a whole bunch—whatever are they called?"

"They are roses."

"Perhaps they are roses. Here they are in a bunch, they remind one of a song, do they not? Almost like the one you two were singing a short time ago? Take them all. I have no idea where you can take them to; do as you like with them—"

The son, to be sure, has nowhere to take them but to his mother, to her rooms. His father is silent when he hears that, but does not shrug his shoulders nor wrinkle his brows—he shows very little interest in the matter and looks at his watch. He suddenly remembers that he has to ride out and look at the forest, and so he must go.

Hm. Yes, to be sure, it was pleasant to have the boy home again; the house was gay, the doors between his parents' apartments were no longer shut all day long. The Lieutenant was very proud of Willatz, although—hm—one or two things had not pleased him this last year. His son had developed a little too quickly, to judge by his letters, and he had begun to sign himself Will. Why? His last letter to his mother was even signed Bill—was that the same as the good old Willatz? And would it perhaps end in the whole name becoming Bill Holmes, a common one like any one else's? The Lieutenant was the head of the dynasty of Willatz Holmsens and would rule it while he lived.

Young Willatz certainly had no idea of derogating from the family name; he was only very young and very English just at present. And oh, how good it was to be at home again! Here were Jomfru Salvesen and all the maids throwing up their hands in surprise over the way he had grown; there was Martin, his father's man, and the other men touching their hats and unable to get a word out for sheer respect. Was not the boy born on a Christmas night?

Young Willatz rode out along the roads and past the cottages, rode quickly and then rode slowly past their doors, and saw faces at every window, and silent, staring children on the thresholds. After a few days this isolation bored him and he left his horse behind and went to see Julius on foot.

Julius had also grown a little, but chiefly his hands and feet—what wonderful hands he had! And besides, Julius was looking rather queer just then—he had clipped off his eyebrows to make them grow more bushy. At the sight of Willatz he behaved as an old comrade should and swore in his mother's hearing:

"What the dev—is that you, Willatz?"

Willatz laughs and says: "Yes, it is!" He pretends to be older than he is and speaks with a deeper voice than he really has.

The woman dusts a chair with her apron and brings it forward:

"Such a great stranger! You must be so good as to take a seat, sir."

Julius' small brothers and sisters stand in the corners and gaze at the stranger; they too have grown, so that their clothes are far too small—ay, how they have grown! There were no such big children in this cottage last time he was here.

"It's wonderful how tall you have grown, sir," says Julius' mother. "I hardly knew you, sir."

"Oh, well, it's a good long time since I last sat here," replies Willatz, in a grown-up tone.

"Yes, time flies!—Don't stand there with your tousled heads," she says to the little ones. "Go and make yourselves tidy!"

Julius stretches his arms out, yawns in a manly way, and says:

"What was I going to ask—have you come from England?"

"Yes, from Harrow in England."

"I am thinking of getting a berth soon and going to sea," says Julius.

"You?" asks his mother. "You ought to be ashamed to tell such a lie."

"Am I lying? Because I haven't said it before? I don't say all I think, I can tell you."

"I'll take down your trousers and beat you!" his mother threatens angrily.

Julius' face falls, he looks crest-fallen and subsides. When he recovers a little be turns to Willatz again:

"Were you seasick on the way home?"

Willatz replies:

"No, I managed all right. But plenty of people were sick."

But Julius sees that he cannot get at anything worth while here in the cottage—his mother is too much in his way. So he manages to get Willatz out with him and feels more at ease at once:

"You were a pig not to write to me as you promised."

Willatz is annoyed at his tone and tries to assert himself. What did this fellow Julius mean! Ought he, perhaps, after all, to have come to the cottage on horseback?

"Perhaps you don't think I had much to do in England?" he asks.

"Well, perhaps you had, but— But what I was going to say is, if you want to see how I have toiled and moiled this summer already, just come here!"

Julius led the way and Willatz followed. They went to the little barn which belonged to the holding, where the goat-fodder was stored. There Julius pointed to a heap of hay which lay in a corner and said:

"I cut that with a hook on the waste land!"

"Oh, did you?"

"And dried it and carried it home on my back. You bet, it was no joke."

"No, I dare say not."

"How many loads would you say it is?"

"That heap?" asks Willatz.

"I cut it for my own goat, but there's far too much for her. I am thinking of selling some of it."

"Are you?"

"If only prices would go up.—I saw you riding; can you ride?"

"Can I? You saw that I could."

"That's nothing anyhow," says Julius, "for I have ridden often.—Well, I must say you might have written to me," he goes on, closing the barn.

"You couldn't have read it in any case. And I had no time to print."

Julius was evidently chafing at feeling so inferior to Willatz, so to mend matters he said:

"As for reading and writing, I can easily get help now. What do you think of Lars?"

Willatz is silent.

"For he's my own brother," adds Julius, "and he knows a precious lot more than either you or I, I can tell you that!"

"I will see whether I can find time to write to you in the winter," says Willatz meekly.

Julius drags out of his trousers pocket a long fid of tobacco and offers it to Willatz.

"No, thanks."

"What, you don't chew?"

"No."

"Oh, well, I don't blame you for that. But I must get used to tobacco before I go to Lofoten. For if I don't I'll get fisherman's sores. You're lucky not to have to go to sea!"

"But you said you wanted to go to sea."

"Well, as to riding, Lars has seen plenty of it at the seminary. And they had a wooden horse to ride on; for a live one would not have stood it."

"A wooden horse? Yes, but I have a real horse," says Willatz.

"Yes, but it's not yours?"

"Not mine? Don't you know it is? It's my own horse."

"I don't believe it," answers Julius curtly and spits.

Willatz suddenly grows red and angry and says:

'You're an ass!"

Then Julius' face falls again and he weathers the storm by keeping silent. At last he says:

"Yes, Lars is next-door to a dean now. He's to be tutor at Holmengraa's. Have you seen Mariane and Felix?"

"No," replies Willatz shortly, still angry.

"Oh, yes you have; you saw them when you came, they were on the pier. They can't speak, only a word or two, for they only know Spanish. There are some who think they are heathens, but that's a damned lie, Lars says."

"How's Gottfred?" asks Willatz.

"Gottfred? I really don't know.—Willatz, have you nothing in your pockets you could sell me?"

"No."

"Not a pipe or a clasp-knife or something?"

Willatz takes from his pocket a little penknife with mother-of-pearl handle. Julius examines it and asks:

"Will you sell it?"

"No, why should I?" answers Willatz.

"What did you give for it?"

"It was given to me."

"I have just a threepenny bit; will you sell the knife for that?"

"No."

"All right," says Julius, "I'll give you fourpence in money and the rest in hay."

"I won't sell the knife," answers Willatz, putting it in his pocket again.

Then he started to go. No! Julius was not as interesting as he used to be—not even a pleasant companion; he had grown coarser as he grew older, he sickened one. There he was spitting hugely again. How disgusting!

"Where are you going? Are you going to Gottfred?" asks Julius.

"Yes, I have half a mind to."

"If you'll take my advice you won't go near Gottfred. I don't have anything to do with him as a rule."

"Oh!"

"No, he's such a thief. 'He's as quick at stealing as a horse at galloping'; you know the saying. I lost one thing after the other, and when I had lost three or four things, I jumped on him one day."

"You jumped on him?"

"Right on to him. You should have been there, Willatz. I tell you, it was something to see."

"Did you thrash him?"

"Thrash him? I should think so. And then he confessed all the tricks he had played me. I swear to you, I heard so much from his own mouth I could have had him put in prison; but I didn't want to do that."

Willatz stands silent for a short time. If only he could get rid of

Julius; but Julius stuck to him and was not easily shaken off. Should he just go?

"Well, good-bye," he said.

"Oh, are you off already?" Julius calls after him. "Shan't we go down to the beach?"

"No."

"Won't you look at my goat? And I have a mouth-organ too."

Julius gets no reply. He stands a moment and watches where Willatz is going, sees that he goes straight in the direction of Gottfred's home, that he will be there in a few minutes. Julius makes as if to shout, then suddenly thinks better of it, spits and goes in again.

Gottfred was thin and big-eyed as of old; Willatz found him standing on the threshold. They greet each other; but as Gottfred is shy of the rich boy, they do not say much to one another. No, there was little to be got now from these companions here at home, Willatz had grown out of touch with them, had left them behind him; they all disappointed him. Gottfred was the best of them, all the same, thin and quiet as he was; but he need not stand like that in the middle of the doorway when a fellow came and might want to go in. Gottfred did not understand these things.

"I was just taking a walk," says Willatz. "I get tired of riding all the time."

"We have seen you ride past many a time," answers Gottfred, glad to be able to say so.

"Yes, I suppose you have. It's my own horse."

"Yes."

"Did you know that?" asks Willatz—for in that case it was a pity that he had boasted of it.

"Yes, father heard that it was."

"Do you think I can have a little water to drink?" asks Willatz and looks past Gottfred into the passage.

"Yes, in the cook-house," answers Gottfred and leads the way.

It was a coal-black hole without a window in a hut adjoining the goat-shed. Here Willatz was given water in a wooden dipper. He had never drunk from a wooden dipper before; it was extremely thick to get your mouth over, and he was awkward in using it and the water ran down over him—besides, he was not particularly thirsty now.

"Are your father and mother at home?" he asked as he went back to the cottage.

Yes, Gottfred's mother was at home.

It was a rude way Gottfred had of placing himself before one in the doorway. Willatz would not have minded it, but as far as he remembered there used to be a little girl here in this cottage—she was not so very little either—and she had eyes she never used but for looking at the ground—but such dark blue eyes.

Gottfred's mother came out now and greeted the stranger and asked him to come in:

"I asked Gottfred to keep you outside, sir, long enough for me to get the floor wiped," she said. "We were in such a mess in here."

Willatz went in; the floor was wet, it had just been washed. But there was no one in the room—only three little boys, so the cottage was empty as far as he was concerned. Willatz declined politely to wait for coffee and got Gottfred out with him again.

"I hardly remember her," he said, "but is your sister at home?"

"Pauline? Yes, but she has gone to the store."

"She is nearly as tall as you now, I expect?"

"Yes."

"Is it true that Julius went for you?" asks Willatz.

Gottfred is a little confused.

"No. When do you mean?"

"He said he went for you and beat you."

"Yes, but didn't he say which time?"

"No. He said you had taken something from him."

"Oh, that time," says Gottfred.

Pause. Willatz does not understand and asks:

"What was it you took?"

"Took? Nothing; I only took back my mouth-organ. He had hidden it at his home."

"He beat you then?"

"Yes."

"Did it hurt?"

"No."

"Has he beaten you often?"

"Oh, yes; now and then he beats me."

Willatz does not understand all this in the least, but he feels angry and says:

"I'd like to see him try to beat me! But did you get the mouth-organ back?"

"Yes. But now he has taken it away from me again."

Willatz stares at him:

"But are you going to let him have it?"

"Well, I don't know. No, I'll try and get it back."

"Surely you don't need to ask it as a favor?"

"He wants twopence for it."

"Twopence for your own mouth-organ?"

"So he said."

Pause. Willatz stands and works himself up to a great resolve:

"Come along and we'll go to Julius!" he says.

Gottfred is more than willing to go and Willatz feels quite the man.

The affair was settled in a moment. Julius had seen the two young gentlemen and met them in the yard with the mouth-organ in his hand. He gave it up at once and declared he had only taken it for fun.

The two young gentlemen go off, away from this person and his door-yard; Gottfred is full of meek and humble admiration.

"Did you see how quick he was to fetch it?" he says.

Willatz swells with satisfaction.

"I'd like to have seen him be slow about it!"

They stand there on the road, meaning to go each to his own home, but there is no hurry and it is not often they are together. Perhaps, if Gottfred waits a little, his sister may come, and he will have company home.

Willatz opens his penknife and begins to whittle a twig. Gottfred looks at the knife, thinking he would like to have it in his hand for a little, to feel it. Suddenly Willatz shuts the knife and gives it to Gottfred.

"Look here, you may have this knife."

Gottfred had never had anything like this happen to him; he feels giddy, he can't believe it. He takes the knife and says:

"May I hold it?"

"You are to have it. You can keep it after I have gone."

Ah! Gottfred had certainly no idea of the kind of man he was dealing with; his eyes were unnaturally big, as he said hesitatingly:

"But dare you give it away? What if your father asks about the knife?"

"But it's my own knife!" cries Willatz with decision.

And now Gottfred wiped his hand well and shook hands in thanks. He was no longer standing there on the road, he was far away; he did not hear Willatz say: "Look, there comes Pauline!" Not that Willatz was any less happy himself; it was a wonderful state of things. And nearer and nearer came Pauline.

Willatz drew himself up and said:

"Gottfred, I shall have to begin to shave soon."

Gottfred is in a dream, and in a dream he answers:

"Why?"

"Why? Don't you see?" asks Willatz, stroking his cheeks.

"But doesn't it hurt?"

"That can't be helped. I can't go about like this."

Here is Pauline. Thin and tall and dressed in her best black—for she has been to the store—with a bundle in a handkerchief in each hand, with wooden clogs on her feet, and with eyes of which she makes no use but to cast them down.

Had she taken care to have her right hand free in time, they might have shaken hands, but she had not. So she just stands there; Willatz says good day casually and she hardly answers him. They did not talk to one another, and she looked only at her brother.

"Look!" says Gottfred and holds out the knife with a queer little laugh. "Who do you think I got that from?"

Pauline looks at Willatz and then she looks down at the ground again.

"You mustn't let Julius have it," Willatz warns him.

"Father shall lock it up," answers Gottfred.

"Then you won't be able to use it?"

"Oh, yes! now and then."

It seems to Willatz that the knife won't be made full use of if they do that, and he says:

"No, you must carry it on you every day. And if Julius takes it, then you must just write to me to England."

"Yes."

What would Pauline think of such power? But Pauline only looked up at him while he was talking, and then looked down again.

"There are two blades in it," says Gottfred to himself, with eyes for his knife only. "And there's a hook too."

"The hook is for buttoning riding-gloves with," explains Willatz. "But I have another hook for that. How have you been all this time?" he asks Pauline.

No, it was no use, he could get no response; Pauline only lifted her eyes once, blushed and answered: "Quite well."

There was nothing more to be said, so Willatz said goodbye.

But then the brother and sister began to talk. Willatz heard their voices far behind him, and when he turned and looked back Pauline had put both bundles down on the road and was standing examining the knife with her brother.

No! He had nothing in common with these old companions any longer; Pauline was like the others and the others like her. Willatz had even had a notion of speaking a little English to them, to give them some idea of the language, but no—it was no use—

XII

"I wonder whether the Coldevins are not coming this year?" Fru Adelheid would remark. And it was impossible to say whether she took much interest in the answer or not.

"No," answers the Lieutenant, "the old folk were so much distressed by the changes here that they are not likely to come again."

Consul Fredrik was not mentioned.

During the summer months nothing much happened, nothing except what was a novelty no longer, that Segelfoss changed little by little and became more and more built over. That was why Per of Bua had not been able to wait till the New Year for the petty license he was to have, but had begun already to sell bottles on the sly, there were such numbers that asked for liquor. And this business lent considerable life and jollity to tedious Sunday evenings.

People built houses here and there about the steamboat-pier, everything gathered about that, so that the lower part of Segelfoss began already to look like a little town of cottages where not long before there had been nothing but beach and a couple of boat-sheds. There was no doubt that life had changed its complexion for people since King Tobias had come to the place. Lars Manuelsen's cottage now—had not curtains appeared in its windows? It seemed, as was only to be expected, that his son, the graduate, had not been able to endure seeing his home without curtains. And from that day on did not Per of Bua have more and more enquiries as to the price of curtains?

And the question arose: was it worth a decent Christian's while any longer to hold a tenant-farm? No, a thousand times no! with its scraps of fields; the right of cutting fodder on the outlying lands, the trouble of bringing winter-fuel from the depth of the forest—! No, a tenant-farmer's life was not worth living now. Why, bless you! you could get flour at the wharf ready ground—flour that was sifted and snow-white into the bargain. Except for the potatoes, people would have been just as pleased to let the ground lie fallow, and were it not for the drop of milk for one's coffee, who would trouble to scrape together goat-fodder in the forest? That is how it was. It was the day-labourers that were having such a good time of it now! They got work from Holmengraa and were in Holmengraa's pay. On Saturday evening they got a ticket from the foreman, presented it to the wharf-manager, and received flour or money as they chose. That was the life for a human being! There were labourers who ran into debt so as to buy a horse and cart and did carting for the mill—why not? In a short time, no doubt, they would be able to pay for both the horse and the cart if they liked, for they earned good money and rattled money in their pockets as they stood at Per of Bua's counter. Altogether, money, ready money, was no longer a rarity. You could see this, too, by the farmers round about; bless you! they were growing rich at this carting. It was an unheard-of thing; they could even indulge in an extra cup of coffee after supper, and go about in the middle of summer in grand top-boots. Things reached such a point that the district-doctor, Ole Riis, began to regret that he had got a post in the south—he had made so much in the last weeks he was here. "The devil!" said Ole Riis. "People who could not afford to have a doctor for typhoid before, will fetch me fourteen miles now for a swollen finger."

Nor was the new doctor heard to complain. He was at once in great demand and was called out late and early; it became the fashion to try him, and it was a strange household that had not enough sickness about it to make it necessary to call in the new doctor. The wise-men and women, who before had been called in in case of sickness, had a very hard time of it now; indeed, they had so little to live on, it was pitiful to see them.

The new district-doctor had no doubt long meant to call on the Holmsens at Segelfoss, but his time had been too much taken up. It was not from want of politeness that he had not done so before, so he said when at last he came one day; "no, indeed, it was not from want of politeness!"

The mistress of the house received him; she was always the one to receive visitors; for she minded it least, in fact she probably rather enjoyed it, she was so lonely.

The man bore the incredible name of Muus,* but to see him was to believe it. A queer little doctor, well versed in medicine no doubt, certainly sallow enough to be dyspeptic; a face worn by hard study, a big nose, large, misshapen ears, and a scanty beard. He was asked to join the party—there was a little celebration to-day, a farewell dinner for *Master* Willatz, who was going back to England again.

The father and son come in, both dressed in their best in honour of one another. The Lieutenant shakes hands with the doctor and makes a few conventional remarks. Herr Holmengraa comes in with his two children—the two Indians, as he calls them.

"Poor children, why do you call them Indians?" says Fru Holmsen.

*Translator's note: Muus = mouse.

"My little Indians," replies Holmengraa. "Oh, they, don't mind it, you may be sure, for it makes them out descendants of Kuohtemoc, which indeed they are in some degree!"

"How is that?"

"They have a little Indian blood in their veins; their mother was a quadroon."

"Then they are quintroons," says the doctor. "Very interesting."

"Well, you are fine children!" says Fru Holmsen, and puts her arms round them both.

The dinner did not last long; Willatz must have time to change into his travelling-clothes, and the mail-boat was expected at any moment. A look-out had been posted on a height to warn the house of its approach.

The Lieutenant lifts his glass and wishes Willatz "a safe journey," and thanks him for a pleasant summer.

"Yes, God bless you!" says his mother; "and work well at school again! Has Papa given you plenty of money?"

"Yes, thank you."

"Well, now go and change your clothes."

Doctor Muus said nothing. Perhaps in his own home he was a connoisseur of wine, for after drinking he smacked his lips appraisingly. It seemed as if he were determined not to let himself be impressed—on special occasions anyone might have things as fine as this; he had been in company where even champagne had been drunk. Perhaps the doctor had taken his cue from information given him by his predecessor, the unlucky Ole Riis; perhaps, too, his delay in paying his respects to the Lieutenant was a deliberate slight.

While coffee is being served, Fru Holmsen had again to do the talking. Her husband was no doubt depressed, thinking of Willatz.

He listened politely to what was being said, and now and again made as if to answer, but then came to a stop. At last he merely sat there. One can be positive in speech, but the Lieutenant was positive in silence—met everything with silence. He was not always so preoccupied; something must surely be the matter with him, whatever it might be.

His wife had to try to keep the conversation going:

"You have come from the north, Doctor?"

"From Finmark, yes. We officials begin there, you know."

"You have been very busy since you came here, I understand?"

"Very. Especially here, round Segelfoss."

"That's the result of Herr Holmengraa's activities. Is that not so, Herr Holmengraa?"

But Doctor Muus is a logician and rises to the occasion:

"He-he; I should hope not. I should hope Herr Holmengraa's activities do not lead to the increase of sickness."

All look at each other. Herr Holmengraa smiles and answers:

"The Doctor grudges me Madam's compliment. However, there can be no doubt that works such as mine demand increased medical attendance, though they also provide the means to defray its cost. That is so everywhere; more people come to the place, and there are bound to be more accidents. There are dangers which people engaged in ordinary country occupations have not learned to guard against; a weight may crush a hand, a crane may get out of control, a winch-handle begin to whirl. Ole Johan was hit by a crank-handle yesterday."

"I have just been with him," says the doctor. "There's not much the matter, no extravasation of blood; it is only what we call a contusion."

Hoping the gentlemen are getting on well together now, Fru

Holmsen hastens up to Willatz for a few minutes. Poor woman! She might well feel sad at losing her son again, and with him all their singing and playing and chat.

When she came down, silence reigned again. She brought some illustrated books with her.

"Look, children! Willatz has lent us these books. And you must eat some cakes—help yourself, Mariane. Yes, you must; and you take this one, Felix. There now!"

"Will he be ready soon?" asks the Lieutenant.

"Very soon. Oh, if only he had not to go so far away. It seems so unnecessary."

"It is not so very far after all, Madam," says Holmengraa reassuringly. "With these fine, big boats he will be over there by Sunday."

Fru Holmsen smiles in spite of herself:

"Yes, and Sunday is just the right day to land in England on!"

Herr Holmengraa smiles too, and agrees: "It is true the English Sunday is not cheerful."

"Cheerful? I know of nothing that is cheerful in that country."

"Fru Holmsen is German," says Doctor Muus.

"Yes, thank Heaven!" she replies, and seems not to hear his next remarks.

On the whole this little man was not as congenial as little men often are. He sat eyeing the pictures critically as if he too came from a home where there were pictures. What was in his head? Fru Holmsen put on the grand manner and said:

"There is something hotel-like about the English home. I have been in many, it was the same everywhere. Servants in evening dress, table-service like an hotel, the ladies fleeing at the end of a meal. There are two signals for dinner. They ring one bell when it is time to go and dress, and then they ring another when dinner is ready. I thought I had a slight acquaintance with great houses before, but—"

"My father," said Doctor Muus, "was at a congress in England when a young lawyer. He could not find words strong enough to praise the life and the people there."

"And then they are an unmusical people," continued Fru Holmsen; "they hire people to play and sing for them in their homes; they hire people to sing in the churches."

The doctor remarks:

"Such a highly cultivated people probably does not go much to church."

"What does an organ cost?" asks Fru Holmsen suddenly—they would be coming to blows soon. "A small organ, very tiny, just a few pipes? If only we had such an organ in the church here!"

"That can surely be managed," answers Holmengraa. "And if one of the teachers could play, the whole thing could easily be arranged."

The Lieutenant strolled across to the window to see whether the ship was signalled. When he came back and sat down, his ring had been changed to his left hand. Then, thinking perhaps that Adelheid had exerted herself enough, and wishing to relieve her, he asked her to go again and see what Willatz was doing. He began to discuss business with Holmengraa:

"I told you once during the summer that I had no more timber here suitable for new buildings. I have been through the forest again, and I think I shall cut some after all. But it is probably too late now for what you wanted?"

"No, not at all; it will come in very handy. We shall require timber for some time to come. What are the measurements?"

"Small. Seven to eight inch by twenty feet."

"That is reckoned heavy timber elsewhere. Fine building-timber. I will buy it any day."

There is a signal from the man on watch—the ship is coming.

Fru Holmsen came down with her son. Willatz was dressed for the journey and said little; they had allowed themselves time to go into the drawing-room for a little music before parting. What a song those two sang, a duet, as was the fashion of the time! The mother swan and her young one pouring out their hearts to heaven!

"Fru Holmsen sings?" said Doctor Muus, listening to the music. "Is it Italian?"

When the Lieutenant was standing in the hall putting on his gloves he had his ring on his right hand again. This strange changing from one finger to another surely could not mean anything when it took place every few minutes; it must be just a habit, a bad habit.

They went down the hill, every one on foot for a change; Willatz walks with the little ones, who begin to run. Was there ever such a long-legged imp as Mariane! The doctor and the Lieutenant come last; the doctor says:

"Segelfoss has changed a good deal, I have heard. Are the changes entirely satisfactory to you, Lieutenant?"

"Oh, is that you, Doctor? Yes, thank you, I am satisfied, Where did you say you come from?"

"From the East-country. Why do you ask?"

"Only because I was reminded of some recruits I once drilled."

"Recruits?"

"Don't misunderstand me—they were fine tall fellows; it is when you speak you remind me of them. What did you say your name is?"

"My name is Muus."

"Muus."

The doctor chews a little at his beard and says:

"And your name is Holmsen?"

"Yes."

"Von Holmsen perhaps?

"No, just Holmsen."

The two men were about even with one another now, but unfortunately the doctor began to laugh, to display amusement, and the Lieutenant could not help looking at him in astonishment. There was a careless disdain in his glance; he seemed a little amazed at the doctor, but he considered it far beneath him to ask the cause of the other's laughter.

Willatz turned back to his father and said:

"You'll look well after Bella, won't you?"

"Oh, yes, my boy."

"Who is Bella?" asked the doctor, unabashed.

"My horse."

"Oh, Lord!"

Willatz looked at the doctor with something of his father's amazement in his eyes.

"My saddle-horse," he explained.

"When I was your age," said the doctor, "I already knew not a little Latin. Big boys like you ought to give their parents cause to be proud of them, you know."

And the doctor nodded in a fatherly manner to Willatz.

But Willatz had never heard such a strange way of talking; it was incomprehensible to him—it was not the language of another country, but of another world.

His father smiles at him:

"I fancy you did not understand what the doctor said. You know you don't always understand what Martin says either."

"Martin—who is that?" asks the doctor.

"One of my serving-men."

They were standing on the quay, the steamer came alongside, the Lieutenant and his wife went on board with their son. And Doctor Muus followed.

"One moment!" he said to the Lieutenant. "I only wanted to say that I would like to meet your man Martin. He must be a cultivated man."

The Lieutenant turned his head slowly and answered:

"The next time you visit Segelfoss, to say good-bye, for instance, you will enter through the yellow building in the courtyard. You will find Martin there."

"Thank you. If when that time comes you still have a yellow building and a man Martin."

❧

Herr Holmengraa has rather a lonely life of it at home; he has no one he can associate with on equal terms. Fru Irgens, the lady who keeps house for him, is a first rate hand in the kitchen, in the larder, and with her needle, besides being excellent with the children, and in looking after the gentleman's linen; but she neither plays nor sings—those are accomplishments beyond Fru Irgens. If Herr Holmengraa wanted a little pleasant society, he had to go over to the manor-house, to the Lieutenant's, where he was in quite a different world. He was not always sure whether the Lieutenant was pleased to see him—how could he know?—for, though the Lieutenant was invariably polite and obliging, he was cool and reserved, like the fine gentleman he was. His high-born wife, on the contrary, would often show pleasure when the visitor came, and it almost seemed as if this was of some consequence to Herr Holmengraa. He permitted himself now and then to pass Fru Adelheid when she was out riding. He did not do this often enough for it to be noticeable, but managed so that it led to an occasional greeting from a distance or a short conversation on the road. Once or twice the Lieutenant and his wife had looked in on him at his house, but only on some casual errand, or to admire his luxurious rooms. On the last occasion the lady had been alone and she had begged Herr Holmengraa to drop in at the manor-house again—he had been there so seldom lately.

"When shall I have the honour of seeing you and the Lieutenant here for an evening, Madame?" Holmengraa had asked.

And Fru Holmsen had thanked him, and promised to come any evening he liked. "And I hope it may be soon!" she had actually added with a smile. She was so amiable.

And now, as Holmengraa stands on the quay, he has everything in readiness for entertaining the Holmsens.

He has planned to invite them to-day, at once, as a little distraction for these parents who are standing gazing seawards, waving farewell to their son. He may have thought of inviting the new district-doctor, Herr Muus, too, but it was pretty clear that the doctor would have no more time to spare to-day, so he would have to ask him another time. Holmengraa had a talent for divining a situation, for doing the right thing; he doubtless took it for granted that the Lieutenant and his wife would prefer to be alone that evening after parting from their son.

He induced the Holmsens to go with him.

Fru Irgens would doubtless have liked it to be a grand supper, but the host would not hear of that; no, there was only a delicate dish of *Bacalo*, and light Spanish wine. Holmengraa had willed it so, he was firm in his modesty, and would not attempt to outdo the gentry at the manor-house.

Fru Holmsen was surprised to find a grand piano in the house, quite new, a heavenly Steinway. "Yes, just arrived," said Holmengraa, "and would Madame do me the great kindness of being the first to try it?" She threw herself upon it like the born musician she was, and poured out floods of harmony into the evening.

Was it possible to understand this woman?—with her wonderful voice, deep and rich in tone as violets. If her husband, with his Arab head, had ever thought her cold, he surely could not think her so now. Of what did she sing? Of fire and ashes, of longing and love. And then she played sonatas, fantasies, chorales: on and on she sang, playing from memory, till at the end of half an hour she stopped because she could remember no more. Was it not wonderful?—how all the time, all through the half-hour, at the end of one song or piece of music she glided without hesitation into the next—was this woman's heart cold? But in truth the Arab had never thought her so, for if he had he could not have cared for her.

Fru Irgens, in passing through the room, thanked her with genuine feeling: "You must really let me thank you, Madam, for this great pleasure," she said.

"Do you not play yourself?"

"No. I only learned a little, like every one else. I had not talent, but I had to learn a little. It was not worth speaking about."

"This is a wonderful piano, Herr Holmengraa."

This was all Fru Holmsen said about the piano, for if she had said more she would have put all sorts of ideas into her husband's head again—she remembered what had happened about the organ. Her husband was actually thinking of getting that unfortunate organ for the church; he had told her so, and it distressed her, for they had more urgent uses for the money. Had she ever complained of the old piano at home? Never! But would she have *liked* a grand such as this one? Yes, better than anything else in the world. But she said nothing. Had she it also in her mind, perhaps, to prevent Herr Holmengraa from offering it to her? He was rich and American in his ways; he might possibly have intended this instrument, so superfluous in his house, for her, just as he had given Willatz the riding-horse. But this man was easily managed; if she gave him this hint he would understand that a grand piano was far too valuable a gift.

Indeed, Fru Holmsen could not help admiring him in many ways. How old was he? About the Lieutenant's age; a little older, perhaps; slightly grey like him, but with a much more ordinary face. In the course of a varied life in the great world outside, he had acquired an agreeable manner; he was full of kindness, of delicate reserve. She remembered the supper party the English captain had once given—this evening she had recognized some of the silver used at that supper. So, no doubt, it was Herr Holmengraa who had arranged that party too, from behind the scenes.

Was she deceiving herself? Had Holmengraa shown them this and all his other almost daily delicately veiled attentions, just in order that he might be discovered? She could not judge; but at least his attentions could not have been more tactful if he had been in love with her. The man was singular and mysterious; what did she know about Kings of the Cordilleras?

But once in a way, on rare occasions, one would get glimpses of a coarser vein in this man—could one wonder at that? No one could make fewer mistakes than he did, considering that he had never had the advantage of culture either by birth or upbringing. Fru Holmsen remembered her journey to England in his company.

His quiet friendliness had been remarkable, he had been an invaluable travelling-companion from morning to night, ready for every emergency, always interesting, always considerate. There were other ladies on board, but he showed attention to none of them; nay, there was a young beauty on board, the captain's niece, who was used to admiration—Fröken Ottesen was her name, she thought—Herr Holmengraa never even seemed to see her. But one evening he had come and told her that the secretary of the Danish Legation in London was on board—a distinguished man, travelling with his suite—would Madam like to speak to him? "No! Why should I?" the lady had answered, looking at Herr Holmengraa in surprise. And he had had nothing to say in reply. She could not help smiling as she thought of it now. She had, however, put things right again by saying to him: "No, thank you; I have the best of company in you!" It seemed, then, that this man had one or two curious traits beneath the surface: he ignored every one on board, but was at once impressed by an old Secretary of Legation. Later on she saw him standing at the foot of the companion-way bowing deeply when the diplomat went up or down.

This unfathomable King Tobias. . . .

"The doctor must have been sent for to one of the cottages," says Herr Holmengraa, looking out of the window; "his boat is only now putting out from the shore."

"Oh, the doctor," says Fru Holmsen. "I am glad no one with us is sick and needs a doctor. I don't know—well, it would not be pleasant."

Her husband looks at her.

"I mean, to have sickness in the house—to have to send so far for the doctor," she adds hastily.

Herr Holmengraa, by way of throwing out a feeler, says: "I have been considering whether I should not appoint my own doctor for the works and the neighbourhood."

"Why?" asks the Lieutenant.

"Doctor Muus is too far away, and perhaps he has too much to do. He does not come quickly enough when any one is ill; my people have been speaking about it for some time."

This set the lady at her ease again, and she leant back with a new conception of Herr Holmengraa's power: he could appoint his own doctor. But she did not wish this to be done on her account.

"You must not do that," she said. "Doctor—what is his name?—Muus is no doubt both clever and conscientious. Don't you agree, Willatz, that Herr Holmengraa should not do that?"

"No," said the Lieutenant.

And Holmengraa let the matter drop, saying:

"Doctor Muus is no doubt clever enough, and that is what I told my people. I hope the trouble will pass over. But there have been complaints."

The Lieutenant begins to amuse himself with the children. He gets them to show him photographs of their mother; there were many of these standing on the piano, very fine portraits; in one the lady was dressed in Indian costume. Did they remember her? Yes. Had not Mariane a beautiful dress like the one her mother was wearing? Oh, yes, and Felix had an Indian dress too. Then they must come over to the manor some day in all their finery.

Fru Adelheid looked up; she noticed for the first time that Holmengraa's eyes were fixed upon her furtively. It was a mere chance, no doubt; and he said at once:

"I was sitting thinking that I would have liked my wife to have heard Madam this evening. She was very musical.

❧

During the winter the Lieutenant not only fells timber to sell to Holmengraa for building, but also saplings to send south, pit-props, the kind England and Belgium use in the mines. Nor was that all; as time passed he seemed to have acquired a taste for ruining himself—for two years on end he cut props in his young forest. What was coming over the man. Yet no doubt the Lieutenant had his reasons for acting as he did; his large household, his father's bank debt, which was still unpaid, his expensive manner of living, expensive tastes, an expensive son in England, all kept the squire of Segelfoss hard pressed for money. He hardly knew himself what became of his money; an inexorable fate sucked it from his grasp. Had he not by degrees become more and more of a philosopher, he would probably have given up the struggle. There was the organ for the church, for instance; could he put off getting it any longer? It was a disgrace that it had not been bought already; Herr Holmengraa might take it into his head to forestall him and that would be a nice business. This church was, after all, a Holmsen church through and through, and was a complete stranger to present it with an organ?

But it seemed impossible that he could ever afford to purchase this little instrument. What would it cost? Some hundreds, for all he knew, three hundred, perhaps more. He spoke to Adelheid about it again:

"With reference to the organ you once expressed a wish for, I have taken some steps about it," he said, as indeed he had. "They want the dimensions; I do not know the dimensions; a loft will have to be built for it, but there is no room for a loft anywhere in the church. The church will have to be enlarged."

"No, certainly not," answered his wife. "I beg you to give up the idea of the organ; there are more important things."

"Are you thinking of anything in particular?"

"No. I am thinking of Willatz, and only of Willatz."

"Willatz is big and clever, he deserves your solicitude. He is doing very well for the present; be is at the best of schools; he is preparing himself for a future worthy of him."

"God knows!" said his wife.

"What do you mean?"

"I am not sure that his school is not altogether too dear."

"It is very dear. But then he is our only child."

The fact was, in many things the lady was by no means lacking in good sense, nor had she fixed ideas which had to be pandered to; perhaps she had noticed that her husband was in difficulties. Dear Willatz ought rather to be in Germany; his companions ran him into first one extravagance and then another; those lords' sons could of course afford a whole household, a tutor, and servants. In the last holidays Willatz had taken part in a costly school-trip to France for the sake of the language; this year he was to make the trip again.

"He writes about new clothes—I don't know; do you think they are necessary? I do not think so. And in any case he ought not to buy the terrier he writes about."

The Lieutenant answered:

"You are no doubt right again, Adelheid. And had I known your wishes before, I would have acted differently. But it is too late. I have sent the money."

"Then I suppose it can't be helped."

"After all it is a trifle. By the by, didn't Willatz write about a knife, that a knife he had given to Gottfred may possibly have been taken from him by another boy?"

"By Julius. He asks me to look into the matter, and I was thinking of doing so to-morrow. You really must not—"

"I am just riding that way and besides I know my way about the cottages; I will see about it at once. To-day is Sunday, the boys will be at home."

The Lieutenant rides to little Gottfred's home, knocks on the window with his whip, and has the boy sent out.

"My son gave you a knife, a penknife; have you got it still?"

"Yes," answers the terrified Gottfred; then he says "No," and can hardly stand on his feet. He glances behind him into the cottage for help.

"Has any one taken it?"

"Yes," answers Gottfred.

His mother has now got herself a little tidy and she comes out.

"It happened in this way," she explains; "father had always kept the knife for Gottfred, but then one day in the autumn—it was an unlucky day,—one afternoon—"

"Has Julius taken it?" asks the Lieutenant curtly.

"Yes," answers Gottfred.

The Lieutenant turns his horse and nods, saying:

"You shall have your knife back again!"

Thereupon the Lieutenant rides to Lars Manuelsen's cottage.

To-day is Sunday; Lars' son, the graduate, who is paying a visit to his home, stands, bowing, on the threshold.

"Call Julius out."

Lars obeys and brings his brother, who looks pale and peakfaced with fear.

"You have a knife of Gottfred's; go in and get it."

Julius does not deny this, but tries to say something, to explain;

the Lieutenant makes an impatient movement as though to dismount, and Julius flies into the cottage.

Lars stands there looking miserable, till his brother comes out again and delivers up the knife.

"You have broken a blade," says the Lieutenant.

"No, that was done before," replies Julius; "indeed it was, sir!"

"The next time you touch anything my son gives to any one you will have a taste of this!" says the Lieutenant, and makes a cut with his whip in the air.

Julius bounds back into the house as quick as lightning, leaving the door open behind him.

Then the Lieutenant, as he sits on horseback, hears Lars Manuelsen, the father, beginning to growl inside. You see, Lars Manuelsen had begun to get up in the world, he was working at the mill, and earning money; there were curtains at his windows; he had a son who had gone through the seminary; his daughter Daverdana was no longer an ordinary servant-girl either, but was walking out with the wharf-manager's assistant. Lars Manuelsen growls and says:

"What's that? Did he hit you, Julius?"

The Lieutenant was about to ride off, but he reined in at once and said to Lars:

"Call your father out."

And Lars obeys again.

The old man comes out in his red shirt-sleeves, made of cloth from Per of Bua's shop; yes, Lars Manuelsen was a somebody now.

"What are you grumbling at?" asks the Lieutenant.

"I? I was just asking the boy—"

"I thought you were grumbling?"

"All the same, if the boy didn't break the blade of the knife, he shouldn't be blamed for it."

"Now listen, Lars; you stole some sheep from my grazing-grounds last autumn again. You'll stop that: I give you this one warning."

"What are you saying? Have I stolen sheep?"

"That might pass. But you sell skins with my brand on them at the store down here, so that my man, Martin, has to buy them again. I won't have skins and hides from Segelfoss mixed up with your dealings."

"You can't say that I have exactly *stolen* sheep, for it is not the truth—"

The Lieutenant makes a cut with his whip in the air:

"One word more and I send you to prison!"

"Oh, sir!" says Lars Manuelsen, his mouth twitching. "If I did have the misfortune to take a sheep, you must think of my large family, sir. It would have been a different thing altogether if I had made a poor man poorer, but you, sir, who can well afford it— But I don't deny that it's the truth that both Lars that stands there and Daverdana cannot thank you enough, sir—"

"Get your father in again!" shouts the Lieutenant in a rage. And then he turns to the son: "What have *you* been standing here for all this time? All this had nothing to do with you; if you behave yourself properly you will have no reason to regret it. What is it you want to say?"

Lars is evidently loath to bring out what he wants; does not know if he dares to. He had stood there throughout the whole scene—a strong, rough fellow, with bent head—looking pinched and humble.

"I can't say anything about this," he says. "It was not my fault."

The Lieutenant begins moving off.

Lars walks a step or two beside him and says:

"I have been reading with the pastor for a year; I want to try and rise in the world; I am going on studying."

A type, the Lieutenant no doubt thinks. The peasant who works himself down to priest. Yes, how he will go on studying! But probably, after all—from a philosophical point of view—it was only the eternal round; nothing was lost; Lars was too lazy physically to be a fisherman.

"I am ashamed to ask you, sir, but if you could see your way to give me a helping hand till—until I can study by myself for a year or so—"

It was perhaps not the right moment for such a request—or was it perhaps just the right moment? After the scene with the two evildoers, the Lieutenant could afford to show magnanimity. Did not everything point that way? The lad Lars was in Holmengraa's service, but it was not to him that he turned; he went to the lord of the manor as before, to the master of Segelfoss who held every one in his hand. Besides the lad was Daverdana's brother, and Daverdana was a good girl.

"I want to take private lessons," Lars concluded.

The Lieutenant nodded and answered:

"I will help you."

Short and to the point, settled. The Lieutenant rode back to Gottfred. What hard work, what a ridiculous fuss for the sake of a penknife! but the Lieutenant did nothing by halves. Mother and son are on the doorstep; Pauline with the big eyes is standing in the doorway.

"Was the knife whole when you lost it?"

"Whole? Yes."

"Whole?" says Gottfred, and looks at his mother. He does not understand it; wasn't the knife whole? had any one broken it?

"Yes, the knife was whole and clean, we had put it away in the box. But it was that day—"

The Lieutenant unbuttons and removes his glove, opens his coat, and takes his own knife out of his pocket. And this one had a silver handle with an animal's head at either end, and it had two glittering blades and a hook to button gloves with. The Lieutenant had bought it himself during his stay in England.

"Willatz sends you this knife instead of the other," says the Lieutenant.

Gottfred is so amazed that he dare not take the knife; he stands there scarlet in the face, putting out his hand once or twice and drawing it back again. He hears his mother utter a cry: "No, it's *too* much!" When at last Gottfred holds the treasure in his hand, he does not say a word of thanks; only when his mother reminds him does he stretch his hand up over the saddle.

The Lieutenant takes the hand and nods—the Lieutenant does more, he holds the hand for a while; such a little hand, but something alive, something that moves in his—the hand of a grateful child. What has come over the Lieutenant.

"Your name is Gottfred?"

"Yes."

"Come to me to-morrow about this time."

"Is he to come to you, sir?" asks his mother. "Was it to-morrow you said?"

"To-morrow at twelve o'clock."

And the Lieutenant rides away.

XIII

And now things go with the rush of an avalanche. Months and years pass by—not with the smooth and uneventful course of ordinary months and years, but with sweeping strides; with changes great and small. Segelfoss and the neighbourhood would not be recognized as the same place as during the Lieutenant's reign; nothing had really gone under, but all—both man and things—had changed in appearance and character, and was changing still.

Take, for example, the Coldevins; they never came now. "Are they not coming this year either?" Fru Adelheid would ask. "No, not this year either." Then she would wait another summer and another winter and say again:

"It is so strange that none of them come. Are *none* of them coming?"

"None," answers the Lieutenant. "Fredrik writes that his parents have grown very old and would rather stay at home. He sends his remembrances."

"And Fru Fredrik and the children?"

"He does not mention them."

Fru Adelheid chances to drop a pin on the floor and takes a long time looking for it. Still searching, she says:

"But Fredrik himself?"

"He has not time. . . . Did you drop a pin? Let me help you."

"Thanks, I have found it."

Yes, everything had changed, even the Coldevins. They came no more. And everything went on changing.

Was there not even a talk of making the rural-district of Segelfoss into a separate parish? But that was probably far off yet; Pastor Windfeld could not support a plan which would reduce his incomings so greatly. "But when my days here in the north are numbered," he said, "you may do what you please!"

His days in the north—then he must have thoughts of leaving. In the life he led he had many blessings; he had a large pastorate and little to do. He had been here for sixteen years, too, and was minded to hold out as long as possible; he had taken firm root here and made his home in this country-side. But he must go south some day; he was a servant of the church and souls in some town or other near the capital had need of him. Should he live and die in the Nordland? In the Nordland? He, C. P. Windfeld, could not be doomed to such ignominy. Had he not been a prominent preacher of God's word, and had he not also been able to add to the parish archives some records of the new church at Segelfoss?—who could have done more? Should not such a man seek a call in the south? With God's help he would not disregard the church's rule that a pastor should change his parish from time to time.

But, with God's help, he seemed likely to have a worthy successor—Lars Manuelsen's son, Lars Larsen, was busy studying for the ministry.

Oh, this Lars! he was a prodigy—a regular glutton for books! He had been in Christiania and passed an examination; had disappeared for a year to lay the foundation for still more culture; and had then come forward again and passed another examination. At the seminary in Tromsö he had begun to call himself Laursen, but here in his home parish, as tutor to Herr Holmengraa's children, he had been unable to keep to this name: for a long time now he had been called Lassen, L. Lassen. Every one talked about his passion for study—it was superhuman. When the Bishop came to the parish on his rounds he said: "If Lassen does not take a little care of himself we shall lose him; they say he has a weak chest already; he will kill himself!"

The parish was proud of its prodigy and people actually began to swear a little less when even the father, Lars Manuelsen, was present. Every time he passed an examination his name went from mouth to mouth, and more than once the boy Lars was the subject of discussion at Per of Bua's counter: "If only he can stand it!" says one. "Yes, if only he does not kill himself, as the Bishop said!" adds another. "He'll be sure of salvation then," says some one, "so what harm if he does?" At this Lars Manuelsen, the father, bursts in: "You talk like a beast, you've had a drop too much!"

How the tongues wag!

Ay, they did get a drop too much on board at Per of Bua's now and then; it was a lively place, what with gossip and the rattle of money and the constant coming and going, and the wine-barrels always on tap. And all the time P. Jensen himself grew closer-fisted and richer and more respectable, though he did not cease to be a peasant and dress in peasant's homespun. Every one should have known now, of course, that a man of his means would never cheat a child; but do you think people suspected him any the less? They went on as before keeping a check on his dealings and objecting and protesting when necessary. However, P. Jensen did his share for the prosperity of the people and the place; no one could deny that. When he failed to get leave to build a dancing-hall, he gave the young folk the run of a boat-shed behind the point; a wooden floor had been laid down in this shed, strange to say, and it did very well for social meetings on Sundays.

But Herr Holmengraa, the man who ruled every one and everything, neither grew thin from hard work, nor fat from prosperity. Gentle in manner and upright in dealing, he went his way and managed his enormous business. He was reckoned to be worth a hundred thousand dollars now; but the year the coinage changed to crowns and ore every one became so muddled about the value of money that Herr Holmengraa was put down straightway as worth a million. Did he complain? Not he. His attitude seemed to be that, thank goodness, he need not complain if they assessed him at two millions of this newfangled currency. He must be made of money. He now owned the outskirts of the Segelfoss estate, the works, the quay, and the wharf; he also owned the store and the bakery down by the sea—though they were carried on under other names. People were certain, too, that he financed several of the dealers along the coast—Henriksen of Utvaer at any rate. Indeed, it was thought that his possessions stopped short only at the estate of old squire Coldevin of Ytteröya, who was altogether too rich to be bought up.

Was there any limit to his activities!

Recently he had been working to get the telegraph to the place, but that had been rather a slow business. The State had intervened and had had the matter under consideration. People were convinced that if the State hesitated even a very little longer, Herr Holmengraa would build the telegraph line at his own expense. And just as if the State had at last recognized this danger, it sent poles, wire, and workmen and began the installation.

And the mill hummed incessantly. Time after time big cargo-boats came with grain from the Baltic and the Black Sea; not long since, a consignment of wheat had arrived, so the people had one more want supplied. Wheat!—a fabulous grain, a product of the south! The mill ground it, the people bought it—in fact, wheat-flour became very popular; white bread appeared in the bakery and white porridge on the poor man's table. It was a wonder that people—especially small children—had been able to keep body and soul together before, when the porridge was not white as snow!

What more could one wish for now? An attorney and notary, too, had settled in the neighbourhood, a young man so primed with legal knowledge that people began to be a little cautious what they said and did. There was no longer any need to take long journeys or actually go to court in order to get justice: District Attorney Rasch could settle the matter on the spot. It was a good thing he had come, and Herr Holmengraa had a small house ready-built for him when he arrived.

Herr Rasch had wished to call on the gentry at the manor, but instead Holmengraa had arranged things so that the introduction to the Lieutenant and his wife took place out of doors—a good idea for which both parties were grateful.

This was how it came about.

The spring flood had burst the Lieutenant's mill-dam and carried his mill with it. As a matter of fact this little mill had been at a standstill for several years, ever since Holmengraa had built his mill; but even as it stood it was one of the minor glories of the estate and now it was gone. But the saw-mill—how about it? It was gone too. And it looked as if the mill and the saw-mill had been cleared away from the river just to suit Herr Holmengraa: it seemed most remarkable, most astonishing—these two buildings had in fact stood in the way of a new scheme of Holmengraa's—and now the river had removed them.

Nor did Herr Holmengraa disguise the fact that he was partly to blame for the misfortune: he had dammed the river up too much in order to float down building-timber from the Lieutenant's forest.

When the Lieutenant went up the river to look at the damage, his wife had really been sorry for him, he felt it so keenly—that his father's and grandfather's flour-mill and saw-mill were gone. He had come home to dinner and was going back to the scene of the disaster, and his wife had asked to be allowed to go with him. At first he bad seemed surprised but had then said: "I thank you for your sympathy. Put on high boots!"

And then Holmengraa on his side had got young Attorney Rasch to accompany him and had gone after the Holmsens. Thus the four people met.

The noise of the river was deafening; they greeted one another, but their words were scarcely audible—Holmengraa had to speak loudly when he presented Herr Rasch. It was strange to see the young man take off his hat and bow while his words were drowned by the roar of the waters.

They all walked away from the spot at a slow pace, the Lieutenant in front; when he halted, Holmengraa said:

"There you see what blunders an amateur can commit! An expert would never have dammed up the river for the sake of those logs."

The Lieutenant pricks up his ears:

"Did you dam up the river? Why?"

"Out of stupidity, I am sorry to say. I am very unhappy about it. Now, if you will only give me the necessary time, I hope to be able to repair the damage."

"What will you do?"

"You had a dam there, a flour-mill and a saw-mill, I will rebuild them all."

Pause.

"As a matter of fact they were old buildings and of no use," says the Lieutenant. "No, you must not rebuild them."

Did Holmengraa expect this answer? No one knows, he said nothing about it. But he said to the Lieutenant very respectfully:

"Then there is another way. I have made your half of the river useless to you and I will pay you its value."

Pause. The Lieutenant is putting two and two together and coming to a conclusion:

"You wish to own the whole river?"

"If you have no objection."

The Lieutenant begins to walk on; they all walk on. When they came to where their ways parted he stopped and said—and by that time he had had good time for reflection:

"I will not do that; I will not sell more of the river."

Had Holmengraa expected this answer? He was not at all disconcerted, but said with his usual complaisance:

"There is a third way out: I will offer you whatever compensation you think fit."

❧

A couple of days later Herr Holmengraa walked up along his own side of the river. He probably had his new scheme in mind and was taking measurements with his eye, pacing out the ground and making estimates. The new scheme? Yes, a new scheme.

A short time after, the Lieutenant came the same way; he was on foot. As he had gone over to Holmengraa's side of the river, and as he never did anything covertly, he was no doubt looking for Holmengraa. Now and again he paused in thought.

Yes, how he had thought and thought, these last two days, and was still thinking! When he rejected Herr Holmengraa's offer to buy the rest of the river, it might well have seemed a piece of folly, a whim; but the Lieutenant knew that he had good reasons for what he did. The bank, to safeguard its own interests, and after consultation with the Bergen guarantors, had requested him to desist for the present from further sales of Segelfoss rights and property.

It was a patient bank to have let things go on for so long. But, none the less, this was an affront to the owner of Segelfoss, and he had been greatly annoyed. An awful possibility began to dawn upon him in these days—that house and land might be taken from him. How was he to justify this to his successor in the Willatz Holmsen dynasty? All his cogitation had left him where he was; perhaps he had not as yet concentrated his thoughts sufficiently. This was only the beginning, mere trifling! He might have seen a picture of himself in the behaviour of the hens on his farm: when a hen gets an idea she cocks her head first on one side and then on the other, considering whether the posture of things in general is suitable to her carrying out what she has in mind. Then she flutters at it in a feeble and futile manner, and only stops if she gets some new piece of folly into her head. Nothing in the world will induce her to turn right round of her own accord; she may turn aside, she may follow a slanting course, but turn round she will not.

Why should the Lieutenant turn? He had not squandered his money—he had not even bought the organ yet, worse luck! No, he was the victim of a law, a force of nature; and how could one struggle against that? As an old soldier he knew how to obey, he obeyed when the retreat sounded! He was not ruined, of course; he himself and no one else owned Segelfoss estate, he himself and no one else owned the big house with its many valuables. But his property was burdened with debt; and in itself the idea of debt to others was the most intolerable thing he knew. True, he might now save himself once again by accepting Herr Holmengraa's offer of compensation, but how much would that amount to? It would not even silence the bank, and afterwards he himself would have nothing left to go on living for. He made no excuses for himself, not a bit of it; all that could be said was that he did not understand the thing, and that there must be some force working against him. He might have said to himself that no one could go on throwing money about when none was coming in, but he did not. Of course there had been no need to discard almost unused patience cards—that was too ridiculous; and, strictly speaking, he had had no need for the expensive cloak he indulged in for his journey to England. Such things, however, did not amount to much, and they were about the only extravagances he could think of. There hung the cloak now; he never went to court, there was nothing to bring the general to the Nordland, so when was the cloak to be used? If he were to suffer a great and unavoidable downfall, it was possible that his wife, Fru Adelheid, might reproach him with one or two things—would that the cloak had lain at the tailor's—a large, uncut piece of cloth—to this very day. It was true he had had to put up with some things from Adelheid—among others, she had made a bachelor of him in the midst of their married life—but he could bear that as long as he knew himself free of blame—what if she now were to be able to reproach him with good reason! He was so constituted that he could bear undeserved blame, but not such as he felt that he deserved.

He was now on his way up to Herr Holmengraa to offer him a small apology. His blunt refusal had taken a form which he had since regretted. He wished to explain that the truth was that certain circumstances prevented him from selling any more of the river. Nor would he have given such a curt answer on that occasion if Adelheid had not been present; it was for her sake that he had had to assume his old role of lord of the manor.

He saw Herr Holmengraa's hat and back up there by the river; well, he would not allow any propositions to be made to him; he would make them himself—if it were possible. Holmengraa? His life had become deeply involved with that of this stranger. The Lieutenant must needs count him his equal in many things and his superior in much; but who was Holmengraa? A man from the antipodes.

Now he is turning and coming down again, coming towards the Lieutenant. Who was this man? He came of no family, had no home; he was a man of mystery, a cosmopolitan—perhaps a symbol, perhaps a force of nature. He greets the Lieutenant as usual and the Lieutenant responds. Their relations are unchanged, but the lord of the manor is, at this moment, the less confident of the two. Had Holmengraa been waiting for him?

The Lieutenant goes straight to the point, as is his custom:

"When we last spoke, you mentioned three methods of procedure. There is a fourth: to leave everything as it is."

"I cannot do that," answers Holmengraa.

"I cannot sell more of the river or the land. Certain obligations dating from my father's time prevent me."

"Surely not from accepting compensation for damage done?"

"Hm. The idea does not appeal to me. You have gained no advantage through my loss."

"Lieutenant, I have just been having a look round up there again. Two things stood in my way on the river—they are gone now. It may sound strange, but they stood in my way and they are gone now."

The Lieutenant is still in the dark and says:

"I do not know—I hardly think I understand what you say."

"It is this way," explains Holmengraa; "if I could rebuild your dam here, on my side of the river, I would be able to work a very necessary machine. May I ask you to come with me?—and I will show you what I mean."

They walk up the river talking as they go:

"What sort of a machine is it?"

"An arrangement with cables which would save me all the expense of cartage to and from the mill."

The Lieutenant asks some questions about rails and a locomotive, but Holmengraa adds in explanation:

"Oh, yes, I would lay rails from the wharf to the mill, a double track. But I would make the waterfall draw the trucks up and down."

They stop, and Holmengraa points out the different places: "*There* would be the dam, *there* the turbine." The noise of the fall forces the two men to stand close together in order to hear one another; and this is not to the Lieutenant's taste. He gathers the impression that there is no longer any obstacle to the plan and at once draws back from the river.

"There is nothing to prevent your going ahead and building," he said.

"What? Oh, no. But we can find some form of settlement that would satisfy us both?"

"I do not know. The bank forbids me to sell."

"A bank forbids?" says Holmengraa in an offhand manner. "I will release you from your obligations to the bank."

The Lieutenant stood still. He seemed to see a ray of light; it appealed to his lordly spirit to be able to give the bank an answer that would silence them.

"It is a big sum," he said, "but all my land stands as security. I have paid off something; there is fourteen thousand left."

"Of the old currency?

"Yes, unfortunately, fourteen thousand in the old money, the dollar coinage."

No doubt Holmengraa had come in course of time to know a little even about the Lieutenant's affairs—he became more and more laconic in his speech:

"Is it a bill of exchange?"

"Yes. With endorsers who are also secured on the property."

"I will take up the bill."

Remarkable—it was a great and very important affair that was being arranged, but only the few indispensably necessary words were spoken. When the two men parted all was in order; and they had agreed on a sum for the whole river and the whole lake up in the mountains. Herr Holmengraa bought it outright from the Segelfoss property and became the sole owner.

Probably the Lieutenant felt a desire to inspect one or other of his forest tracts on the west side of the river since he was there in any case; he turned and walked up the river again to the ruins of his dam, passed it and followed the river right up to the mountain lake. Yes!. there was good timber up here—in fifty years there would be big timber, valuable timber, here too; Willatz might be easy about that! On the whole—things were improving! A fairly important piece of business settled this afternoon; the bank paid off and money in his hands once more—a goodly sum, sufficient for a long time. Whoever Herr Holmengraa was—there was something providential about him. He knew how to find a way out of difficulties; the Lieutenant could not but marvel. And the best of it all was that he had received no gratis service at Herr Holmengraa's hands, he had simply done business with him. That was as it should be. Could one lay oneself under a perpetual obligation by accepting an unrequited service? No, nothing costs so dear as a gift.

So we see the Lieutenant had grown wiser and wiser. Where was now the intractability, the obstinacy of his younger days? Only at rare moments did he still show that there was fire beneath the ashes. That was as it should be.

He sits down for an hour and thinks—he is a philosopher and is not in any hurry, When he gets up again, he walks further up into the forest and looks round: here and there, he is sorry to see, are fresh-cut stumps, left from the last felling of props; but much healthy young timber is left as well—time would mature it and make Willatz rich!

He made a circuit and happened to halt where he could look down on the courtyard of Holmengraa's house: a large house, but new and outlandish in appearance, with an enormous roof which jutted far out—meant to give shade; as if that were necessary!—and was supported on pillars at its extremity. It all looked raw, like a new settler's place.

The hens were poking about in the yard; in the garden there was hardly anything but currant bushes. Look! there came Adelheid out at the back of the house; she had no doubt been there playing on the grand piano again.

Herr Holmengraa accompanied her and led her along the wall to the little alley through the garden. Strange—he was walking with his arm round her waist. They sat down among the currant bushes.

From here downwards, too, there was fine timber, but somewhat mixed—foliage trees among the pines. Now why, if it really was the air of the pine-woods that Herr Holmengraa wanted, had he built his house in a wood of mixed trees? The Lieutenant had not thought of this before, but it occurred to him now. He went on, came down to the river again, and stopped on the bridge. So there stood the tile-works still; there they stood, forgotten, forgotten even by the great flood—the only thing left to him of the river and the old works.

When the Lieutenant lies upon the sofa in his room he no longer jumps up to ring for Daverdana; he has given up many of his old habits, he is disciplining himself. But things have not gone at all badly with the Lieutenant; he is growing grey, but that is with years; he reads the humanists, but that is from inclination. When, as rarely happens now, the Lieutenant rings, Gottfred comes.

Little Gottfred with the small limbs and the child's hands.

He was ordered, you remember, a couple of years ago to come up to the house. He had been dreadfully afraid, and his mother had had to go with him. But the Lieutenant had been kind and spoken mildly to him, and told him he was to stay. A strange man the Lieutenant! Afterwards he had taken the boy into his wife's room and asked whether she, too, did not think he might stay, and his wife had said yes, she thought just the same as her husband. So Gottfred had stayed. He is dressed in good clothes now and has had good food all the time, so he looks like a little gentleman, though he is dressed like a page with a round jacket and bright buttons. His special duty is to keep the master's and mistress's riding-horses and saddles free of dust, but he has to make himself generally useful as well. He was exclusively the servant of the master and mistress; no one else had any authority over him, and he divided his services between them. The high-born lady was by no means the one who needed him least; how easily, for example, she might take a fancy to teach some one a little French, and who could be a more suitable pupil than Gottfred? Then again, when she was tired of her own company and wished to talk to some one, Gottfred was not far away. Probably she was thinking all the time of Willatz and, indeed, she talked about little else than him; now and again she would read something out of her son's letters to Gottfred, and that was a great treat.

The Lieutenant used the boy more for out-of-door work, such as taking the post to and from the office on the wharf, or feeding the pigeons with peas. That also had to be done. One way and another there were many duties in the big house; when the master or the mistress went out or came home, Gottfred stood in the hall and was at hand if he were wanted. That, too, had to be done. But on the whole the Lieutenant's service was an easy one and did not overtax the servants, and besides Gottfred was so little. When the Lieutenant himself rang for him, it might be, for instance, because he wanted Gottfred to go down to the front steps and look at the thermometer; then when the boy came back and told him the reading, the Lieutenant would nod to show that he wanted nothing more.

So things went well with Gottfred. And now Pauline, Gottfred's sister with the downcast eyes, wished to come into the Lieutenant's service too. And there could be no particular objection to that It was her mother who came and offered the girl's services. "I will ask the mistress," answered the housekeeper. "I will speak to my husband," answered the lady of the house. "If you can make use of her, I have no objection," answered her husband. "Bring the girl in," said his wife. "What's your name? Pauline? We will keep you here. How old are you? Look up, Pauline!"

And so Pauline stayed on too. There were so many at Segelfoss already, one more or less made no difference.

And time went on.

The Lieutenant rides his daily rounds and inspects his fields and his fences, his ditches and his woods; as before, he arranges with his man, Martin, what work is to be done on the estate, at times he calls out the cottagers for extra day-labour, and altogether he goes on in his good old way.

But the winters were long and dreary. Now, when he paces his room of an evening, he hears no other sound in the whole house but his own muffled tread on the carpet. Ah, the winters were long and dreary. Willatz was still at school in England and Adelheid played on the grand piano at Herr Holmengraa's house.

An odd man, that Holmengraa. He owned the river now and could build his dam and his turbine, but he did not do it. For two years he did nothing towards it. One day he explained to the Lieutenant that unfortunately he had had to abandon the plan; his people would suffer greatly through it, the carters would be thrown out of work. "My plan must wait!" said Herr Holmengraa. All very well. But this plan about a turbine—had he ever been in earnest about it?

But much had happened: Herr Holmengraa had become master of Segelfoss, of the river, the forest, and all the land—the Lieutenant knew that.

When first this fact came home to him in all its monstrous reality, the Lieutenant had, indeed, been appalled, and his hair had grown suddenly greyer. He arranged matters one day so that he could not help running up against Herr Holmengraa down on the road; he was impelled to this meeting by his own fear, he wanted to read the truth in his creditor's eyes. But Herr Holmengraa had been exactly the same as before, polite and considerate towards the squire of Segelfoss just as on the first day. Then the feeling of terror passed away, months and years went by and no cataclysm took place—why, did not Holmengraa's household even go on getting its milk down at the manor and paying for it? But it must not be forgotten either that the Lieutenant on his side paid the interest and the installments on his debt punctually, though, to be sure, it was Holmengraa who in one way and another found him the money for it.

But after all—all this did not matter so very much; there were worse things. How, for example, can a man quite forget an organ he has decided to buy? And, in the first place, when would the money be forthcoming for the enlargement of the church, for the loft in which the organ was to stand? The Lieutenant reproached himself for being so slow about settling the matter—it must actually look to people as if he had not sufficient funds for it. Had he begun to lose his energy? At the first good opportunity he would tackle it in earnest.

And perhaps there were other things, too, about which he had shown himself remiss. The Lieutenant did not disguise from himself that he would have to talk seriously to Willatz when he came home for the holidays. The young lad was a fine tall young fellow, but he had not yet the firmness of will and character which a Willatz Holmsen must have. What had come over the boy? He wished to take lessons in drawing and painting, he wanted to be an artist. —"Well, be an artist!" He would rather be a sailor—a naval officer.—"Still better, much better still, my boy! Be a sailor for a time, till you take over Segelfoss!" But Willatz had many fancies and wanted to try all sorts of things; he had even, to his father's regret, hinted at wishing to devote himself entirely to music; but that had probably been the vaguest of all his ideas—he did not mention it again.

But, if his father had only known it, it was just music and nothing else that the good Willatz was wasting his time on both night and day. For that was the one thing he had in his blood—that was what his mother had taught him.

XIV

Willatz comes home.

He is tall and elegant, wears spats and grey clothes, quite like an Englishman. When his mother saw this tall youth who was her son, it was quite a shock to her: a great many years must have passed since his birth, years that must have left their mark on her too—she must have grown old. What a strange and unpleasant thought! "Good gracious, I do believe the boy is growing a beard already!" she thought. For some days this mother actually felt displeasure at seeing that down was beginning to appear on her son's cheeks.

He had with him as a companion another young gentleman, whom he had known well in his childhood, Anton Coldevin, son of Consul Fredrik. Young Anton had for several years been at school at Saint-Cyr, where his father had been before him; he was having a commercial education and was to go into his father's business.

Now at last a Coldevin had come to Segelfoss again; Consul Fredrik sent as his representative—an all but grown-up son. Alas! how many years must have gone by; Fru Adelheid looked with as much displeasure at young Anton's well-grown figure as at her son's.

The two young men had otherwise no resemblance to each other, though they were friends; if one took one thing into his head, the other could hit upon something else: both were self-willed.

Anton wandered round everywhere, in the mill, on the wharf, up at Holmengraa's house, round about the tenants' cottages. Willatz went with him out of politeness now and then, but he had become English enough to prefer to stand still by the hour idiotically busy in fishing in the river for trout. Willatz was still a mixture of many elements; he could play and sing with his mother, but he could also converse in a grown-up manner with his father. He brought out in private some of his own compositions—romances, trifles—; had not his mother known that he was a genius, a Christmas child! She sang this youthful music, lifting it to heaven with her beautiful mezzo-soprano. She forgot that he had grown too fast and made her feel old, she made a friend of him, and now and again she would take him with her up to Holmengraa's to try the grand piano, and to meet the children.

They were tall youngsters now, the little Indians, and their yellow skins and black hair and shining brown eyes gave them an unfamiliar appearance. Truth to tell, they looked even more Indian than their father had stated; there was a gliding motion, too, about Mariane's walk like that of a savage, and she had lazy-looking hands that seemed an inheritance from the idle, vagrant folk she was descended from. She struck young Willatz with surprise, and before long he began to fall in love.

What a strange sensation that was! He was paralysed by the happiness which seemed to penetrate his being and send pangs of sweetness through it. She, on her side, though a child of thirteen, was perhaps even more in love; she would stand beside him, stroke his waistcoat; and gaze at him. What did it all mean? They smiled at each other and both blushed scarlet; he kissed her lightly—hardly touching her with his lips—yet aware of a delicious fragrance. But what painful embarrassment followed this daring—he felt ready to die! to sink into the ground! He could not tear himself away from her again, but held her close and hid his face; they hid their faces on each other's shoulders. Now they would have to let go and meet each other's glances—impossible! How could they ever look one another in the face again after to-day? Impossible! If it had only been dark! Was there no escape? "There's a man down there on the road, I see," he says. "Where?" she asks and turns round a little. "Down there, he is carrying something. Yes, he is carrying a sack! don't you see it is a sack?" By this time they have drawn apart from one another. "What a big cock that is of yours," he says, still looking away from her. Indeed, it will be a long time before they can look at one another again. "Where is the cock?" she asks, looking everywhere but at him; "where is it?" Then Willatz has to allow that it was another day he had seen it—"but it was a large cock." "Yes, and so handsome!" says Mariane; "its comb stands straight up on end and it's not all combs that do that!"

But now Felix joined them and they were safe—for this time.

What a time that was, beautiful, unearthly! When Willatz went riding now it was no longer that he might be seen from the cottages as he passed—he rode a long way simply and solely that he might sit and look up at Mariane's house and garden. Soft summer-time and shining eyes! He lived in a world of sweetness and bashfulness; driven aimlessly into the woods, to the mountains, back home again. Where did he rest at night? Where could one rest at night? In the grass, in the hay, in a garden-swing he had used as a child, anywhere; a little here, a little there—sometimes even in bed with his clothes on, curled up, exhausted.—What a time it was!

And how unsettled and restless he grew, without time to finish anything. As for fishing in the river for hours at a time—no more of that for him! Perhaps he had been giving himself airs a little, and pretending to be more English than he was, when he seemed so keen on that tedious business. Gottfred's company meant much to him at this time: he was a patient listener and could sympathize with a man's tribulations. And Pauline? Oh, well! Pauline, like her brother, was neatly dressed now, and she was well fed, too, like him, and had a clear, healthy complexion. But she was still so subdued and flower-like, she would not even ask the time to give Willatz a chance of showing her his watch. But Gottfred, at least, asked questions about England in all good faith, so that Willatz had a chance to talk about it, and little Gottfred had really learnt some French, too, and so he was not to be despised as a companion.

"I saw Anton going off to Holmengraa's again," says Willatz indifferently.

"Oh, did you?'" answers Gottfred.

"He was there yesterday too. I don't understand what he goes there every day for: Mariane herself told me that she does not care about him."

"Then he goes to see Felix, I suppose."

"Yes, but I saw him meet Mariane a short time ago. Half an hour ago. And they are behind the hen-house, I expect."

"I will go up and see if you like."

"No, what do I care! Leave them alone. What was I going to say? Oh, yes! Bella is a very handsome mare, don't you think so?"

"Yes, and she is so good-tempered, too," says Gottfred, and tells of his visits to her. "She stands so still when I wash her hoofs, and turns and looks after me when I go away."

Willatz seems not to be listening; he is thinking of something else, and asks suddenly:

"Can you hold your tongue?"

"Hold my tongue?"

"Be as silent as the grave? If you can, I will ask you to do me a great service."

"Oh, yes!" replies Gottfred obediently.

"But you mustn't say yes if you can't be sure of yourself. For it is an important matter, It is to deliver this letter."

"Yes, I'll do that."

"And deliver it into her own hands. You see the name on it?"

"Yes."

"But you must be quick. And most important of all, you must keep it secret. Did I say quick? That's not what I meant; I don't remember what I meant, I've forgotten what I meant exactly. But, Gottfred, you understand, then, that it's important. And if Anton is there then you'll make signs to her to send him away."

"Yes."

"But you must on no account let Anton see you doing it."

"No."

Gottfred was away a horribly long time; there was no end to it, and Willatz had to go to meet him. He met him at the bridge; Gottfred was cautious; he lay down under the bushes, and brought out a letter.

"Did you give it to her?" asked Willatz anxiously.

"Yes. And she asked me to give you this one into your own hands."

An answer—she had sent an answer! Gottfred was splendid!

They started to go home again—Willatz would have liked to run, but that would not have done. What in the world could be in the letter?

"I have a walking-stick you shall have," he said. "Do you know what's in the letter?"

"No."

"Oh, well! it doesn't matter a bit what is in it. Did you see Anton?"

"No, he was gone."

Willatz hurries up to his room, stays there a minute or two, hurries down again trembling with delight, in an ecstasy, finds Gottfred and gives him the stick;—"No, thank you, you mustn't do that!" "Yes, take it; no nonsense!"—hurries up to his room again, stays away some time, comes down the stairs singing, stops in the courtyard and looks about him, turns round and goes upstairs again; this is the third time he has done this and it looks as if he means now to lock himself in to study some difficult task. But in half an hour's time he has evidently done his tasks, for he appears again on the stairs coming down the steps. What is he to do now? He has become calm and a little listless. His mother passes him in the hall, she is going for a walk no doubt; they exchange a few words, but she does not ask him to go with her. Then he hears his father walking to and fro in his study—his good father, a comrade and a gentleman—he knocks and goes in to him.

"Are you not fishing?" asks his father. "Anton is up the river, I expect."

"Yes, probably he is. No, I don't care about it. You have grown very grey, father."

His father starts.

"Grey? Not so very. Where is your mother? Are you and she not going to play?"

"Yes, later. That last song we sang had English words, but Norwegian music; did you hear it?"

"Yes. Very beautiful."

"I did not mean to tell you, but it was my music."

His father starts again.

"Willatz—not but that—exceedingly pretty. I heard it in here. So you yourself—? Indeed. Does your mother know?"

"Yes."

"Music is very well in its way, I quite admit that. What does your mother think of it?"

"She thinks it is pretty."

His father suddenly says:

"Have you thought of what you wish to be, my boy?"

Pause.

"Artist or naval officer? One must decide definitely on something. I don't say this to hurry you, but it is best for yourself. Music, of course, is only a pastime. But that was uncommonly pretty; I was walking up and down here listening to it. Did your mother think so too?"

"Yes."

His father puts on a determined air and says:

"But then, music is one thing, the serious side of life another; I fancy we are agreed about that? Make up your mind firmly what you want to be and then we can discuss the matter. I have nothing against your becoming a sculptor or a painter; perhaps our family needs a new departure of the kind at this point—I cannot say. Think it over and tell me your views some other time."

So Willatz had a reprieve and was glad of it. But he might expect the question to be raised again soon; what if he gave a hint now?

"I suppose it is your intention that I should go through the whole course at Harrow?" he asked.

God knows whether his father had intended it, whether this grey, elderly man, who was pacing up and down the floor, had quite made up his mind about this—God knows. But he answered at once:

"Through the whole school? Certainly—if you wish it. So you

will have time to think over what you want to take up. Oh, yes! go through the whole school."

Ah, but this was not what Willatz wanted. His most fervent wish was to get away from the school at Harrow, where he was unspeakably ill at ease, and which was only hindering him. But his father was a splendid man and Mariane was lovely—

"I could play the songs for you again now if you would like?" he said.

"Now? Oh, no, thanks; wait till your mother comes; I have something to do just now. But thanks all the same."

With that he nodded and Willatz went out.

The Lieutenant is left in peace again, but what he has to do just now seems to be nothing but to pace up and down once more. Through the whole school? That school in Harrow seemed to be a mysterious place, it must be looked into. Was it a university? Year after year at a grand school at Harrow—was he going to settle down there? He must write to Xavier Moore about it; he must consult with Adelheid.

He rings and asks if his wife is out.

Yes, Gottfred had seen the mistress go over to Holmengraa's.

"Tell me when she comes back."

He waited a long time, an hour; yes, indeed, Adelheid forgot everything when she was playing the piano! Two hours later she came. What—had she been weeping? She was extraordinarily friendly, humble; this surprised him, and he asked:

"Has anything disagreeable happened to you?"

"To me? Why? No, not that I know of, thank you."

They spoke of Willatz; Adelheid composed herself and gave excellent reasons for her opinions: there was no sense in keeping him longer at that school a Harrow; it was fashionable and expensive, select, but that was all.

"That is no consequence. He is our only child!"

"But it is no use his staying there any longer; the boy is working at nothing but music."

This turn for music was something he had inherited from his mother, there was nothing of that sort on the Holmsen side of the family; the Lieutenant could therefore make a somewhat contemptuous remark without feeling unjust.

But Adelheid—what had come over her this evening? In the old days she would have paid him back in his own coin; now she grew even more humble: "Oh, no I don't say that," she begged him. "He can't help it; it is just that he is musical through and through. If you only knew—I hardly dare tell you—"

"That he has composed songs? He has told me himself."

"Thank God! that was right of him. Ah! that boy, he is full of melody; I assure you I sing his music with the greatest joy. I suppose you did not hear it yesterday?"

"I was walking up and down in my study listening to it yesterday. I have heard it for several days."

"What do you think of it?"

"Your singing is always beautiful."

"Do you think so? But the melody is really so musical—he is no ordinary boy, I beg you to remember that."

The Lieutenant himself thought that his son was far from ordinary; had he said anything to the contrary? His mother was no ordinary woman either, for that matter.

"Hm. I have no objection to being reminded of it. Though it is superfluous to do so."

"I beg your pardon!"

More humility, more meekness; how is this? The Lieutenant saw clearly that something had happened to her, otherwise she would not have been so unlike herself. It was not unpleasing to him that she should show respect for his opinion; she was right, too, in saying that the school at Harrow was extortionately dear. There stood Adelheid, no longer young, but, as it were, untouched still, unworn, with a figure straight as a dart, that any woman might envy. Hm. And for once he decides to take part with his wife against his son; he will show his authority and set his face against Willatz's wishes Perhaps it will be good for him.

"I had thought of writing to Xavier Moore," he said, "but that will not be necessary now; Willatz shall leave Harrow. But what was it you were going to say?"

"What was I going to say? I was going to intercede for him with you," she said.

This tone again! The Lieutenant says:

"Will you tell Willatz, Adelheid, that for reasons which I have only now learnt, I must oppose his return to school at Harrow?"

"Yes. And he will not be disappointed, he will thank you."

Better and better, everything seemed in a whirl—only the Lieutenant's comprehension was at a standstill. It is no joke to have both mother and son against one! So what was the upshot of it all? Why, that Willatz should go to Germany. He was to become as great a musician as his abilities would permit—that was the upshot.

"On your responsibility," the Lieutenant had said. "He is our only child; but this matter is one that you understand best—you are responsible."

She made a movement as if to step forward or stretch out her hand, but checked it again. It was prettily done and he was touched by it—this slight impulse towards him, this movement of her almost girl-like body.

"Thank you; then that is happily settled," she said; "happily for him, and more happily for me than I deserve."

They played and sang that evening.

A couple of days later it was Willatz who was his mother's spokesman with the Lieutenant. This was such an unusual proceeding that something must be behind it: Adelheid wished to go with her son to Berlin.

As she used an intermediary, she must wish to avoid giving definite reasons, there was no doubt of that. The Lieutenant asked his son:

"Did you understand your mother aright?"

"Yes."

"Tell her that if I had not wished to spare her the fatigue, I would have asked her myself to go with you. For various reasons. She is the one who understands such matters best, and she can help you most."

Willatz suddenly felt a wave of sadness pass over him, and he had to struggle for self-control. Was it love, was it pity? Something of a grey, bereaved look had come over his father, something forlorn, that filled him with sorrow.

When Willatz could speak he said:

"But you and I must travel together again some day, father. It was such fun travelling with you."

"All right," his father nodded, "some other time. But now go and tell your mother what I have said. And say that I have no doubt things will go badly here at home while she is away, but it cannot be helped. When will you start?"

"Anton wants to go now."

"Anton. But you and your mother?"

"Mother thinks we should start at once."

"At once?"

"Mother says there are no holidays in music."

Pause.

"Good; she is the one who understands the matter."

❧

Young Willatz had no mind to meet Julius this time, for Gottfred had told him of the trick Julius had played him about the penknife and it made a deep impression on Willatz. Julius had been up near the manor several times, and had characteristically hung about, watching what was going on; also he had asked Gottfred to give Willatz a message from him. But Willatz had not come to see him. Julius could not understand it—they were such good friends—and after all, he was the brother of a man who would soon be a full-fledged parson.

Besides, Julius was no worse than he had been; on the contrary, he had grown, in his own way, a much more important person—a tiger to work when he wanted to, and altogether superior in bodily strength to his parents when trouble arose at home in the cottage. Gottfred said that it was so, and he had it from Julius himself. He had always had ability—much more than his brother—though he did not bother about reading, only he had nothing to bring out his talents. How should he?—living at home in the cottage and hearing and seeing nothing. His mental powers were put to such tasks as separating self from half-dried fish, and distinguishing billy-goats from nanny-goats. But Julius had grown to be a much more capable fellow lately; he had been to the Lofoten fishing for two winters now, and often worked for Herr Holmengraa. He had also become good friends with Felix, who was like-minded in regard to happy ignorance and hatred of books. Felix was a thorough heathen.

One day Willatz and Anton are walking along the road and there stands Julius, just opposite his father's cottage. That Felix is not far away, there can be no doubt, for he is to be heard whistling somewhere down by the out-houses.

The two young gentlemen nod good day and are about to pass on.

But Julius had evidently taken it for granted that the said young gentlemen had at last come to see him—if not, why should they be walking this way?—and that was why he was standing there.

"What do you mean—don't you know me, Willatz?" he asks.

"Yes," answers Willatz.

"Isn't it me you're looking for?"

"No," answers Willatz in surprise.

Julius is very much hurt that the two gentlemen's business is not what he expected it to be, and he says:

"Oh, isn't it? All right."

But in the meantime the two young men have stopped and Anton has burst out laughing. Was Julius going to stand still and let himself be laughed at? Not he! He was tall and heavy, his eyebrows had grown thick again, and what fists he had!

"What's that ass standing there grinning at?" he asks.

But, as it happened, Anton Coldevin was a man who had more than once had fights with the cadets at Saint-Cyr—he wasn't the man to let himself be called an ass.

"Perhaps you would like a licking?" he said.

Could it be that, far from taking two steps back, Julius stepped forward a little? How did that come about? What could have given him such courage, and would any one give him credit for it? He held his ground and, for very shame, had to let it be understood that as far as a licking went, he was ready; but his face had a strange drawn look.

Pause.

Willatz had no objection on principle to a tidy little fight, but it would not do here in the middle of the road. "No, shut up, you fellows!" he said. Felix—the little Indian—came strolling up—how interested he was at once in what was going on; it was clear that Julius' cause was his; he slipped quietly between the foes and looked at Anton with glittering eyes. The little devil might be dangerous enough, and no mistake. Willatz had to use a lot of persuasion, and at last threaten to go off alone, before he could get Anton away with him.

But then Julius grew indeed in stature: "Come back!" he shouted. Oh, he became a warrior, a hero, and spat streams of tobacco; the language of this brother of a parson waxed stronger and stronger and he roared: "I have seen the Kvæns* fight; just come back and I'll show you! Do you think I'm afraid of you? I'll send six inches of steel right through you; I'll make buttonholes all over you!"

And Felix gave vent to little howls to show his approval of Julius' proposals.

*Translator's note: Kvæns, the name given by the Norwegians to the Finns, in distinction to the Lapps, whom they call Finns.

XV

Willatz and his mother are gone. There had been the customary dinner at the Lieutenant's and the Holmengraas were there. As this was a turning-point in Willatz's career his father's speech in his honour was much more serious than usual: There were two ways of handing down one's name to posterity, he said; one might lay it in an air-tight grave, so that some one might find it in two thousand years; or one might live it out in a storm before mankind, and then history would record it! They ate hurriedly, and though there was no District-doctor Muus this time to disturb the harmony, the silence was almost worse—all were so affected by the leave-taking. On the quay Herr Holmengraa—thoughtful and sympathetic as usual—had held Fru Adelheid's hand in his and said almost in a whisper: "Come back soon!"

Several months had passed now and Fru Holmsen had not yet come back; what could be the reason? The Lieutenant received letters asking for a postponement of her return—well, so be it, there was no need for her to over-exert herself in order to hurry home. And the Lieutenant thought that if she did not wish to come, there was no use worrying about it; he began to make up his mind to it, and one day he began to hum again. Daverdana, who was his parlour-maid once more, brought this news to the kitchen and all the servants set themselves to listen. They heard nothing, the Lieutenant hummed so softly, so inaudibly—more strictly for his private satisfaction than the last time even. And what if he did? Very likely the only reason why he did it was that his household was now recognized as a musical one.

After a time a letter came saying that his wife begged to be allowed to stay the whole autumn. A humble letter, an entreaty; and now, indeed, the Lieutenant had a feeling that something must be wrong. What, the whole autumn? And when that was over, the whole winter perhaps? There was something behind this. Their married life had been no better than that of many others; no actual disaster had befallen, but a constant unhappiness had brooded over it. That was how it had been. A disaster—that would be nothing! A disaster has an end, it is over and done with; it is worse to go without happiness day in, day out, year after year. Even an angel may turn bad-tempered and bite—only natural! But when an angel never bites, only murmurs; when an angel's lips curl perpetually with an empty smile? That is all right too! One is a philosopher, thank God, and something of a humanist. A gnat is a great nuisance; with the shrill drone of its gauzy wings; "z—z—z," it says; at first it is a trial to one's reason—at first only. After all, what is happiness? One must learn to recognize its unimportance. Besides, the Holmsens' married life had really become quite endurable; it went more smoothly, had become comparatively happy, thank God! Mutual respect there always had been, and now there had come to be good feeling as well; they might even exchange a frank smile now and then. The Lieutenant had begun to hope for a kind of atonement for them both, a new life now in their old age—had not Adelheid shown during the last weeks at home an evident affection for him, as though she no longer preferred his absence to his presence, as she used to?—yes, a new life in their old age. And then she goes away and wishes to stay away!

There dawns on the Lieutenant a possibility that she has gone through some experience which has become more insupportable than her married life.

What could it be? God only knows; but it can certainly be no small thing. She had said in her last letter that she had done him wrong—that meant nothing; it was only a piece of flattery, to obtain a postponement of her homecoming; yet it was clear that Adelheid had some trouble on her mind. And the Lieutenant stopped humming all at once; he no longer felt inclined to. Yes, indeed, it had been but a short bout of humming, and surely as innocent a thing as a man could take to in his wife's absence.

But the Lieutenant was determined to do more, he did nothing by halves. If Adelheid were in some trouble or other, it would not do for him to be unsympathetic; he would have a pleasant surprise for her when she came home, he really would take up the matter of the organ again. That organ must be got—if it were his last act.

Ah! if it had been only the organ! But where was the loft to carry it? And where was there room for a loft? The church must be altered. Could the Lieutenant take timber for it from his own mortgaged forest without permission? His hands were tied; he must go out and read Herr Holmengraa's face once more.

Autumn passed and his wife did not come. She wrote now begging leave to stay longer—some time longer—over the winter; Willatz would otherwise be lonely—yes, and she would, too. Besides, they had made very judicious arrangements, were spending little money, and working hard at music.

Perhaps fate had willed it so; the Lieutenant was to have time for his building operations before Adelheid came home.

Herr Holmengraa would often ask after the two, mother and son, in Berlin, and that was strange for two reasons: in the first place, he had not asked after Willatz when he was in England; in the second, little Gottfred now and again went over to the Holmengraas' with letters from Willatz to Mariane. "Are they well and happy?" Herr Holmengraa would ask. "They are well and happy," the Lieutenant had always replied. To-day he made the same reply and added: "My wife wishes to stay in Berlin some time yet."

He began to talk of the church, saying:

"This little church here—your undertakings have so much increased the congregation here that the church has grown too small."

"Yes," said Herr Holmengraa, "yes, that is so—"

But his mind was evidently occupied with something else, and the expression on his face was dark and inscrutable. The Lieutenant spoke no more of the church; this man of fine perceptions stopped short as though he had been given a sign.

Yes, but was it not a fact that the church was preposterously small? Think of the Sundays when there were great christenings or when people assembled in force! One could easily foresee, too, how things would go at the next service, when that new servant of the Lord, L. Lassen, was to come and preach to his fellow-parishioners for the first time. Yet all Herr Holmengraa answered was: "Yes, that is so." The Lieutenant perhaps thought in his obstinate way that if he had had his old power he would simply have ridden out into his league-long tracts of forest, and given orders to the woodsmen to fell timber enough for half a church. And he possibly thought besides: if I acted according to my rights I would telegraph this very day for timber from Namsen! And it was no doubt this thought which gave him for the moment a lofty air of prosperity. He was still in good case, he felt; he had the money for the river; and were it not for those two, the mother and son, in Berlin, he would not care if he spent every penny of it. These ridiculous crowns, these piles of small coin, which were not even dollars.

Herr Holmengraa's final question and the reply he received were fully worthy of both gentlemen:

"I have not been in Berlin; is it not expensive for your wife to live there?" said Holmengraa to the Lieutenant.

"It is *not* expensive for my wife to live in Berlin," said the Lieutenant to Holmengraa.

❧

There was no mistake about it, in the following weeks a slightly different tone crept into the relations of the squire of Segelfoss and the new-come Herr Holmengraa. Outsiders did not notice it, but the Lieutenant was in no doubt about it; and now there arose in his precipitous Arab head a plan which he brooded over night and day: he walked on mortgaged ground and lived in a mortgaged house; he would move away. It was well that Adelheid and Willatz were abroad. He would ask them to stay where they were; then he would only have himself to prepare a new life for.

It is stated towards the end of Pastor Windfeld's history that Fru Holmsen went abroad and stayed away because she and her husband did not agree. Well! on this question at least they did agree. "Remain where you are for the present!" wrote the Lieutenant to his wife. And, that she might not feel oppressed by gratitude for this, he declared, as was true, that he wished to carry out a plan, to effect which he must be alone.

Where was he to move to? There was the old tile-works; he had not sold them, they were not included in the bargain about the river. The tile-works were mortgaged like the rest, it was true, but they might be released from the mortgage; they were leaky and draughty, but they could be made weather-tight and fit for habitation.

The Lieutenant took up the idea in earnest. In all these years of decline he had never taken things easily and just let them drift—that was far from his nature. He was tortured by his distresses, but he could not remedy them. How was he to remedy them? By earning something, by making something? He? This man who could only spend, only pay, pay; a spendthrift without riches to draw upon, a man of negative qualities, a genius at creating expenses. He was the son of his fathers, and lived in the shadow of his ancestors.

From the day when he had received that real or imaginary hint from Herr Holmengraa, his difficulties seemed to tower up higher and higher before him: he forgot or intentionally ignored all his movable property, his over-filled house, the furniture, the works of art, the library, the cattle, horses, boats, tools, machinery—of these he did not think. Being, as he was, the soul of order, it was inevitable that he should think himself a few steps only from bankruptcy.

This old Lieutenant—was he not fighting against a force of nature! Should he turn to his sisters in Sweden? Such an idea never occurred to him; between him and them there had been no regular communication for twenty years, and since their mother had died they had not even written to one another. He might perhaps retrench his manner of living, reduce the number of his servants, cut down the yearly account from the merchants in Bergen? This, he would tell himself, was unheard-of nonsense; and he would not even consider it. Were the two abroad to get an inkling from home that things were at a low ebb at Segelfoss! They were not used to consider ways and means, and did not deserve to be obliged to. Little Willatz must not have a different idea of his father from what the Lieutenant had had of his: he must feel that one was in a position always to be ready to help, to give, to buy; could always be a gentleman, a Willatz Holmsen. And as to the servants? Were there more men and girls in the servants' hall than in his father's days? Little Gottfred—was he in any one's way? And his sister Pauline—was she not the only one who had pretty little answers for the Lieutenant and who curtsied as if to a father when he passed her? Nor could he, in his wife's absence, get rid of the housekeeper. Nothing could be changed.

The housekeeper? An active and diligent person—trained by his wife herself for many years—so that now she had the management of the house at her finger-ends. Did not everything go as if by clockwork under her hands? No! no!

Nor did Jomfru Salvesen herself seem to feel any shortage. She had, in fact, ample stores to draw upon; the big estate supplied most of what was needed, and wine and groceries and delicacies came from Bergen, just as before. There was nothing lacking. And that was why Jomfru Salvesen was never anything but gay and contented with her lot, and often screwed up her face and cracked jokes with the maids.

Was she not the head of Segelfoss? But that was not all. The wharf-manager was courting her, and wanted to marry her. That was a fact. And he sang such amusing songs too. They had as good as settled it between them that spring; but then Attorney Rasch began to make love to her and wanted to marry her—and that was quite another matter. You see, Herr Rasch wanted to do as his father and grandfather and his grandfather's father had done before him: found a family and seek an official post and lead a cultured existence. The wharf-manager's career would be more uncertain; he was a business man and could not start a business without money. No, the wharf-manager was not to be compared with the other, though one could not help screwing one's mouth almost out of joint laughing at him. But Jomfru Salvesen, the housekeeper, had no objection to having two strings to her bow.

She had become friendly with Fru Irgens, née Geelmuyden, and often took an evening walk over to Holmengraa's house to have a chat with her. Being the widow of a solicitor, Fru Irgens was in favour of Rasch—"What are you thinking about!" she would say. "A man of culture, while the other could, at the utmost, never be more than a shopkeeper. No! Don't send Rasch away!"

"He may go off of his own accord," says Jomfru Salvesen.

"Go off—an educated man? Never. Such a man doesn't act like that. Irgens didn't go off."

"How do you like being in this house?" asks Jomfru Salvesen.

"Here?" Fru Irgens indicates by a movement of her head that her place is a paradise. "I have never had such a time, it is quite out-of-the-way. I only wish Irgens could have been here."

"Do you know what I believe, Fru lrgens? I believe Herr Holmengraa is not all he seems to be."

"What do you mean? What isn't he?"

"Has he never put his arm round you?"

"What in heaven's name are you saying, Jomfru Salvesen!"

"Well, he has done it to me."

"Put his arm round you?"

"Yes. A couple of evenings ago."

But now Fru Irgens is hurt and says:

"I should think that he has not put his arm round any one more than round me, but it has only been the last few weeks that he has done so—he has somehow seemed a little changed. But this I will say to his credit, that he does not go too far. Never! And with you who do not know him, he cannot have gone even so far. What did he do to you, do you say? I am shocked at you."

The two ladies' conversation goes on and Jomfru Salvesen is hurt in her turn. For Fru Irgens comes out with the remark that there are so many ways of being embraced; "one might stand right in the way of a man who wanted to pass, and then what is he to do with his arms, Jomfru Salvesen?"

"No, don't come to me with such tales. But what is it like at the manor now? I should really like to know that!" says Fru Irgens.

"With us?" answers Jomfru Salvesen, much hurt this time, terribly hurt. "I can tell you, you may be as Spanish and rich as you like over here, but you can't compare with us at the manor, you can tell Herr Holmengraa so from me. I have not seen plates and bowls and trays of solid silver in his house, but we have them; and I haven't seen gilt handles to the silver cake-dishes either, but *we* have *them*. Yes, indeed!"

"But, my dear Jomfru Salvesen, you know she has left him?"

"Has she? It's your tongue that God should preserve from gossip and scandal, Fru Irgens, not mine. What *are* you saying? She has gone with her own son to Germany and he is studying to be a composer. I don't know what you mean. I can quite believe you have all changed a little over here. But I, for my part, hope to live and die a respectable woman; and for the matter of that, Consul Coldevin never put his arm round me, you can tell Herr Holmengraa that from me."

And so the two ladies went on chatting, their talk a strange mixture of foolishness and sharpness. When these women talked to each other there was no need for them to curb their tongues, and so nature got the upper hand; their speech smacked of their original upbringing; they said incredible things.

❧

At last Pastor Windfeld had obeyed the law of official migration and sought a charge in the south. He had done it reluctantly, this old, worn-out man, for he had in the main a pleasant and comfortable life here—a full church and a peaceful congregation. But what choice had he? Why, bless you! were there not people down there in the Eastland hungering for a share of what was left of Pastor Windfeld? Could he fail them longer? He had obtained a charge in the flat but beautiful Smaalenene region.

Then his substitute arrived. It was not the curate of the diocese; he unfortunately had not been appointed yet. No! it was a self-sacrificing soul who was willing to serve in the parish temporarily. The people had to take what they could get and be thankful that any pastor would take the duty up north here for just a few weeks.

And such a pastor! A splendid man in black coat and starched linen. No one could mistake him; the hands worn thin with turning the leaves of books and manuscripts; the solid frame fit to carry a sheep on each shoulder into the fold; the roomy boots—large enough for two pairs of socks; and over these, galoshes. He had no bishop's crosier—not yet; but he had long hair and learned-looking spectacles, for was he not a great scholar? It was Lars Manuelsen's son, L. Lassen.

He was a full-fledged priest now. He had come home to show himself off. One cannot shine in the Cordilleras—it is only at home that one can shine!

He came with a housekeeper and some cases of furniture and

went straight to the parsonage in the head-parish. The vestrymen had assembled to meet him and from now on they assisted him with the utmost zeal; for, indeed, his fame had run before him for many years past—who had not heard of L. Lassen!

"May you prosper here and stay with us a long time!" said the vestrymen.

"No, no. I shall not stay here long," answered the pastor. "But I felt it my duty to take up the temporary duty here."

"Ah, no, sir; it's but natural you shouldn't feel at home here among us any more."

"Do not say that of me, my friends; but we are so remote here, and I cannot live in an out-of-the-way corner. My scholarly pursuits seem to indicate a position in the south for me."

"Yes, no doubt that is so. But, supposing you were to seek a call here, sir, you would get it for the asking."

"The pastorship of this parish? Yes, but I will not seek it. My doctor forbids me to live here; I cannot stand the climate, he says; it is too far north."

Then he preached in the parish church, and it was too small for his congregation; but he gave orders that the windows should be taken out so that those outside might hear him too. And, well—the like of the sermon he preached—!

But Segelfoss church of course was even smaller, and when Herr Lassen preached there, there was not an inch of space to spare. Bless you! every one went to church even Per of Bua went—and there they stood unable to get in. "Take the windows out," the pastor again ordered, "and with God's help my voice will reach even those who are furthest off!" And, as sure as fate, his voice carried as far as the wharf, as far as the cottages. It was not even worth while to go to the church; and so a young couple, following an old Sunday habit, went down to the boat-shed behind the point. The girl was Daverdana, the pastor's sister, and the lad was the assistant to the storekeeper at the wharf.

But after the service the pastor was hungry, and since no invitation came from the Lieutenant at the manor or from Herr Holmengraa, Herr Lassen, in his humility, went to his father's cottage and had a meal there.

There he sat once more, the boy Lars, the blessing and the miracle of the parish. His little brothers and sisters bad grown bigger, and his mother greyer, but his father was the same red-bearded, brawny old fellow, and Julius was a man.

"Now I wonder whether you can eat what we have," said his mother.

"Oh, yes! thank you; it is fresh meat, I see, and it is fresh meat I am ordered to eat."

"We killed a goat," said his mother.

He was particular in his manners, tucking his handkerchief under his chin and helping himself to bread with his fork; Julius muttered to himself below his breath: "The devil!" By and by they went out one after another that Lars might be left in peace; the small brothers and sisters, who knew no better than to stand about in the corner, were called out by their father.

The father, indeed, was quite overcome to-day; he was almost struck dumb by the solemnity of the occasion; besides which he owed it to his son to show how the sermon had attuned his mood to meditation; for that reason, too, he was silent. But Julius, the rascal, the sinner, stole up to the attic, where he had made himself a peephole in the floor beforehand, and lay there watching his brother in the room below. Just look how he's behaving now! Why, all his manners are gone; he gobbles, he eats enormously, he eats coarsely, blindly, makes a pig of himself, spills fat all round him. And he does it all as hurriedly as if it was a case of getting as much as possible into himself before any one comes. Julius, no doubt, decides after this that his brother had not become too grand altogether for him to talk to.

When the pastor has eaten he lies down on his parents' bed and sleeps. When he wakens, his mother takes coffee in to him. The pastor is refreshed now, he yawns loudly and thanks his mother for the coffee; he takes down from the shelf under the rafter the two old, well-known books which the cottage possesses, one a book of sermons, the other a "Mirror of the Human Heart," which his father had once brought home from Lofoten.

Then the others come in again, one at a time; the little ones come in, and Daverdana too comes in at last. The pastor does not see and does not hear, he is deep in the books. What a fellow for books that Lars! And how he could turn the leaves, without even wetting a finger; and how he would hold a book as though it were a treasure. But his mother saw from well-known marks on his hands and neck that he was just as dirty as he used to be.

Then he tears himself away from the books and begins to talk to the others; he notices Daverdana and asks after the Lieutenant.

"Thank you, he is well."

"I must have a little talk with him, I suppose," says the pastor. "His wife has gone off, I hear."

He asks for Willatz.

"He's studying to be a musician," answers Daverdana.

"Mere worldliness!"

"Just what I have thought the whole time," puts in his father, Lars Manuelsen. "I am an ignorant man in all that's got to do with books and newspapers, but I have always understood that music and playing and dancing and dicing are all of them works of the devil—God forgive my sins."

"How long are you going to stay here in the parish?" asks Julius.

"I do not know; no longer than absolutely necessary," answers the pastor. "My bishop has promised me a speedy relief."

"Why can't you apply for the charge?"

"Because I am overwrought with study and I cannot stand the air here. I must live in the south."

"The air? What the devil's the matter with the air here?"

"You are so coarse, Julius," says the pastor to his brother.

But Julius was not really so far wrong; he simply asked what on earth was wrong with the air here? And whether a pastor was not wanted in this parish.

"All north-country cures are the same in that respect; there is not a pastor who willingly comes to the Nordland. It was purely out of kindness that I came."

Pious folly and learned folly sometimes join hands; his mother seemed as if she would burst with pride over her great son:

"Oh, yes! it was grand of you to be willing to come home again!"

But Julius did not give in:

"Well, then, there are not to be any pastors in the Nordland, I suppose?"

"You're talking rubbish, Julius," mutters his father.

The pastor coughs and answers:

"My bishop thinks that people here in the north ought to be able to get along with pastors who are not such thorough scholars. And you must submit to his judgment, Julius."

Julius never submitted if he were not frightened into it, and he was in no danger here. Besides, his respect had received a blow—it was awful the way that fellow Lars had stuffed himself with goat's meat.

"What's up—are you sick?" he said, as though he heard this now for the first time.

"Yes, unfortunately I have studied too much. My chest is affected."

But Julius, who remembered his brother's lion-like voice in the pulpit that day, asked again in astonishment:

"Your chest?"

"Yes, and my eyes. My sight is weak."

"Now, just you leave Lars alone, Julius," his father admonished.

"What's the matter with your eyes?" asks Julius.

"Something that concave spectacles are needed for. You would not understand."

No, Julius did not understand, so he said nothing.

The pastor laid his hand on the books and said:

"You don't use these books much at home here, I suppose?"

"No, worse luck," answered his father; "there's much too little reading of God's word."

"Then, perhaps I may take them with me?" said the pastor.

"What do you want with them?" asked Julius.

His father looked as if he would not miss the books and said:

"Just take them if you want them."

"Your eyes will get still worse if you do," said Julius.

But to that the pastor replied: "Ah, no! with God's help I shall not get worse. My doctor says my sight is better now than it was a while ago."

"I know of another book," said Julius. "Ole Johan has an old book written by Jesper Brochmand."

"Can you get me the book?" asked his brother.

"Yes, I think so," said Julius, and went out.

Then the pastor began to speak of Herr Holmengraa, saying that he was a worldly man who thought of nothing but business. "Is it true that he has taken to drink?"

"Holmengraa?"

The pastor nods.

"I have been told so."

His mother wags her head again. Lord! what a lot her son knew!

"I shall have to speak to him, too, one of these days," said the pastor. "And the children, I suppose, are running about at home and getting more and more heathenish since I left?"

"Yes, Felix won't learn anything. And now his father is going to send him back to Mexico," Daverdana has heard.

Her brother pricks up his ears:

"To Mexico? And Mariane too?"

"No, only Felix, Mariane is to go to Christiania later on."

"To Christiania? Indeed."

The talk turned upon Per of Bua—the pastor knew something about every one, the vestrymen had been so zealous in their assistance. Per of Bua was getting fatter and fatter, he might be called before his Judge at any moment; he ought to give up his reprehensible sleight of hand in weighing and measuring goods.

And then the telegraphist, did he not go after girls at night? And the wharf-manager, was it true that there was something between him and the housekeeper, Jomfru Salvesen?

Daverdana sat there on pins and needles; there would be questions next about the assistant wharf-manager who was her sweetheart of the boat-shed. Ah! she would never look at him again!

Then Julius came hurrying in again; he had been over at Ole Johan's and he now flung a bulky and horribly dirty book upon the table. Good gracious—he surely had not stolen it?

"There's the book," he said.

"Am I to have it?" asked the pastor.

"You're to have it."

And his mother wagged her head: Dear me! what a fellow for books Lars was, what a fellow for learning.

The pastor laid the three books together and patted them. What did he want with them? Why, L. Lassen had begun to collect a library, and to strip the cottages to furnish it. Here now were three new volumes; and this Jesper Brochmand in particular would look so well on his shelves.

Then Julius says:

"Ole Johan begged that you would come and hold a prayer-meeting at his cottage before you left."

"At Ole Johan's? He hasn't a large enough room, has he?"

"We could take out the windows there too."

Pause.

His mother then says:

"I can never believe you will make yourself so cheap as to hold a prayer-meeting at Ole Johan's, so that all his people could go about boasting of it."

"No," says the pastor. "And besides I have had enough for to-day. My throat—hm!" The pastor put his hand to his mouth and gave a cautious, smothered cough.

"No! don't you pay any heed to him," says his father, Lars Manuelsen. "Just let Ole Johan abide by what he's heard to-day already!"

But Julius is a regular demon:

"As far as that goes, and if you're hoarse," said he, "mother can just lift that tongue at the back of your throat with a silver spoon. She did it to me."

"You are so horribly coarse, Julius," said the pastor to his brother.

He pulled on an extra coat over his bulky frame, put on his

galoshes, and went out. No doubt he wanted to take a turn round his old haunts before he set out homewards to the parsonage. Daverdana and her small brothers and sisters ran to the windows to look at him.

There went L. Lassen up the well-known road, his head drooping slightly, because it was so heavy he could not hold it erect. It did not look as if anything could make him step aside from the path now, he evidently felt so sure of himself, and when he met people his only fear was that they might not take off their hats to him. For it was surely not for him to take off his hat first; was he not a pastor? There were so many people; and some were strangers to him—workmen at Holmengraa's no doubt. He stared hard at these people till they had got quite close to him, and sometimes he went on so long with this that he got no greeting at all. That, of course, was not what he wanted. But rather that than that he should be the first to salute.

In truth, L. Lassen had in him the makings of a great churchman, and he would no doubt go far yet. One could even imagine that he might, in time, get the length of slapping Lieutenant Willatz Holmsen on the shoulder.

And then something would certainly happen.

The telegraph operator is sitting at his instrument receiving messages. There comes an urgent telegram from Berlin; it is not long, but so important that the operator decides to deliver it himself. He signals three dots and a dash, gets up and takes a pull at a bottle he has standing on a shelf behind a curtain, locks the office in defiance of the regulations, and goes out. He takes the road to the manor. He is a tall, heavily built man, and he swings his shoulders as he walks.

As he had never been at the manor before, he goes by the back way so that he may meet some one. He asks a girl for the Lieutenant; the girl brings the housekeeper; and only after an insistent demand from the telegraphist is the Lieutenant fetched. He seemed greatly surprised, and asked if one of his people could not give a receipt for a telegram. "Oh, yes, they can. That is not it. I only wished to let the Lieutenant know beforehand that this is a very important message."

The Lieutenant is on the point of tearing it open and reading it, when the operator intervenes, saying:

"Wait a moment, take it gently. It is not a cheerful telegram."

In ordinary circumstances the Lieutenant would probably have struck at the man, now he paused confounded, and looked at him. He knew him slightly through seeing him at the telegraph office—a willing and a pleasant fellow whose name was Baardsen. That he should come now and behave in this merely foolish fashion bewildered the Lieutenant, and this was perhaps the telegraphist's object. When the Lieutenant at last got the telegram open and read it, the impression it made at first was comparatively faint.

"Mother had accident," he read. "Oh!" said the Lieutenant and leaned against the doorpost. "Had accident while bathing," he read. Strange!—could one have a serious accident while bathing? There was more, but it was of no importance.

"I must answer. Wait a little; I will go with you," said the Lieutenant.

He took up his cap in the passage, and the two men went down to the telegraph office.

"While bathing?" said the Lieutenant to his companion, as if he did not understand.

"The lady has probably hurt herself. But it does sound odd," replied the other. The telegraphist looked, however, as though he had a suspicion of the truth; and he said a little later—again, perhaps, by way of leading gently up to it: "There must be something behind it."

When they reached the office the Lieutenant sat down to write an answer to Willatz, putting many questions. While he is occupied with this the operator sits at his table and receives another message.

"Wait a little," he said over his shoulder; "here is another telegram coming." And as he wrote he gradually prepared the Lieutenant: "It is more intelligible now—I'm sorry, this is a message to say—"

Fru Adelheid had been drowned while bathing.

A couple of days later the Lieutenant goes south by the mailboat; he is to meet his son, who is already on his way to Norway with his mother's body. So after all the Lieutenant found a use for the new cloak he had bought for his journey to England. Ah! but he did not wear it now with such Arab-like jauntiness.

XVI

The sad news from Berlin had a strange effect upon Herr Holmengraa; he seemed to go a little off his head. At first he was plunged into deep mourning and grief; the mistress of Segelfoss had been so exceptionally kind to him from the very first: indeed, very likely it was she that he had to thank for having been able to start his great undertakings here at all.

But when a few days had passed, a change came over Herr Holmengraa and he began to look at the bright side of life again—it seemed incomprehensible! He was seen to smile, to laugh—he must surely be drinking his Spanish wine at dinner; there could be no other explanation. And this being so, the vestrymen would hurry to Pastor Lessen with more tales, no doubt.

Who was Herr Holmengraa? A cross in the sky, a symbol? But perhaps there was nothing mysterious about him, perhaps he was only a transitional type who happened to possess superior abilities? Was he not a man who had earned money, but had lived obscurely and as a stranger upon the plateaus of Mexico and now wished to come home and reap the honours he had earned? He came; the reports of his fame had rolled and thundered from afar, but out on that grey holm there were no possible means of keeping his glory alive—he must get away from the island at all costs. He came to Segelfoss, and there he found the very place he needed.

There were fine people here and splendid prospects for business—from here one might shine over the whole Nordland.

What happened then? He carried out all his plans, perhaps more than he first thought of; but he continued to lead a modest life—the only noise he made was with his machines. Was there anything artificial in this sobriety? Might not his self-control fail once in a way? Never. When could it be said to have failed? In his relations with the Holmsens at the manor he was delicate and frank, he was indulgent to his employees, generous and good-natured with all men. Did he make his way by fraud, did he practise deceit? His dealings with all were open-handed and irreproachable. If the Lieutenant had any suspicions about this singular stranger, he must have his own peculiarities to thank for them. What about the incident of the mill-dam which was washed away? Was it not to make up for that that Herr Holmengraa took up the heavy bills owing to the bank? That he at the same time became the sole owner of the whole river and of the whole mountain lake was a chance; a fortunate chance, but at any rate he paid hard cash for it. Was there, then, any real ground for suspicion? Take the fact that there were pine forests in Mexico too; quite true, but not where Herr Holmengraa lived—though he had a saw-mill at work there. He suffered from a break-down in health and took pills, until he had his operations in full swing; since then nothing more had been heard of his break-down—strange, how curative was the effect of the air here upon Herr Holmengraa, while its action was so lamentably the reverse upon another of life's warriors, Pastor Lassen!

Where was such tact as Herr Holmengraa's to be found? And he showed it in such a natural way, as though he had not learned it, but had been born with it. Late and early, at all times. Fru Adelheid, who was a connoisseur in such things, had never once felt any doubt about it. What a feeling of safety and content he gave her! Was he in love with her? In love? Surely he would have chosen some one younger. That he should have made so much of her and quite broken down when she died—could hardly be because he was in love? Why should it be? Was it not a fine thing in itself for Tobias of the holm to go out and in of Segelfoss and be the mistress's friend? There is no glory in showing off to people whose doors are always open; a red flannel vest will impress the rabble. Herr Holmengraa, we may presume, showed his devotion to Fru Adelheid; as he had shown his respect for a Danish ambassador. He was a peasant from his cradle and thus belonged to a race for whom life had as yet done nothing except barely to keep them from death. All he knew he had picked up for himself, all that distinguishes the intercourse of cultured human beings, their speech included, he had made a personal possession—well done, Herr Holmengraa, brilliantly done! But he was two hundred years younger than the inmates of Segelfoss; he had learned to bow, but his bow was that of a slave.

Were there private reasons for his grieving over Fru Adelheid's death? Jomfru Salvesen and Fru Irgens, née Geelmuyden, sit and discuss this question when they have their confabulations; maybe the lady of Segelfoss herself will reveal it some day if her diary is published. A she-wolf may visit a dog!

In any case Herr Holmengraa did indeed grieve at the lady's death; this showed itself by his face and even his nose seeming to grow longer—probably because he grew thinner. But when he changed round again and became gay, it was no doubt because he had, so to speak, no one to consider any longer, now that the fine lady, Fru Adelheid, was dead.

For Herr Holmengraa did change, as was shown by the fact that he went too far for Fru lrgens, so that she really had to stop him, saying: "No—some one might come!" It showed itself still more when one evening he got hold of Jomfru Salvesen and wanted to marry her: "Think it over," he said; "I am in earnest. Come and have a look round the house; come upstairs!"

He was quite off his head.

For a week he played the fool for his own amusement, he had completely lost his balance. It was as though he had gone in chains for years, and was now free. He let the hens out in the evening and then stole down to the girl Marcilie's window; as Marcilie was not alone he pretended to have come to say that the hens had got out and must be put in again. He did not leave her alone, but followed her to the henhouse, kissed her, and gave her money. That was a fine state of affairs! He had shown some inclination before to pay little pranks, but only in reason, nothing like this. As he was so rich he felt no qualms and he probably cared very little about what people thought. During the time the Lieutenant was away Herr Holmengraa even went down to the manor and got hold of Daverdana. She, to be sure, was engaged to the wharf-assistant and in no need of a lover; but when Herr Holmengraa got wind of this he became jealous, fell in love with her, dressed himself up, and put the gold chain doubled over his waistcoat. It was realty pitiable to see him—this old man was in a condition unsuitable to any one past his youth.

District-doctor Muus came into his mind and he got him to his house. Why not? It was common politeness. The doctor was richly entertained, with plenty of strong liquor; it promised to be an interesting day for him. This man from the west was indeed an excellent host; there was no exception to be taken to his silver, and his wine was that of a man of wealth; Doctor Muus crossed one leg over the other and was very well pleased with things.

"I hope Attorney Rasch will look in later," said Herr Holmengraa, "and then you will have more company."

So the solicitor had not been asked to dinner, but only to a little conviviality afterwards. The doctor appreciated this mark of honour. Not but that Attorney Rasch was of official standing too, and in a way of equal rank; but, after all, a solicitor is not the same as a doctor; neither is a pastor. Herr Holmengraa doubtless still retained in his blood the ideas of degrees of rank as understood by the people of the holm; these were to the advantage of Doctor Muus, and Doctor Muus made the most of them.

But he should not have made so much of them; it did him no real good. What did any one in this house know of the official hierarchy!

The doctor, oddly enough, cherished the belief that he, too, had a right to pride of rank; hence, no doubt, his clash with the Lieutenant on their first meeting. Herr Muus was the product of five generations of industrious school life and ordinary ability, of that and nothing more; how then could the man give an opinion on the subject of music and of the new pieces of music which lay on the grand piano? It was Fru Adelheid who had mentioned these pieces, and this had induced Herr Holmengraa to purchase them. They now lay there and waited in vain for her who would never come, but they should have his esteem—that was not too much to expect of him. However, the point was that Herr Muus still held by Italian music—his parents had told him he ought to do so—and this was only Beethoven—for, as we know, Fru Holmsen was so very German in everything.

"A sad loss, this that you have had down here," says the doctor.

Herr Holmengraa bends his head low and answers:

"A heavy blow."

"How does he take it?"

"The Lieutenant? He is a sensible man, a superior man. But I fancy it was almost more than he could bear."

"What do you say? That he is a superior man?"

Herr Holmengraa answers:

"Yes, that is my impression."

The doctor says:

"Then I think your impression leads you astray."

These are the doctor's very words.

Now, while it is true that in the popular mind a doctor ranks above many other folk, yet it happened that Herr Holmengraa had seen a doctor before; there were doctors even in the Cordilleras; they were not rare. Herr Holmengraa probably thought, too, that some respect was due to his impressions. He had now and again during his life had to depend upon his impressions, and they had not led him astray; for they had made him Holmengraa—the man he was to-day.

"I believe, all the same, that the Lieutenant is a superior man," he said.

This did not impress Herr Muus, for he was one of the upper classes and a man of scientific culture:

"I make a distinction between a man who is brought to his knees by misfortune and one who steers systematically and madly to ruin," said he. "The Lieutenant belongs to the latter class. I have heard it said that it is you who own his property."

Now, would it do to make Fru Adelheid and the Lieutenant out to be quite ordinary persons, whom any one might criticize? What glory would Herr Holmengraa reap, in that case, from having been their great and good friend all these years?

"That's just gossip," he said.

"Gossip? It is what responsible people say."

"Then you must have misunderstood the responsible people."

"I did not misunderstand them. But it would appear, then, that their fears for the Lieutenant are unfounded. So much the better!"

Then the attorney arrived and the gentlemen settled down to the bottle. The attorney was a man who kept more to everyday matters and was not so learned and argumentative. With his coming the talk took a practical turn, and it was not long before he and Herr Holmengraa were talking business. And then he drank far more lustily than the doctor, indeed he even led his host on to drink heavily—God knows why, unless it was that he wished his benefactor to deny himself nothing. Attorney Rasch had much to thank Herr Holmengraa for; house, land, and help at the beginning of his career—and now he was established in a flourishing business and had both an inner office for himself and an outer one for his clerks. It was wonderful how things had prospered with him. For a long time past he had wished to buy the ground his house stood on, as well as a strip of land adjoining; but Herr Holmengraa had always answered that the Lieutenant did not wish to part with any more of Segelfoss.

He asked about it now and received the same answer.

On this the attorney again respectfully invited Herr Holmengraa to drink with him.

What was this leading to? Herr Holmengraa, the peasant from the holm, his tongue loosened by wine, aired, in the course of the afternoon, many great plans, the last of which was that of joining in the Spanish sardine fishery and fitting out a Norwegian fishing-fleet in Santander.

"Norwegian fishermen will not be allowed to fish there, will they?"

"Then I'll naturalize them."

Perhaps he wished to shine before his two guests; he hinted something about a discovery of metal in two more or less precisely indicated parts of the country; he thought of buying mines. Yes, perhaps he wished to show off, but what did it all mean? It was not his custom to make a parade of his ideas, but to keep them to himself. He spoke quietly and without boasting as was his habit, but great plans were seething in his brain. It was interesting to listen to him. "Your health, gentlemen," he said; "it was kind of you to look in upon me!"

Tall little Mariane came gliding in and showed that she could curtsy with her long thin legs. How strikingly well developed she was, how ripe her curling lips! She handed her father the letters she had brought and said as she did so: "Letters from home!" It was almost a surprise to hear Norse words from one with that low forehead and Indian hair and sensitive nose. "That was all," she said.

"Thank you," said her father.

Yes, that was all, she herself had got nothing. The letters from young Willatz had stopped.

"Excuse me a moment!" said Holmengraa, and opened a letter with foreign stamps on it. He glanced rapidly through it and said to his daughter: "Greetings to you, too, my dear!"

Herr Holmengraa put the letters aside and said:

"If you gentlemen think the sherry too cold or too hot—we have not an the same taste, of course—oh, you don't?"

Polite and good-humoured as usual. He began to tease the attorney about Jomfru Salvesen: it was on that account he was so keen about the piece of ground, about pasture for a cow? Ah, those young people!

The doctor took the opportunity to say:

"Could you not sell Attorney Rasch the ground, Herr Holmengraa? That would prove on the spot that you own Segelfoss."

"How can I sell ground belonging to the Lieutenant's estate? Per of Bua wants to buy ground too; I suppose he has become so full of money that now he wants to buy a bit of meadow big enough for a couple of cows. I have not even mentioned it to the Lieutenant. Besides, it is all so trifling; it is a matter of no consequence which of us owns pasturage for two cows. Pasturage for two hundred cows would be a different matter."

The attorney asks:

"But why shouldn't the Lieutenant want to sell? He gets money for it, doesn't he? I know another who would gladly become his own landlord: Lars Manuelsen. He came to me and expressed himself openly on the subject: as he had a son who had become a parson, and what's more, a noted parson, he could not well remain a tenant-cottager; he wanted to buy his own place and a moderate-sized piece of arable land as well."

"Is that the father of Pastor Lassen?" asks the doctor.

"Yes. And of course it is the pastor who is behind it. Do you know him?"

"No. He paid me a visit; I thought him a very modest fellow. A peasant, of course, but he has worked his way up to culture."

"Yes, it's his father, a man worthy of respect, since he has a son who is a pastor," says the attorney, turning again to Holmengraa. "And I know several others who want to buy land. Your own baker wants to buy land, Herr Holmengraa."

"My baker? I have no baker!" And now it seemed as if Herr Holmengraa had heard enough small talk from these two dapper and absurd little persons for that afternoon—as if all of a sudden he could not be bothered with any more, but meant to say just exactly what he pleased. "My baker? You seem to take for granted that I am very rich, just as you look at this chain of mine and think it is real. Of course it isn't real. Why should I waste my money? I am not so rich as all that. The chain is gilt, it is stronger than gold, it shines like gold—doesn't it shine?"

Would he give the two gentlemen another dose of this kind of talk, or would he, in the desire to shine, resume his romantic character? After a moment's pause he said, putting it in the form of a compliment:

"I have a son, Felix. It was my dream to make him a cultivated man like you gentlemen, but he will not study. Now I must send him back to Mexico."

"Has he any one to go to in Mexico? I thought—"

"I can put him into the care of some one. Besides, he might find relations there—his mother, for instance."

Pause. The attorney and the doctor look very much amazed.

"I thought—I was told you were a widower."

Herr Holmengraa looks at the doctor with indifference and again pays no attention to him, but goes on with what he was saying:

"No, nothing can be done with Felix here; he will probably find his way back to his tribe again. But Mariane, my daughter, stays with me."

When Herr Holmengraa accompanied his guests to the door in the evening he was after all not so drunk but that his feet could lead him into forbidden paths. It was late in the evening and the gentlemen had dined well and drunk deep, nor had they any fault to find with their entertainment. But Doctor Muus remarked that when their host had contradicted him now and then during the evening, he had plainly perceived the hatred of the uneducated man of the lower class for the upper class to which he and Attorney

Rasch belonged. And Attorney Rasch had noticed it too.

With this evening Herr Holmengraa's strange excesses ended. During the days that followed he became master of himself again and King over all. He made arrangements for the funeral, he telegraphed for a wreath for Fru Adelheid's coffin, and at the moment when the mail-boat swung in from the fiord with its flag at half-mast, he had the quay and the road thickly strewn with pine-twigs. Was it out of respect for the Lieutenant that he stopped his mad pranks? Or was it from a sense of shame? Whatever the cause, Herr Holmengraa had done much harm in the last two weeks, and if he had not been the man he was it would have taken him a long time to repair it—it took Herr Holmengraa no time at all. No! he was such a legendary being already that anything might be expected of him.

Fredrik Coldevin came to the funeral too with his wife—at last he had found time to come to Segelfoss again; it was a long time since he had been there. And the old Coldevins came from their island—they looked like small white curios now, and they had no voices left. They were like wrinkled albino children. Colonel von Platz of Hanover sent a representative, and flowers which, however, arrived a week too late.

Even on this occasion the Lieutenant could not help acting in a strange and self-willed way: he had arranged by telegram that the pastor of the neighbouring parish should come and officiate at the funeral. Was there anything the Lieutenant was not capable of! One would have thought that now at least he had received a heavy blow to stun him—but no.

But the evening before the funeral the pastor's boatmen arrived without him; they brought a letter with excuses and explained that the pastor had been prevented from coming. Most likely he had been seized with scruples at the last moment; he did not dare, perhaps, to offend his colleague, L. Lassen, who was in the good graces of the bishop. That was probably it.

The Lieutenant smiled and said to his son:

"It will have to be a Lars after all. And really it does not matter, your mother will not hear him. Will you give Martin orders to fetch Lars in good time to-morrow morning?"

When the pastor came Consul Fredrik had to act as intermediary between him and the Lieutenant. It was the Lieutenant's wish to avoid an address by Lars, but the pastor could not agree to that altogether; however, out of respect for the Lieutenant, he would make the address short, and he waived his right to meet the bier at the gate of the churchyard.

The Lieutenant said:

"Then I shall stay at home."

Consul Fredrik made a show of considering the matter in order not to excite his friend; but he had no doubts on the subject.

"Yes, that's a way out of it," he said, nodding his head. "If only you do not come to regret it afterwards."

"Doubtless I shall."

"In that case the question arises whether it is not better to endure an hour's unpleasantness now, rather than suffer for the rest of one's life."

The Lieutenant gave up the idea of staying at home. He dressed as if for parade, with epaulettes and sword and gold lace, and over all he wore his expensive cloak. He was more splendid than any one had ever seen him. Young Willatz was in a new black suit with crepe round his silk hat. Both father and son, strange to say, wore white gloves without any black about them.

All Holmengraa's people had been given a day off, the mill was stopped; all the cottagers and the tenants assembled in the churchyard, which was black with human beings, as on a great baptismal Sunday. The coffin was quite hidden under flowers; there were wreaths from England, from Germany, from the Holmengraas, from all the Coldevins, from the merchants in Bergen—it seemed nothing but a mass of flowers that went down into the: grave.

Then came the address. Paster Lassen was certainly not quite sure of himself; but this was too good a chance to deliver himself in some detail on spiritual matters, and he could not refrain from his original intention of giving a long oration. Any other sorrowing relative would have been grateful for his solemn words of comfort, but the Lieutenant, true to himself, gazed straight in front of him, absent-mindedly, and probably did not listen. When the address had lasted half an hour and the Lieutenant could stand no more, he suddenly took the little wooden spade from the sexton and handed it to the pastor—not even with the handle first. The pastor was forced to pause; he looked at the Lieutenant, and seeing that it was time to stop, he took the spade and threw the three spadefuls of sand down upon the flowers.

And then the grave was filled up.

But people who had noticed the episode of the spade did not approve of the Lieutenant's action: Lars Manuelsen disapproved of it, Per of Bua disapproved of it; they had never before seen such behaviour to a minister preaching God's word—"and that was what our Lars was." But the pastor knew better than to take the spade and thrust it back into the Lieutenant's face, for he was a cultivated man. He showed that right up to the end: no sooner was the ceremony over than he was about to address a few private words of consolation to the relatives—a beautiful custom among the clergy on such occasions; but, not being quite sure of himself, he turned to young Willatz first, because he stood nearest. Pastor Lassen held out his hand to the lad and said: "You have suffered a heavy loss, Willatz, but the Lord will help you to bear it!"

Yes, indeed! the Lord would certainly do that; Pastor Lassen had only to bring it to his notice, to exhort him to it.

Then the Lieutenant's voice was heard—and the pastor saw two grey eyes looking at him with icy disdain:

"Are you addressing my son by his Christian name? None of that, please!"

Whereupon the Lieutenant took his way home from the funeral.

❧

The old Coldevins only stayed two days this time, then they went home again in their boat. It was like a boat out of a bygone age, with shades on board. They could not quite take it all in—the old folks! "There was no road *there* before," said they; "there was no house *there* before," they said. Then they shook their heads as if they did not know where they were they were not quite sure that it was Segelfoss they had come to this time. Then they went home again; they had not taken any walks in the young forest; they had scarcely spoken.

Consul Fredrik and his wife stayed four days, then the south-bound mail-boat came and took them with it. Even Consul Fredrik was no longer so full of life as he used to be; he had grown very grey and there were pouches under his eyes. His wife was fat and homely and had even become interested in missions lately, and she was there with him. The Lieutenant was much occupied with his own affairs; his grief was very great, quite remarkably great. One would not have expected the Lieutenant to suffer from sleeplessness because he had lost Adelheid—whom he had lost before. And so there was nothing this time to make the Consul's stay pleasant; and he was longing to get away all the four days he was there.

He spent the evenings as of old drinking wine with his old friend; but they were so formal together, the conversation was far from enlivening, and Consul Fredrik had no opportunity to stand or fall by his philosophy of life.

Hardly a word was said about all the sweeping changes on the estate; when the Consul suggested that he feared he was, unfortunately, not without blame for these changes, the Lieutenant at once repudiated any such view, saying:

"No, I am grateful to you; you are not without credit for them."

Then the Consul tried the subject of Willatz—was Willatz to stay in Berlin?

"Certainly," answered the Lieutenant. "He goes south again on the same boat as you."

"My daughter Thea," says the Consul—"you remember Thea? She took the mate."

"Margaret did right."

"The mate is a captain now."

"There you see!"

"Captain of the steamship *Horsefly*, fifty-two feet long. Well, it can't be helped."

Pause.

Then the Consul actually tried a little pleasantry even on this mournful occasion.

"You mentioned your responsibility for there being a lazy fisherman the less in your parish?"

"Yes, I regret it, for the fellow's own sake."

"What do you say to this, then? You remember that many years ago a mulatto was born in our town? Well, I don't know why, but people began to make out that I was responsible for the mulatto. Did you ever hear such a thing! There was supposed to be a connection between him and a certain entertainment in my garden, ha, ha, ha! But at last I got tired of it and sent the boy away. Now he's at a commercial school in Philadelphia."

"At any rate your guilt is less than mine," said the Lieutenant.

How melancholy it was talking to his friend now; Consul Fredrik almost regretted that he had come to the funeral. Indeed, to tell the truth, he had lived the life of a small town for so many years now that he was beginning to think it quite good enough. Was not his business doing well? Were not the pens in his office kept busy? And had he not for society the best families in the town? In the club, too; they found many an interesting subject for discussion, as, for instance, this summer, when a daughter of the house-owner, Bommen, died from dancing too violently on board the German man-of-war in the harbour. Ha, ha! the crazy girl! French officers would never have let her dance herself to death.

But Consul Fredrik, who talked so gaily and laughed so much, sometimes went off by himself and fell into deep thought. Possibly he did it for the sake of appearances. And one day, when, perhaps, it was not quiet enough elsewhere, he went into Fru Adelheid's bedroom and stood there a short time. He looked tired and worn out now, and the pouches under his eyes were very large. He took up a hair-comb which lay there among other trinkets, looked at it, and seemed to think it beautiful, for he gazed at it long. And then it seemed to occur to him that perhaps it was not quite the thing for him to sit down in this place and fall into a reverie; so he went quietly out of the room again.

He went down to the hot-house. He might have gone there to begin with; it was lonely enough there. What?—had he brought the comb with him? How absurd! Well, since he had done it—it was a trifle; he would not even trouble the Lieutenant about it. It seems as if it still has a slight perfume—can it be the perfume of her hair? Imagination! it smells of tortoise-shell. But suppose she were suddenly to begin singing again up there in the music-room, were to sing down to these flowers here? Ah yes!—how she would fling open her passionate heart, as one flings open a fan, in a rapture of song. Poor woman! Poor all of us! . . .

Consul Fredrik seized a chance, too, of having a little farewell chat with the housekeeper, Jomfru Salvesen. It was not until the day before the last that he was able to take his stand outside her pantry window, knowing that his wife was away at Fru Irgens'.

"Is that you!" said Jomfru Salvesen.

"It is me—more or less, Jomfru."

You see, Jomfru Salvesen had been under the shadow of the mourning in the house until now, and it was long since she had screwed up her mouth in laughter; now she heard by the Consul's tone that she might venture to lay aside solemnity for a moment:

"I suppose you have come to make an end of it again, Consul?"

Consul Fredrik gulps once or twice and says:

"Jomfru Salvesen, I have heard all!"

"All!"

"Yes, can you tell me yet more?"

"No, you see I don't want to drive you mad."

"Woman, you have betrothed yourself to two others besides me. Does the wharf-manager and does the attorney know how you have treated me, Jomfru Salvesen?"

But this was, perhaps, carrying the joke a little too far, for Jomfru Salvesen answered:

"I will tell my betrothed, Herr Rasch."

Suddenly Consul Fredrik became really interested; this was almost as important as Fröken Bommen dancing herself to death. He lifted his eyebrows and asked:

"May I congratulate you? Really?"

"Yes, I almost think you may," said Jomfru Salvesen, smiling.

"That's splendid. That is really a great piece of news. When are you to be married?"

"I don't know. In about a year, perhaps."

"Who will look after the Lieutenant then?"

"Some one else. I won't leave him before he gets somebody else."

"Shall you live here?"

"Yes, for a time at any rate; Rasch has a good business here, you know. But later he intends to look for a post in the south."

"Then you may perhaps come to my part of the country, Jomfru Salvesen; and if so you must not forget to pay me a visit."

"Thanks for your kindness, Consul Coldevin."

"For I am fond of having cultivated people about me, I am making a collection of cultured people. Well, this is a great piece of news! May I be allowed to press your hand, Jomfru Salvesen?"

"Yes—just wait a moment!" answers Jomfru Salvesen, drying her hands. "Now!"

But when the Consul held her hand he put on the jester again and began to make a speech:

"As I am now holding this hand for the last time—"

"Ha, ha!"

"I mean: while you are still innocent—I mean: while we are

both still innocent. As I am now holding this hand which I did not obtain—"

"Let me go now, Consul."

"Which was not destined to be mine—have you a dram or anything to drink in there, Jomfru?"

"No, really—" answers the housekeeper, looking about her. "But let me go and I will go into the dining-room for something."

"Oh, no, thank you; I will do without it. But, Jomfru Salvesen, you ask whether I have come to make an end of it once more? No. I have come for the one and only purpose of telling you the form it will take; that I have now settled upon the form. But it really ought to be sung, to be proclaimed with my dearest breath: at the very moment Pastor Lassen calls down the blessing of heaven on you and Attorney Rasch, I shall be found with a rope in my hands and gazing with blue eyes up at a nail—"

"Ha, ha! really, you are quite impossible!"

"Do you know what it is that is about to happen?"

"There's your wife coming!" says Jomfru Salvesen suddenly.

Then Consul Fredrik let go her hand.

And he knew his wife so well that he at once went to meet her and explained to her that Jomfru Salvesen had become engaged to Attorney Rasch and that he had just been congratulating her.

"Did you need to hold her hand to do that?" said his wife.

And Consul Fredrik answered:

"I wished to be polite. She will take up a different position now, of course. It is quite possible that in time she may come to move in our circle."

Young Willatz had a bad conscience about having given up writing to Mariane. How had it come about? Little by little, because he had had so much to do. Then, besides, the pangs of lovesickness had driven him to confide in his mother and she had been greatly troubled about it and would not hear of any more letter-writing. When he had insisted that he would love Mariane till he died, his mother said: "Wait ten years, and we shall see! You have first to do something worth while and please your father; you know!"

But when he saw Marlane again on the wharf and later in the graveyard, there was nothing better to do than to give her his hand, while she looked straight up in his face and slipped close up to him and stood almost touching him as she gazed. Mariane was so thoughtless in her tenderness.

They met at last. Young Willatz felt obliged for some reason to go down to the high-road, and there she was standing; as there was a good thick clump of osiers a little above the bridge, they hastened there. Young Willatz was ready dressed for his journey, and as soon as the ship came in he was to go on board; but though he had so little time he could find nothing to say. What had become of all the words in his head and his heart? Mariane was silent too. They each took up a twig to pull to pieces.

"I am going away again to-day," said he.

"Yes."

"It is not a very long journey," he said.

"Felix is going away too," she answered. "He is going to Mexico."

"Oh! is he?"

"Yes, because he will not learn his lessons. And I am to go away too, to Christiania," said Mariane. "Sometimes I want to, and sometimes I don't."

"To Christiania! that is not even as far as Berlin, so it's nothing to be afraid of."

"Can't you write to me any more?" said she.

"Yes. But I won't have time to, not if I am to do anything worth while, mother said."

And Mariane was not in the least hurt by this; she only thought of her side of the matter, and asked ingenuously if he could not write on Sundays, on Sunday evenings.

But no, he could not do that.

"I have written many letters to you; I wrote both yesterday and to-day too. Look here," she said, and handed him a couple of letters. "Take them!" said she.

And Willatz gave the girl his hand and thanked her, and put the letters away in his pocket, and was dumb with joy and bashfulness.

And then, how did it happen?—she was tall and sweet, with her Indian hair down her back and her skin of brown and red—well, however it happened, Mariane pressed close to him again and he held her in his arms without knowing what he was doing. As they stood looking at one another's necks he managed to say:

"Let me kiss you—for the letters—may I?"

And as a little quiver of assent passed through her, their lips met in an endless kiss and they both closed their eyes.

But after this their meeting did not last long. For they could not look at each other any more, and their talk was directed to the ground.

"Well, good-bye," said he.

"Good-bye," said she. . . .

When young Willatz got home, Gottfred took him to his father's study. His old, bent father was very solemn. He said:

"I have been waiting for you."

"I am sorry, I—"

"Never mind. Hm. Your name is Willatz Wilhelm Moritz von Platz Holmsen."

"Yes?" asked his son.

"It is. That is your name. Hm. And Willatz for everyday use."

"Yes?"

"You can use Moritz for every day if you like!"

"No, why should I?"

"If you like, I say."

"Yes, but I don't want to.".

"Is it not better to be called Moritz in Germany? Your mother—we owe her as much as that."

"I am registered as Willatz," objected his son.

"Your mother called you Moritz."

"I don't remember hearing her."

"Yes, when you were little."

"She never did so of late years."

"Well, then there is nothing more to be said. Hm. You must forgive me for not having invited any one to dinner with you to-day."

"Why, of course—"

"We could not this time. We owed it to your mother."

"If only you could have come with me to-day, father!"

"I have not time, my boy. Besides, you are a grown man now. Take care of yourself, Willatz, and a good journey to you!"

XVII

Had things been now as in the old days, the Lieutenant would have put up a monument on Adelheid's grave; what could he do now? To be sure he had already found the money for a large and imposing bronze tablet; but that was no monument, no memorial stone. And, naturally, he would have presented the church with silver-gilt vessels in Adelheid's name, if he could in any way have raised the funds required.

So funds were beginning to run low, were they?

How should they not be running low?

He had already had to give in about the organ. And had he been in a position to have Adelheid's and his own portraits painted for the collection of ancestors? It hurt this man's inborn sense of order that an important matter of this kind had been left undone. Besides, there was little Gottfred here—something must be done for him. And little Pauline—was she not to be properly provided for? And Halflapp Petter, who, it must be remembered, had once been Adelheid's groom.

Ah! in some ways it was well that Adelheid had gone when she did; she could not have borne it, she would have sung no more. Some of the misfortunes of a family turn to blessings: heaven dispenses mercies in the guise of buffets.

So one may say, being a humanist.

But when Fredrik Coldevin had asked whether young Willatz was to go back to Berlin, the question was too ridiculous. Where else should he go? Was it likely that he would be kept at home and have his eyes opened to his father's distresses? Life had dealt hardly with poor Fredrik; he had not even sense enough left to understand that here it was a question of a Willatz Holmsen who usually lived abroad, but now and again came home on a visit.

A man did not let himself he cowed; a man should be silent and proud, warrior and man of the world, strong in his will-power. Was life a thing in which the old Lieutenant had no part any more? Ay! then he would not seek for it by day and lie tossing and turning in longing for it by night. The year of mourning was not over and he felt that he ought to be as punctilious about this as he was about everything else, but at the same time there was a limit to his patience: he would start the evening readings again.

Little Pauline was his parlour-maid now—some one had to be—and she had those pretty, gentle ways, and that velvety look in her blue eyes. It seemed that for a change the Lieutenant wanted to be a pasha again. He rang for Daverdana.

It was some time before she came; he lay there on the sofa and thought with satisfaction that she was washing her hands now. And she would swing her body from the hips when she crossed the floor, she would rouse the most dangerous longings in him. He lay with both hands clenched in his trouser pockets, thinking wicked, crazy thoughts. Then she would go and get the book over there, then she would come back, swaying, and swaying—

But as it was a bright summer evening, his eyes began to wander round the room; he looked at the furniture and the pictures: *there* was a large photograph of Adelheid, and *there* was the alphabet and all Willatz's toys—old things now; how time had passed!

Yes, time had passed.

His hands relaxed again in his pockets and he went on thinking of how the time had passed. How many years had he still to live? Ah, God! how he had been cheated and plundered!

When he hears Daverdana coming he suddenly springs to his feet and stands stiff and straight. Was it rage or distraction? One of his fits of passion must have seized him; he stood there rigid, without moving, and when Daverdana came in he only made some remarks about her conduct—said that she was a good girl, hm, that she had always been a good girl, in short—hm. His seizure passed off, and he ended by saying: "Wait a little, stop there!" Then he hunted out a bank-note from his desk and gave it to her.

Daverdana curtsied, blushing and pleased, and thanked him. A word of praise or blame from the Lieutenant meant a great deal. But Daverdana was so astonished that she did not go after he had nodded: was she not to read? was she not to play draughts? And the Lieutenant had to nod a second time and say: "That was all I wanted you for."

There, it was done!

As he had once made up his mind in the case of his wife: this is the last time! so now he made up his mind in the case of life itself. Why had all these years of his manhood been wasted? Well—he could do the only thing there was for an old man to do without becoming loathsome to himself and others: he could hold himself erect. Should he start now and make a meagre meal at the great feast of life? He was a guest who had been set apart from the others and who would not sit down with the serving-folk now for the sake of a mouthful on the sly—he would hold himself aloof, stubborn and erect. Yes! he scorned to provide the little there was left of him with sweetmeats; they had not been offered to him before, he would not seek them for himself now. Was this taking vengeance on himself? Yes, on himself, on everything, on the whole system of things. He would stand erect—

This was the last time.

❧

Little Pauline was not dismissed from her post as parlour-maid; Oh, dear no! But as the Lieutenant had an unrivalled knack of creating opportunities for spending money, Pauline must, of course, have a bank-note too, now that Daverdana had had one. And after all it was only one of these small new notes which he felt almost ashamed to give away.

"Well, are you pleased with it?" he says to Pauline—for the Lieutenant chats a little with her now and then.

"Yes, thank you," says Pauline.

"Would you like another?"

"Oh, no I thank you, no—"

Then he talked to her about what she should be trained for; what had she thought of herself? Did she like sewing?

No, Pauline would rather learn to be a housekeeper.

Would she? A housekeeper? Very well. Jomfru Salvesen could teach her; that was not a bad idea. He would speak to Jomfru Salvesen. . . .

And he talked to the telegraphist, Baardsen, too, about Little Gottfred, saying that the boy might learn telegraphy perhaps. You see, Gottfred was not big and strong enough ever to be an efficient fisherman, whereas the mistress had taught him a good deal of his own and other languages.

This telegraphist, Baardsen, was a remarkable fellow. He was sitting playing the cello—deep-toned and almost black—when the Lieutenant entered. He rose and bowed, and when he had heard the object of the visit he answered:

"Of course, sir, if you wish it."

This was not irony, it was politeness; he treated the Lieutenant as if he were still the great lord of the Segelfoss manor.

Whereupon the Lieutenant became equally polite and said he was very grateful.

When the Lieutenant had gone the telegraphist crossed over to the curtained shelf, took a pull at the bottle that stood there, and sat down to his cello again, his great shoulders working as he played.

❧

As the days went by, the Lieutenant aged more and more, but he still held himself erect. On the other hand, what could be weighing upon Herr Holmengraa, who had no cares, and turning his hair and beard grey? It was strange. Those two weeks of dissipation could not have had such a bad effect on him surely; and Fru Adelheid's death did not concern him—she was not his wife.

Felix was gone now. For Felix would not learn anything, his father explained, and so he must go back to his relations in Mexico. It was quite pitiful to see how sad this made Herr Holmengraa—as indeed was only natural. It was no longer all sunshine with every one at Segelfoss—even Daverdana had begun to droop her head and look sorrowful. Daverdana with the red hair, and still so young. She was standing one day close by the stable-well, at the back of the other buildings, and, strange as it may seem, Herr Holmengraa was standing by the side of the well too, and Daverdana was weeping up into his very face. Jomfru Salvesen happened to pass by and saw them. What?—was the world out of joint? No! the world was moving along just as usual, and Jomfru Salvesen is seized with a horrible suspicion and thinks: how easily it might have been me standing there weeping before Herr Holmengraa!

All sunshine? Why, even a man like Per of Bua had had a stroke —fat Per of Bua, who every now and again had to reweigh the goods he had sold, because he had given short measure; and now he had had a stroke. Nor was it a slight stroke either; he was paralysed all down one side, and District-doctor Muus said that if he had one more stroke he would be done for—such was Herr Muus' verdict. It seemed to Per of Bua as if the whole world had gone awry with him; he did not understand it. What?—was one side of him lying there in bed with him, dead? It is true he had been a stirring and active man all his days till now, but he had had no intention whatever of being inactive in his old age, and what could be the use of crushing him? He was, in a way, at the very summit of his powers now; never had he been such an expert at profitable errors and omissions, and since he had got his liquor license, his sales of fine and costly goods to the cottagers had been quite fabulous. Curtains? Yes, but silk handkerchiefs too, machine-made stockings, hanging lamps with glass drops. Was that all? No, indeed! what was the good of slaving and making things in the winter evenings when anything whatever was to be had at Per of Bua's for money? He sold ready-made rakes and ax-helves from the factory; he sold roasted and ground coffee in tasteful wrappings; he sold margarine in kegs and pork from America. In the olden days one had to cut up one's own tobacco. That was all over—no more of that drudgery!—Per of Bua kept shredded tobacco. And what about boots? In olden days Nils, the shoemaker, came to the farms and crofts and made all the footgear the house needed for a year, and he blocked his own leather and waxed his own thread, and monstrously strong his sewing was, was Nils the shoemaker's. Now Per of Bua sold footgear from the town, and it was thin as cloth, and shone like glass.

So no one could say that Per of Bua had not been an active man, and he did not understand why he should have to lie on his bed now. But, all the same, he still carried on his trade through his wife and children, and he directed them with a firm hand from his bed; nothing went wrong. Before his illness he had known how to keep people about him in their places. He did it still; he made use of a stick to knock with when he wanted to call any one. He had the doctor, he had wise-men and women, he had drunk cod liver-oil, he had tried opodeldoc and cold water bandages—these, by the way, had been the worst of all—and one day he knocked with his stick and demanded the pastor, to see if that would do him any good.

"Here, sir, you see the worst that ever happened to a man in his life on earth," he said.

Pastor Lassen tried to comfort him by saying that he still had one good side, that he was still alive.

"Alive? No-ho, indeed! Do you see this stick here? I am just as much alive as it is."

By the way of soothing him, Pastor Lassen spoke to him of Jesus and his sufferings; what were his compared to them! He ought to be thankful to God for the good side.

"You keep talking about the good side," answered the sick man; "but it isn't so very good either any more, let me tell you." And Per of Bua mentioned various defects on the part of his good side—altogether he seemed to be quite a connoisseur in sides.

"But just look at this side," said he, and he took hold of his dead arm and threw it over to the wall that the pastor might see what it was like. "This is the side I'm talking about. There it lies; but if I didn't see it, I wouldn't know it was there. What's the use of such a thing? It isn't worth its food!" Then he took hold of the dead hand with the other and held it aloft and twisted and turned it: "And there's the hand that belongs to it," said he; "curse it—that I should say so!" and he threw the hand back to the wall again.

Pastor Lassen again tried to console him—and this time he called him Jensen, to see if that would do any good—saying: "It is not every one who has had so much success in life as you, my dear Jensen, and now you should try to make up your mind to resign yourself to a little adversity for a time."

The sick man writhes with impatience and asks:

"Can't *you* help me either, then? Is there no cure you know about—supplication or whatever it may be?"

"Supplication?"

"Isn't it true that pastors like you know a lot of things we others know nothing about?"

So that, it seemed, was what Per of Bua had been thinking of when he asked for the pastor.

"Oh, yes! no doubt that is so, to a certain extent," answered Herr Lassen—it was not for him to deny that he knew a thing or two. The fisher-boy from the cottage had the upper hand now, and he determined to use it—in the good cause, of course. It would be interesting, too, to know just how much of a rogue this Per of Bua was; would it not be possible to get him to confess?

Pastor Lassen went to the door and fastened it tight, though it was already shut; then he sat down by the sick man and looked at him. Per of Bua no doubt looked upon all this as preliminary to the supplication, so he was full of hope.

Then Herr Lassen said:

"Could it be possible I am asking as your spiritual adviser, Jensen—could it be possible that you have been too clever with this very same dead hand of yours, Jensen?"

Per of Bua gaped—and he had quite two weeks' growth of beard round his mouth.

"What?" he said. "Clever with it?"

"In giving false weight and measure?" said Herr Lassen. "I ask in God's own name."

Per of Bua's mouth closed; his expectancy changed in a moment to rage, he reached for his stick:

"Clever this, clever that!" he said. "I'll teach you to 'clever' me!—Is that what you've come for? Go home and preach to your father and your own folk. The boy must be mad!"

How he raged at Herr Lassen, at his spiritual adviser! He even dropped his title and called him Lars to his face.

At this the pastor left him.

But even as he went, the sick man shouted after him:

"And ask your father, with my compliments, to see to it that he pays what he's down in my books for! Rascally crew!"

Pastor Lassen went straightway to his parents' cottage and went into matters a little: how about Daverdana?—was she to go about for weeks longer and not get married? And how about his father himself?—was he going to sit still here and stay in debt to the Lord knows how many people? Per of Bua wanted his money!

"You must find a way out of all this," he said. "I haven't anything to help you with, or you should have it—to the last stiver. But all I earn goes into books and study. You must find a way out yourself."

"Yes," said his father. "But it's not so easy, and where am I to get the money from? The Lieutenant won't sell me the plot, and here I have to stay."

"Have you asked him?"

"I have asked Holmengraa."

Pause. The son is thinking.

"Holmengraa is the very one to do it," he said. "At any rate, I won't have my career spoilt by you people here."

"Of course not," said his father. "What was it you wouldn't have spoilt?"

"My career."

"Yes, that's just what I've said all the time that you wouldn't have spoilt. I'll go this very day to Holmengraa and offer to settle what's between us in a friendly way."

❧

The Lieutenant does not make his daily rounds on horseback any longer, he has begun to go on foot. This surprised every one but himself: were not the horses standing in the stables as before, and had not Halflapp Petter to take them out for exercise every now and again? Why did not the Lieutenant ride them himself?

He had his own ideas; perhaps he wished to accustom himself in good time to do without horses. He was troubled with sleeplessness; he walked about deep in thought, and often and often he wandered round down at the tile-works, measuring, pacing distances, and nodding to himself. He seemed to have chosen a corner of this big structure of upright logs for some special use; he marked out windows on the lining-boards. But now and then he would give this up for days, and at these times he would go about with a pickax and spade and a number of flower-pots and dig in the ground. And he dug in such strange places that people had their own thoughts about it: could it be that the Lieutenant too—the third Willatz Holmsen—had begun to search for his ancestor's treasure? If this were so, this proud and sceptical man had changed much. Perhaps want of sleep had clouded his mind. But as for the flower-pots from the hot-house, which he kept filling and emptying again everywhere he dug, they seemed to be a mere pretence at any rate.

There was nothing unusual in his appearance; if anything was weighing on his mind he bore it well. Since this old horseman had taken to walking so much, his bandy legs had become more noticeable, and he seemed bent because he kept his eyes fixed on the ground. He weak and frail! He! Why, he was made of steel!

When he heard that the housekeeper was going to be married he became eager for the event to take place, though it was to his own disadvantage: "By all means," he said; "what day have you fixed? Don't put it of!" But, when it occurred to him that this eagerness might be misunderstood, he added: "Though, indeed, I don't know how I shall keep the place going without you!"

His praise was greatly valued by Jomfru Salvesen, and in her gratitude she said that she would never think of leaving him until he had some one to replace her. "But, to be sure, little Pauline has become clever at the work these last weeks," she said.

"Indeed. I am glad to hear that. Hm. Sooner or later I mean to arrange a couple of rooms for myself somewhere. You must not postpone your wedding for a day on my account."

"Will you not go on living here in the manor-house, sir? Excuse me, but where will young Willatz stay when he comes home?"

"He is not coming home, he has no time."

"But surely he will come some time?"

"No. I have more time to spare; I will go to him. Have you not read about him in the papers? He is a musician, he composes."

"Would you not like me at least to wait a year, sir?"

"No. But I thank you all the same. What is it you wish to ask about?"

So the housekeeper comes out with it, saying:

"My betrothed thinks that we cannot very well marry on the little bit of money we have saved. And except that, we have nothing but the house. There is no land with it."

"Land?"

"If we had just enough for two cows, sir; just enough for the milk we need."

"We must see about that. Hm."

"Oh dear! if only you could!" said Jomfru Salvesen. "My betrothed has often asked Herr Holmengraa to speak to you, sir, but Herr Holmengraa has always answered that you will not sell."

He pricked up his ears, and, though he did not speak, his questioning look led Jomfru Salvesen to repeat what she had said. Then he nodded and said:

"We must see about getting a piece of ground for you, Jomfru Salvesen."

The Lieutenant wanders away, wanders down to the old tile-works, and measures and nods. Why did he not begin fitting up his quarters? Keeping oneself erect is no easy matter in these days, and very likely he is at his wit's end—but he measures and nods to himself as though what he has just heard had no particular interest for him. So—Herr Holmengraa had assumed control of the Segelfoss lands already, and declared in the name of the landowner that he would not sell! Hm. And here is Jomfru Salvesen, who has been in his and Adelheid's service for many, many years—she cannot get a bit of land from her old master!

The Lieutenant changed his ring on to his left hand. For months now this strange man had stopped changing his ring about—it had become impossible to do so—it ought by rights to have been worn upon his left hand all the time, and he did not want to do that, out of respect for Adelheid's memory. He changed it now as though he still had something to remember, something to give orders about, to remedy. It was a little comedy he played for his own benefit—an innocent piece of bravado to which his unbending will gave some value, even some real significance.

He would go home and make an inventory of his furniture.

He left the tile-works, but, when he had gone a little way, turned and looked at them and nodded. And this, too, was probably a comedy; he had a hundred times already thought out each little detail of the alteration of these tile-works into a human habitation—and this was as far as he had got.

He walked with his eyes bent on the ground as usual; he noticed the prints of a man's boots on the way to the house. He had time to imagine some new misfortune and to resolve to meet it in a manner worthy of him.

Herr Holmengraa was standing waiting for him.

The gentlemen greet one another; there is great politeness on both sides, even friendliness. They go in and sit down and begin by speaking of quite unimportant things. Herr Holmengraa has fallen away somewhat, he is pale and grey; he does not say what he has come for, and as the Lieutenant want to come to the point be helps him out:

"I am glad you came, Herr Holmengraa. There is a matter I should like to speak to you about."

Holmengraa bows.

"My housekeeper is engaged and is going to be married; she and her betrothed wish to buy a piece of land from—from Segelfoss.

Hm. I should have agreed to this sale in other circumstances, in recognition of Jomfru Salvesen's long service in this house. But as things are I cannot sell."

Herr Holmengraa thinks a moment, then he smiles and says: "Surely it depends entirely on you, Lieutenant."

"No. I cannot reduce the value of the mortgage."

"Oh, the mortgage—as far as that goes, you can perfectly well sell."

Who in heaven's name could make out this fellow Holmengraa? The Lieutenant had so accustomed himself to expect the worst—perhaps even to be turned out—that he now felt a glow of pleasure; his face brightened, he furtively slipped his ring over to his right hand again. And there sat Herr Holmengraa; he had spoken, he had shown his higher side again.

Herr Holmengraa himself seemed to be pleased—what could be passing in his head? Not much, hardly anything; it was only that the Lieutenant had made his own errand easier, had indeed made it almost unnecessary. Herr Holmengraa had been so hard hit lately: the great cargo of rye, which he had too certainly bought all too dear by telegram during those days of debauchery, was weighing him to the ground and driving him out at night in despair. And, as if that were not enough, the girl Daverdana came and wept up in his face. And then, to make matters worse, her father, Lars Manuelsen, had grown to be a man of importance—he could say what he thought, he could even threaten. Where would it all end? Lars Manuelsen had stopped Herr Holmengraa on the road to-day and demanded a settlement.

"I am again—as so often before—under an obligation to you, Herr Holmengraa," said the Lieutenant. "Of course the purchase money will go to reduce my debt to you."

"No, thank you. I do not consider the security to be reduced in the very least by this little transaction."

"In that case the transaction cannot take place," says the Lieutenant, and the two gentlemen try to outdo one another in generosity. How was it to end?

"I have received lately," says Holmengraa, "several requests that I should speak to you about the sale of land;. four or five at least. I answered that you did not wish to sell at present; I wanted to prevent these people from coming and annoying you just now when you are in need of quiet."

"Thank you, I appreciate your kindness."

"But there is one of these people for whom I wish to put in a good word—if I may?"

"Certainly."

"Thank you. It is Lars Manuelsen. He has got it into his head that he cannot continue as a tenant, now that he has a son who is pastor; he wishes to own his land."

"Indeed. Lars Manuelsen?"

"Yes. Lars Manuelsen. He has worried me a good deal about it; he stops me on the roads to talk about it."

"That is too bad!"

"But if you would let me get rid of this man, Lieutenant, I would settle the whole thing. The money would be paid by Lars through me."

"I will do exactly as you think best in the matter, Herr Holmengraa."

"What Lars Manuelsen wants is not so very little—land, I mean—full pasture for two cows. That is to say, the whole of the field between him and Ole Johan."

"Indeed. Lars Manuelsen. Is that son of his in a position to find the money already?"

"So it would seem," answers Holmengraa. "I will measure the ground and arrange everything; you will not be troubled in any way. Allow me at the same time to apologize for taking up your time with this question; I thought I would mention it as we were already on the subject. The price—what shall we say?"

"The same as usual."

"Well, I don't know. Segelfoss land must be worth more now."

The Lieutenant thinks for a little and says:

"I should be obliged if no alteration were made in these two cases, at any rate. That is to say, in the case of my housekeeper and my tenant-cottager."

Holmengraa bows.

"Do you wish me to arrange for the sale to the attorney, too, Lieutenant?"

"I shall be obliged if you will do so."

Holmengraa bows.

When he is about to go he remembers that he has not yet given any reason for coming, so he says:

"Oh, by the way, I had an errand, but I will not trouble you with it, I can see Jomfru Salvesen about it. I also wanted to pay my respects to you. I hope young Willatz is getting on well in Berlin?"

"Excellently."

The two gentlemen part.

Herr Holmengraa's business with Jomfru Salvesen was that he wanted to know on behalf of his wharf-assistant whether Daverdana could be allowed to leave service and marry. Herr Holmengraa, as he was here at any rate talking to the Lieutenant, thought he might as well do the bridegroom this little service at the same time.

And Jomfru Salvesen understood perfectly.

❧

The Lieutenant did not give up his intention of picking out the articles of furniture he could best do without and making an inventory of the whole. Money he must have and, as he had not any, it must be procured. It was a sad task he now set about: in order to make a sum that would be worth while, he foresaw that he must include one or more of his precious family heirlooms—and which of them should be sacrificed? A writing-desk here, a cabinet there, all rare specimens with richly gilt bronze fittings—could he bear to part with them? And, after all, how was he to convert them into money? An auction was hateful and, besides, might get to Willatz's ears. But whether Herr Holmengraa would help him again was a very doubtful question.

However, Holmengraa actually appeared a few days later with papers relating to the sale of the lots of land and laid the money on the table. Once more there was a contest of generosity about the money; neither of the gentlemen wished to keep it—it was a trifle for them both, to be sure. At last, in accordance with a half playful suggestion of Herr Holmengraa's, the money was equally divided between them.

And so the affair was settled.

Owing to this unexpected occurrence the Lieutenant once more had money in his pocket; not much, not any large sum, but enough for the alteration of the tile-works. He got materials from Namsen—this windfall could not be used for anything better. Herr Holmengraa had again acted the part of providence; but for his kindness not a single crown would have found its way to any one but himself. But it soon appeared that Herr Holmengraa had given his help for the last time.

The next thing was to get men to do the building and fitting up—and they were not to be had! The weather had, in the meanwhile, grown wintry and cold, and people really could not stand and freeze to death any more for the sake of the Lieutenant; they were more their own masters than heretofore. He got hold of Bertel of Sagvika, the father of little Gottfred and Pauline—he came at once, of course; but Bertel could not do much alone. So the Lieutenant's man, Martin, had to come down from the manor and help as much as he could.

Would the people not work for the Lieutenant any longer?—these people who were his own cottagers and tenants and none of whom had even paid the rent of their land, nor, for that matter, had ever been asked for it. Had not these people, too, received many benefits from him while he was still prosperous? Lars Manuelsen had a big son, Julius, but he did not come. It was well to have learned a little from the humanists and to be able to call up a smile to one's lips.

So Bertel of Sagvika and Martin sawed and planed and nailed and stopped up chinks. They made two rooms with windows and double floors and double roof—it was wonderful to see how thorough all their work was. But the foundation-wall had to wait till spring, when the frost should be out of the ground.

It did not promise to be a cheerful winter. The Lofoten fishery had been bad so far, and Per of Bua lay there bedridden and would not let people have any more goods on credit. So there was only Herr Holmengraa to go to; he was good-natured and helpful up to a certain point, to be sure—but the point had been reached now. For he had made such a heavy loss on a big cargo of rye purchased abroad, and he made no secret of it—he was probably unused to reverses and could not bear them by himself, but had to share them with others. It was certainly a staggering loss; but what could even a staggering loss matter to Tobias Holmengraa, the King? The fishermen were in Lofoten now, and their wives and children came to Holmengraa and did not always get help from him—what were they to understand by that? Take, for instance, Ole Johan's wife, who had such urgent need for a sack of wheat-flour, for the children's sake—and also no doubt that she might not lag behind her neighbours, who had white porridge. But Herr Holmengraa only gave her common meal. For a long time, too, she had wanted a muff like the one Lars Manuelsen's wife had—it would not have cost Herr Holmengraa more than a line to Per of Bua; but Herr Holmengraa said "No." He no longer behaved as one had a right to expect.

When the fishermen came home at Easter, the girl Daverdana was married, and her own brother, Pastor L. Lassen, performed the ceremony. In this case Herr Holmengraa showed himself kind and open-handed again, making the newly married couple a present of a little house to live in—was not the bridegroom his own employee at the wharf?

But a little wedding like this could not liven people up for long; they were in a gloomy mood and grew yet gloomier. No one could quite make it out; the mill was working night and day as before; the mail-boat, which at first had only run every third week, now called every single week in the year; Baardsen, at the telegraph office, and his assistant, little Gottfred, were busy sending telegrams about herring and fish and the buying and selling of goods, and all sorts of business—so that there was plenty going on at Segelfoss. But the atmosphere was gloomy. Of all the people in the place the wharf-manager was the one who took life most cheerfully. This was odd, for he, if any one, had good reason to be melancholy, and yet he sang. Maybe God had given him an unusually light-hearted nature. There was his own assistant safely and suitably married, while he himself, the head of the wharf, had been disdained. Very well, Jomfru Salvesen! Very well, Kristine! Keep your attorney, Kristine! God knows whether it wasn't out of sheer sorrow, but in the very darkest time of winter, the wharf-manager started a musical club at Segelfoss.

The Lieutenant had made his man, Martin, cart the piano and the necessary furniture down to his rooms in the tile-works by degrees, and he took the rooms into use by degrees too. This was a good plan, an excellent plan—it was not really like moving. He began by sleeping there one night; that did him no harm: he kept a fire in the stove, had lamps and candles, clenched his teeth, and slept. Then he did it a week later again—it was novel, an odd sensation, and the river roared disagreeably near; but he forced himself to sleep. Now the Lieutenant was sleeping in the tile-works every night and was at the manor only at meal-times. He said to Jomfru Salvesen, and he wrote to his son in Berlin, that, thank God, he had found a cure for his sleeplessness.

Spring came. The Lieutenant would not ask the men to work for him again; he got his man, Martin, to find a good stone here and a good stone there and cart them down for the foundation-wall; he himself worked at the excavation for it. While he was thus occupied a letter came one day from young Willatz saying that he was in a fix. It was a mere accident; he happened to be at an auction and found a lady there weeping over her valuable grand piano, her only means of livelihood. What else could young Willatz do? he gave her back her piano, it was a point of honour and a deed of charity. "Dear father, it is quite a sum of money, a big sum—perhaps I should not have done it? It was a mere chance. We had gone to an auction—several of us musicians—where pawned musical instruments were being sold. And the lady wept—she was a teacher, I think—and we musicians stood looking at her. Then I did it, I thought of you and did it—with two words; the money must be paid within a month. What else could I have done, dear father?"

"Stop!" says the Lieutenant to himself and to the letter, "—not another word!" he said. "Money? Assuredly."

He goes to Herr Holmengraa. On the way be becomes aware that he is greatly moved; his son has done him credit, he is proud of him, his eyes grow dim at the thought of him. Young Willatz—yes, he was a true scion of the race, a Willatz Holmsen such as his own father, that gallant gentleman, had been. "With two words—I see him—"

The Lieutenant was wise enough not to hope for too much from Holmengraa this time; from various signs and indications he had gathered that the great mill-owner had begun to hold himself aloof. For example, Herr Holmengraa must have seen very well that the Lieutenant was in need of work-people for the masonry work, but he did nothing—did not send a man. And yet this same Herr Holmengraa had shown himself before so exceedingly helpful—who was to know what he might do?

"I must beg leave to apply to you on a personal matter to-day," says the Lieutenant. "In order not to detain you longer than necessary I will be brief: I shall be obliged if you will read this paper; it is a catalogue of certain portions of my furniture which I wish to dispose of."

"That can probably be done best by auction," answers Herr Holmengraa quickly.

The Lieutenant understood at once that he had come on a fruitless errand, and Herr Holmengraa made his rebuff unnecessarily plain by declining even to take the catalogue.

"It is true I have not included the most valuable of my possessions in this list," the Lieutenant said, not giving the matter up at once, "but I could do so. Paintings by old masters which you may have seen in my house, the large marble figures, the silver statuettes. And you remember, presumably, the tall female figure with the amphora on her shoulder; perhaps, too, the Four Seasons—very valuable works of art."

"I do not doubt it!" said Herr Holmengraa. "But for the time being, I am not in a position to saddle myself with further expenditure."

The Lieutenant grew pale. Had Herr Holmengraa "saddled himself with expenditure" for him? In that case there was no more to be said.

And now Herr Holmengraa began to talk, to dilate on his own affairs: things had gone so badly with him; he had lost large sums of money—he was not speaking now of trifles, but of a fortune. He need not have gone so deeply into his troubles perhaps, or at least he need not have laid them quite so bare, but probably he thought that for once in a way he would make a clean breast of it; who knows? perhaps he was not so steadfast in adversity as he should have been—that might well be. But this man from the holm was a king for all that. Must a king be without a blemish? Even a king may lose his balance!

And besides, a weakness for rank and distinction seemed to be one of Herr Holmengraa's inmost characteristics. It had been a satisfaction to him to associate with the master and mistress of Segelfoss; but what glory was there in helping this same master of Segelfoss now—this broken-down lord of the manor, a dweller in a tile-factory? Herr Holmengraa was not entirely devoid of the milk of human kindness; but neither was he blind to worldly advantage.

"The best plan I can think of," he said, "is that both of us should reduce our expenses."

This was rather too familiar for the Lieutenant; and he answered: "I have nothing to reduce."

"Somewhat on the lines of what you have done already—you are living in the tile-works, are you not?"

"I sleep at the tile-works," answered the Lieutenant; thank goodness, he had command of himself again. "It is the best cure I have yet found for my sleeplessness!" And now the mine might burst for all he cared; he went on: "By the by—I had not intended to touch upon the subject to-day, but perhaps I had better mention it to the sole mortgagee: I am living much at the tile-works, it is true I am growing old too—and on that account you would perhaps prefer to make other arrangements for the management of Segelfoss?"

"What!" It sounded as if Herr Holmengraa greatly surprised—but did it really surprise him? The following words were then exchanged:

"You want me to take over the estate?"

"It is no longer mine."

"I cannot manage it."

"I can continue to manage it for the time being to the best of my ability."

Herr Holmengraa expressed much gratitude for this—but was he grateful?

As the Lieutenant walked home he nodded to himself and thought: In vain! What is to be done now? He regretted this visit to Holmengraa to-day; the mill-owner's help would have been too easy a way out of his difficulty. One should *not* take it for granted that life is easy, if one does not wish to have a rude awakening.

There was, however, nothing to be said against this same mill-owner; he had so often found a way of escape, so often shown good-will—and he himself had been struck by adversity now.

XVIII

There was nothing unusual to be seen in the Lieutenant's bearing, but he had certainly fallen on evil days. He worked so hard; he began again to dig earth for the flower-pots in the hot-house—it seemed as if he were very much taken up about his flowers, and as if he could not find good enough soil for them anywhere on the place. Many days passed before he gave up.

He had telegraphed to his son that of course he had done right, and that money would be sent. And of course money must be found, even if he had to go to Trondhjem with the silver plate. The annoying and ridiculous thing was that he had not enough money left for the journey even.

Any one else would have collapsed and gone to pieces! the Lieutenant only stiffened. He began to use a walking-stick because he had begun to go on foot—that was the only reason. This stick had been left him by his father—that gallant gentleman; it had a gold knob and a silk cord by which to hang it from one's wrist; it suited the Lieutenant and by no means detracted from his dignity.

Walking thus one day, he met the district-doctor and the attorney on the road; they both greeted the deeply afflicted man—Doctor Muus's greeting showed he knew what good breeding was; for here was this one-time lord of the manor who, according to trustworthy report, had neither yellow building nor man Martin any longer; and yet Doctor Muus took off his hat to him. But the Lieutenant answered their greeting with so much indifference, so absent-mindedly, that he forfeited both the gentlemen's sympathy—the attorney's as well as the doctor's. It is true that Attorney Rasch had just succeeded in buying the piece of meadow—yes, he had succeeded in that, he had got what he wanted, but he had not undertaken to show everlasting gratitude. And next week he would take Jomfru Salvesen away from the manor and marry her; how the Lieutenant would get on without his housekeeper was his own affair after all.

Thus things looked black to the Lieutenant. Under these conditions surely he gave up digging for the foundation-wall? By no means. It was autumn again already, and there must be a stone foundation beneath his rooms by next winter. While his man carted stone, the Lieutenant dug with a single-minded, an almost inspired, determination not to give in.

But in the evenings he sat in the tile-works and rested, and played patience with a pack of cards which he had gummed and patched. And he hid them carefully each time so that Pauline might not see them. His hands have suffered much these last months, they are sore and full of cracks; to see them handling the cards disgusts him, they are ugly and coarse. So he hides the cards away till the next evening and sits musing for an hour or two instead.

Are we to think of him sitting there in his chair shrunken and miserable, mumbling to himself out of sheer weakness?—sitting there with his head almost hidden between his shoulders and his legs drawn up, looking for all the world like a poor, tangled thread-ball with a little voice inside?

Certainly not.

Things have gone badly with him, it is true; he is sixty-nine years old now and heavily burdened with money troubles, but he babbles to himself as little as he has babbled all his life to others—he is silent—with an obstinate, a continuous, an absolute silence. But to Pauline he says—for the Lieutenant chats with her a little now and then when she comes down to the tile-works to tidy his rooms—to her he says: "You think perhaps that I am not looking well, Pauline; but there you are mistaken. I have never slept better than down here!" And then Pauline may tell him that Jomfru Salvesen is to be married next week, on Thursday, and the Lieutenant will answer: "That's right!. I shall certainly remember it!"

And to make sure of this he changes his ring to his left hand once more.

He had introduced an odd economy in his little household down in the tile-works: he liked to save matches—as if that could help him! He would never by any chance light the fire with a match if he could blow the embers into flame—he would go down on his knees and blow. He retained these oddities of behaviour to the very end. But he did not become obtrusively original. One day when he saw that the coat of his uniform had a hole in the elbow, he went up to the manor at once and changed the coat. He was engaged in digging at this time and the hole would have been a fit and proper hole from a philosophic point of view—a hole on which he might have plumed himself a little in his own eyes; but he may have thought: I am too old to put on airs of any sort; he may have thought: There is philosophy in a whole coat too.

He went early to bed, and was up early—perhaps to save lamp-oil; perhaps from a sound instinct that it was right to be up with the lark. Then he went out.

Snow had come already, but the ground was still unfrozen; only a thin crust froze during the night. He goes out walking with his gold-headed stick. It is a coldish morning, here and there a few stars are shining in the sky like fireflies on a blue ground; one or two clear cock-crows come down to him from Segelfoss, from his manor. He takes up his station on the bridge and looks up towards Holmengraa's house—all is dark there. And the river comes rushing, rushing down towards him with its never-ending roar. A wind is blowing—it has risen as he himself has risen—it is blind and invisible, without form, but there it is. When it grows too cold on the bridge, he wanders down towards the wharf, finds a sheltered place, and looks out over the sea.

Now he hears a sound that must come from human beings; probably some one is getting up. Then he hears the sound again. No, it is not some one getting up, it is some one who is up already—only a sound, blind and invisible, without form, but there it is. Soon after, Lars Manuelsen comes out of a door, and after him the wharf-manager's assistant. It is the new-made father and son-in-law; they do not speak, they are lifting a sack between them, and Lars Manuelsen gets it up on to his back. And when he notices the Lieutenant it is too late—too late to go back again, but he bows very deeply and humbly as he passes with the sack. And the assistant disappears into his cottage again. They have probably been at some night-work, thinks the Lieutenant—every one has his own warfare to wage—here it was a man bent double under a sack. . . .

He determines to pack up the silver to-day and go straight on board the mail-boat; he was well known on board and could pay for his ticket when he got to Trondhjem. He decides to dispose of a few valuables, yes, to lock himself in and pack in cotton-wool some table ornaments which necessity compels him to part with. He nods as he stands there, his face inflexibly set. When he goes back homewards to the tile-works it is the grey of dawn, the meadows lie in semi-darkness, he passes like a figure in a ghostly landscape—tall, upright—tenacity embodied.

He had no foreboding of what awaited him.

Now that he was going to Trondhjem, he would, of course, give up the excavation for the foundation-wall? On the contrary, he would finish it to-day and have all in order; he would bring masons home with him from the south. When he had been up to the manor for breakfast, he went down to the tile-works again and set to work.

And then something happened.

He had been digging for a couple of hours at the last corner of the wall, when his pick struck wood. Wood. He dug round the wood, took the spade and threw the earth up, and dug again. A box came into sight, a chest—in a flash he thought: The treasure! If the first Willatz Holmsen had buried a chest, then this was it! The Lieutenant did not believe in legends, but perhaps he had some ground for his hope—a family tradition, a memorandum; it seemed as if he knew the chest. He struggled a long time to get it out of the hole, but had to give it up. Then he broke the lock where it stood and looked down into the dark interior of the chest.

There were caskets and small boxes in it—heavy, full of coin, gold pieces. The Lieutenant set about carrying them into the house; but he was weaker than ever before in his life, his knees trembled more and more each time he went and returned—lucky that he was alone.

His man, Martin, came with another big stone for the wall and then again with another, but the Lieutenant was not to be seen. Midday came and Martin drove home.

But the Lieutenant was not to be seen anywhere; and at last Pauline went down to the tile-works to look for him. There sits the

Lieutenant in his room, his face grey with suffering. Assuredly a great grief would never have crushed him—now that he is so overcome, it is by a great joy. He had to send for his man, Martin, to drive him home.

During the day he drives to and fro between the manor and the tile-works; he has much to arrange, and time presses—to-morrow he sets out. He packs his trunks at the tile-works, stuffs them with mysterious packets, with rolls heavy as lead—ancient gold, Spanish doubloons, English guineas—it is the treasure. Yes, indeed, there are reserves on a great estate even if a war sweeps over it!

The next day the Lieutenant went to Trondhjem. His face was grey with suffering, it seemed as if all the blood had deserted his body, but he stood upright upon the deck—stood leaning upon his gold-headed stick.

The wharf-manager is a very busy man; he conducts practices with his mixed choir, and his own assistant is his leading bass. For the moment the choir is working up chorales and wedding-hymns for performance at Jomfru Salvesen's and Attorney Rasch's wedding. Truly it was a magnanimous trait in the wharf-manager's character that he should wish to lift up his voice on that occasion, in fact that he should take any notice at all of the wedding. But not only did he take an interest in it; he exerted himself to the utmost. "We sing like so many brute beasts," he said, dissatisfied and desperate. "Is this a choir? It is worse than the fog-horn on the mail-boats. We shall never be ready in time."

But one evening the wharf-manager came to the choir with the tidings that the wedding, thank God, had been put off for a week;

there would still be time to learn to sing like human beings! And so he hammered away again at the chorales.

Was the wedding postponed? Yes, out of consideration for Herr Holmengraa. Fate had so ruled matters that Herr Holmengraa, just at this time, was much depressed by his unfortunate speculations, and when he was asked to the wedding he had declined emphatically. He was a rich man and could afford to give a refusal. Good-natured? Of course he was good-natured; but he was a man of business too, and now his business had suffered. "I thank you," said Herr Holmengraa, "but I must ask you to excuse me just now!"

Why should he go on putting himself about for people? He was a self-made man; his refined manners were no doubt largely artificial; and he was quite capable of showing the natural man on occasion; he could afford it.

But the wedding could not take place without Herr Holmengraa. Attorney Rasch talked it over with his betrothed and agreed with her that Herr Holmengraa was indispensable. They had the district-doctor—that was so far good; they had a parson with a well-known name—L. Lassen; they had the sheriff of Ura and his wife; a couple of merchants and their wives; the wharf-manager, and Fru Irgens—that was all. None of the bridal pair's relations would be there—the bride, poor thing, had probably no relations, and the bridegroom's occupied official positions in the south and could not be expected to take the trouble to come north; they were people who had had enough of the Nordland. The telegraph-operator, Baardsen, was not asked, because no one knew him; he had not called on any one. "What a way to behave! Just think of it! Not to pay calls!" And who else was there? The Lieutenant was away, otherwise he would have been a guest at Jomfru Salvesen's wedding—there was no doubt about that, though his health had broken up lately. Herr Holmengraa was also broken in health and asked to be excused. Who else was there?

Clearly Herr Holmengraa was indispensable.

And in fact, when the great man heard that the wedding had been put off for a week on his account and no other, so that he might have time to recover, the natural man came to the front again, and being flattered by the attention, he accepted the invitation.

So the wedding took place. It was quite simple, but really most pretty and genteel, with wine and speeches and telegrams and a song outside the windows by the wharf-manager's choir.

And Pastor Lassen had been so agreeable. It is true that he was not very clean, and, in fact, it was misusing dirt to have it lying so thick round one's neck as Pastor Lassen had. This was the reason that Doctor Muus was reserved towards him at first; but then who, at his best, could bear comparison with Doctor Muus?—a man refined to his finger-tips! But after the dinner the doctor quite changed his opinion and had an enjoyable talk about books and examinations with this excellent pastor. Their principles agreed so entirely, the only wonder was that the pastor did not come from a refined home as did Doctor Muus.

"How do you get on here in my native place, Doctor?" asked Herr Lassen.

"Oh, well!—you know it is not the same as in the south. But of course I have my work. I must put up with it for a time."

"Yes, that is the way with us officials. I do not see how I could endure it here for any length of time; however, thank God, my relief has been arranged and my time here is at an end."

The doctor said:

"I should have thought, however, that you who belong to this part of the country and have only been away for some few years—

but your health suffers here in the north, I have heard?"

"I am not well for a single day; the air here does not suit me. That is the way with any one who has been south for any length of time—all one's student years. And besides, there is the purely psychic or spiritual attraction towards the main centres of life. In my opinion it is only men of exceptional personality who can endure life in the Nordland. My bishop says the same."

But at this the doctor coughed a little and in quite a friendly way intimated that he could not accept such a naive view without reservations.

"To a certain extent," he said; "but that does not apply to every one. Are you leaving at once?"

"In a few days. I am packing already. . . ."

The wedding gifts took the form of furniture and silverware. Thanks to the week's postponement, they had all arrived in time; even the Lieutenant had sent the bride a gold watch and chain; it seemed a fitting reward for long and faithful service, and Jomfru Salvesen wept with gratitude. Just think, there was the Lieutenant far away in Trondhjem, and he had thought of her! There was no one like the Lieutenant! But Attorney Rasch, who from the standpoint of his social position, felt that he had reason to be somewhat dissatisfied with the whole marriage celebration, felt that he must account for these tears of joy in a delicate manner and said:. "It is one of your many good points that you are so easily pleased, dear Kristine!"

"Have you seen the watch the Lieutenant has sent, Herr Pastor?" asks the doctor. "To judge by it, the man must have plenty of money."

"Oh, yes, the Lieutenant—no one knows the truth about that man. I saw he had a stick with a gold head, costlier than any bishop's staff."

Doctor Muus shrugged his shoulders. And wishing to give both the Lieutenant and Pastor Lassen a dig, he said:

"The watch must certainly have cost a good deal; but I never heard of any one sending a watch as a wedding present to a bridal couple."

"No, that is quite true now that you mention it, Doctor. I did not think of that."

And Herr Holmengraa? Yes, he was there. He came late, but there he sat now, benevolent and respected by all. Perhaps he was not enjoying himself particularly, perhaps he found nothing to interest him, nothing worth listening to—no one talked about anything big; the word million was not even mentioned. The bridegroom proposed his health—well, he didn't mind that!—the bridegroom thanked him for having helped two people to obtain a piece of meadow from the Segelfoss estate—thanked him on his wife's behalf as well as his own!

And Holmengraa drank, but afterwards he declined all undeserved credit—he had nothing to do with Segelfoss estate.

"By the way," says the bridegroom, sticking to the subject, "there's the baker wanting to buy ground now, and then there's Per of Bua. There that poor fellow P. Jensen lies in his bed 'done for,' as he puts it, but directing everything with the one side left him. Just think of him, Herr Holmengraa. My interest is natural, for of course some little crumbs fall to a poor solicitor at a sale of property, however small they may be."

Herr Holmengraa made no further reply, probably because he took no interest in the matter. He had not betrayed by so much as a look that he remembered having had the bridegroom and Doctor Muus as companions in a drinking-bout, or had made advances to the bride last year when he had openly gone woman-hunting for a couple of weeks. And now here is this room full of small things and small talk—and here he is, the man of mystery, the king, making himself small, though the greatest there.

Fru Irgens, who is watching her master, sees very clearly that he finds it is time to be going. As he disappears through the door she thinks: Ah, yes! the girl Marcilie is sitting at home waiting!

The bridegroom drinks with the two merchants for whom he has recovered debt—it falls to him almost entirely to play the amiable host, for the bride has had no experience in the manners of society. He had remarked to the bride: "Those telegrams are hardly worthy of a festal occasion, Kristine!" The fact was, the bridegroom was hurt that they were not written out by the head telegraphist, Baardsen himself, but by little Gottfred, who had just learnt to telegraph and was not yet even on the permanent staff. His schoolboy hand gave offence to the bridegroom, for the telegrams were of course to be bound and to lie on the parlour table.

Then the guests left. When Pastor Lassen went, he said: "Peace be in this house!" A very appropriate saying; and the doctor felt respect for this fisher-lad's inborn tact.

"Books again! You are always carrying about books, Herr Pastor!"

And Herr Lassen answered: yes, that was true, they had taught him so much. He had been in a cottage to-day and got these two books for his library; the one was a genuine Bertha Canutte Aarflot and the other a Christian tale about a pastor's daughter; it was called "The Latter End of the Pastor's Daughter, etc., etc."

❧

The Lieutenant came back from his journey completely broken down; he was driven from the wharf to the tile-works and put to bed. Would he have the district-doctor? No. Should Young Willatz be informed? No. The Lieutenant wished for nothing, he merely wished to lie still and get better, he said.

But the Lieutenant did not get better, he got worse; and it was lucky he had not brought the masons with him. They could not come before March. When Pauline came down from the manor with food for him, Mariane would often come to meet her to learn how he was; she stood outside the tile-works and waited and always received the same report: "He is worse to-day!" And one day when the Lieutenant asked, not for the doctor, not for the pastor, but for the telegraphist, Baardsen, it was Mariane who ran over to the station and fetched him.

"I am beginning to doubt if I shall recover," said the Lieutenant. "I caught such a bad cold on the way home from Trondhjem."

To this Baardsen only answered that perhaps the Lieutenant's will might do something—

"I shall be grateful to you if you will make out a telegram to my son. Though indeed he will probably not arrive in time."

Baardsen answered:

"I have reason to believe that your son is on his way."

The old Lieutenant hides his joyful surprise and asks gruffly:

"Then has some one informed him?"

"Yes. I did."

Pause.

"Hm. I thank you—in this case I thank you—hm. Though indeed he will probably not arrive in time. When can he be here?"

"With the first boat going north."

The Lieutenant counts the days and says:

"There's a letter on the table—I wrote it on board the boat. You have a safe in the station, you could keep it safely there."

"Yes."

"And I will ask you to hand it over to my son in the event—in case—you understand."

"I shall do so!" is all Baardsen says as he takes the letter.

The Lieutenant thanks him again and nods to show that that is all he wants.

"Will you permit me to look in and see you again?" asks the telegraphist.

"I will not only—have you time to do so?"

"Plenty of time. Gottfred is doing the work."

"Then I will be grateful if you will look in."

Baardsen went out and found Mariane standing waiting outside the door. A strangely faithful, untutored child! she surely could find no pleasure in standing waiting there every day, but she had got it into her head that these visits, which she knew Pauline had told him of, did the sick man some good. The telegraphist nods to her and says:

"Little Mariane, Young Willatz is on his way home."

Mariane's brown face grows red, but she only says:

"Oh!—is he—"

The telegraphist came regularly to the tile-works; the sick man made no objection, and Baardsen never grew tired of coming. He brought his cello with him and played a little; he spoke seldom and his silences were full of good sense. Without him the Lieutenant would have missed the company of a kindly man during his last days. Baardsen kept the sick man informed where Young Willatz would probably be at any particular moment, and the Lieutenant was grateful. There he lay, grey and exhausted, waiting for his son;

his eyes seemed already to have an inward look, his temples were sunken—so death does its work.

"Wait a little, Mariane!" said Baarsden one day as he entered the tile-works. In that way he conveyed to the sick man that Mariane was standing outside.

"How is it the child comes here every day?" he said. "Call her in!"

"I am to leave for Christiania soon," Mariane tells him, "and I don't know if you will be well by that time."

"Oh! and so you have come to say good-bye. That is kind of you. Your father is very busy?"

"Yes. He is expecting another ship with rye."

"Remember me to him!"

At that moment the door opens and District-doctor Muus steps in. He had not knocked, so as not to disturb the sick man, but when he was safely inside he at once took off his overcoat and coughed audibly in an authoritative manner.

"I hear you are ill," said the doctor, preparing to feel the Lieutenant's pulse. When the sick man tried to prevent him, the doctor persisted and said with firmness:

"Now we must have no nonsense. You must submit to me this time."

The man was doing his duty—even more than his duty—and it was really most kind of him; but the Lieutenant had never been able to submit and now he was doubtless too old to learn. He sought help with his eyes and brought Baardsen to his side.

"Show him out!" he said.

"I am to show you out," said the telegraphist Baardsen, helping the doctor on with his overcoat again. Telegraphist Baardsen had such swinging shoulders, he almost lifted the doctor from the floor when he pushed the overcoat up over his arms.

❧

The days went by and Young Willatz did not come. The mail-boat was drawing near, but it drew near too slowly, and it seemed that the Lieutenant had his great will-power no longer at command—no, the hand of death pressed heaviest there.

"In case," he said, "I die to-day or to-morrow—one can never know—I have a message for my son. A couple of family portraits are coming from Trondhjem—of my wife and of me—they are not good, but they must be hung up—among the others. Will you tell him that?"

"It shall be done!"

"And in the spring an organ is coming—a small organ for the church. It has been delayed; it was his mother who asked for it. He can widen the end of the church—thirty feet will be enough—and build a loft for the organ. Timber is coming from Namsen. Then there will be an organ—"

Steadfast and firm of purpose to the end!

The next day Pastor Lassen too must needs come to do his duty. It was an autumn day, and bright sunshine flooded the Lieutenant's room when the pastor entered.

At the sight of him the sick man smiled. This man who was already in the grip of death gave a wry smile, and then closed his eyes. He opened them no more.

Telegraphist Baardsen locked the door of the tile-works.

❧

When two days later Young Willatz's ship came steaming up towards Segelfoss, flags were flying at half-mast at the manor and Holmengraa's house; he knew at once what had happened.

It was so strange—even more strange than when his mother had died. Nothing seemed changed, but everything was strangely different. He has just swung past the boat-shed behind the point, which Per of Bua made into a dancing-hall—the boat-shed was standing there still, painted and in good repair; as he entered the bay he heard the hum of the mill. Under the crane on the wharf a big Black Sea boat was lying, discharging rye. The sailors were moving about on the deck at their work. Life, human beings, the world, were everywhere—but the flags were flying at half-mast and his father was dead. Young Willatz stood and gazed landwards, tall and grown up, with gold buttons in his waistcoat. He had hoped to come in time—and as he gazed his mind seemed to wander; he saw everything, but could not fix his thoughts. He remembered that he bore greetings to his father from Fredrik Coldevin, who had not had time to visit Segelfoss just now, but would come next summer.

On the quay Martin and Pauline met him. Herr Holmengraa came and gave him his hand; Fru Rasch, who had been Jomfru Salvesen, was so red about the eyes. And there stood Mariane, far away, clasping her wrists and looking at him.

When he reached the tile-works, the telegraphist, Baardsen, was there waiting for him. They went into the sitting-room—a large, bright room, with furniture and pictures; then they went into the next large room—there was his father, laid out in his uniform, gaunt, Arab-like, dead. A military cloak lay upon the body—Baardsen had placed it there because it was in keeping with the rest. And so the Lieutenant found a last use for his costly cloak.

The telegraphist, Baarsden went out and Young Willatz was left alone. He had been given an account of his father's last days, had received his father's letter and read it. Yes, he would free the mortgaged estate; the money was ready, lodged, some of it here, some there—thank God, his father had been rich the whole time! If he had only been able to take his hand once more and hear his voice again! There sat Young Willatz, still wearing the gold buttons in his waistcoat. These gold buttons his father had bought himself, and given to him when on his visit to England, and to-day he had put them on that he might give his father pleasure.

He went out. The roar of the river came down to him, the rattle from the big Black Sea boat discharging rye. And he could see Mariane climbing the hill on her way home, alone.

THE END

Acknowledgments

Profound thanks are extended to the following for their generous financial support which helped to defray some of this book's production costs:

Stephanie A., Kevin Adams, Adhvika & Ananya, Ash, Eloise Ruth Auld, B. D. Austin, Matthew Beckham, Martha Benco, Thomas Young Barmore Jr, Nicholas Barry, Joseph Benincase, Matthew Boe, Brian R. Boisvert, Thomas Bull, Tobias Carroll, Scott Chiddister, Adam Cloutier, C. Colla, Jonathan Collins, Jangus Cooper, Joshua Lee Cooper, Sheri Costa, Randy Cox, Walter F. Croft, Malcolm & Parker Curtis, Albie D., Daniel M Dion, Isaac Ehrlich, Steve Elsberry, Danielle D. Evans, Pops Feibel, John Feins, Andrew E Fisher, Luke Frazier, Nathan Friedman, GMarkC, Dr. Natalie Grand, David Greenberg, Elizabeth Hackler, Mahan Harirsaz, Kyle P Havenhill, Billy Hayes, Erik Hemming, Aric Herzog, Sarah E. Hiatt, Antonio Inaniel, Erik T Johnson, Kristiana Josifi, Haya .K., Larry Kerschner, Jesse Knepper, M.D. Kuehn, Chaz Larson, Lesli Lembcke, Frank Loose, LordHog, Theodore Marks, Sergio Mendez-Torres, Dr. Melvin "Steve" Mesophagus, Serpent Moon, Geoffrey Moses, Gregory Moses, Diane Mountford, Matt Murray, Tom N., Richard Ohnemus, Michael O'Shaughnessy,

Andrew Pearson, Ry Pickard, Stephen Press, Robert Price, Patrick M Regner, Asierleigh H. Richards, Michael J. Richmond, Frank V. Saltarelli, Connor Shirley, Mindie Jeanne Simmons, Ethan Stahl, K.L. Stokes, Jack Waters, Crystal Weber, Conrad Wendland, Christopher Wheeling, Isaiah Whisner, Jordy Williams, Matt Williams, David S. Wills, Morgan Witkowski, T.R. Wolfe, Mai Xiong, The Zemenides Family, znf, and Anonymous

Lightning Source UK Ltd.
Milton Keynes UK
UKHW042339120421
381885UK00001B/109